FULL COURT
PRESSURE

Also by Lynn Galli

Wasted Heart

Imagining Reality

Uncommon Emotions

Blessed Twice

FULL COURT PRESSURE

LYNN GALLI

Penikila Press

FULL COURT PRESSURE
Published by Penikila Press, LLC

ISBN: 978-1-935611-30-1

Printed in the United States of America.

Author's Note

It should go without saying that this is a fictional story, and therefore, I've taken liberties with Graysen's basketball background and coaching career. The universities named are out of respect. In no way am I expressing unhappiness with their current or former head coaches. Lake Merritt University does not exist, so I've done whatever I please with that place. Also, when I started this book, Sacramento had a WNBA team. Ah, the things that can change in a year. I spend a great deal of time purposefully not thinking about what could change in ten.

CHAPTER 1

When I woke up this morning, I knew my life was going to change. I could feel it as pronounced as my heartbeat. It wasn't an entirely foreign sensation. I'd experienced landmark events in my life: the day I was awarded my basketball scholarship, when my team took the NCAA title, when I played in my first Olympic game, won my first WNBA title, and got my first head coaching job. Yes, I'd gone through wonderful experiences before, on grand scales even, but this time felt different. It would first require a six-hour flight, something I'd grown sick of during the past twenty-two years of my life, but for a life change as exciting as this could be, I'd take any number of those flights.

"Aren't you Graysen Viola?" a voice interrupted my musings when I found myself at the end of the required trip on my way through Lake Merritt University's campus.

I looked down at an eager student sporting a vintage t-shirt. Pretty young thing with her perky smile, perky bounce, perky, well, you get the picture. Thus far on my stroll through campus, I'd been stopped by three others, but none as pretty as this one.

"Yes," I admitted, smiling at the flash of braces on her otherwise flawless face.

"Oh, wow, this is so cool! You're like my favorite basketball player ever."

Really? Over Michael Jordan or Cheryl Miller? That seemed unlikely. Of course she was so young she might not even know either of them. Pushing that depressing thought away, I offered, "That's so nice of you to say. Do you play?"

"Not since high school. The team here is way out of my league."

I took a second to size her up by her stance and the way she'd walked. Yeah, she wasn't a natural athlete, and the team here was a top-five club. A tradition I hoped to continue, even as baffled as I was by the current coach's impending retirement. I wasn't about to look a gift horse in the mouth, though.

"Well, you've made a wise choice for your school anyway. It was nice meeting you." I made a move around her.

"Could I, like, get a picture?"

"Sure." I smiled while groaning internally. I really shouldn't have to do this, not since I'd retired from the WNBA and finished my contract with ESPN. Coming back to California where I'd played professional basketball probably increased the likelihood of running into former fans. Not that such a small inconvenience would keep me from taking this job. At least this one knew how to properly pronounce my last name with a hard "i" and the stress on the first syllable, not like the musical instrument. That told me she was a true fan.

She shrieked and dug into her massive bag to find her cell phone then swung around to slam her body up against mine. She looked up at me with pleading eyes. I took the hint, stooping so that our faces were closer together for the picture. Flash. Torture over. And with an airy thanks and shake of her tush, she took off on her way across the beautiful quad.

By the time I reached the athletic department's gorgeous glass and steel structure, I was fifteen minutes early for my interview. I glanced over at the equally elegant arena where my new team would be playing. I couldn't wait to get my hands on them.

Entering through the revolving door, I skipped the elevators and trotted up the steel and timber steps to the athletic director's suite of offices. As much excitement as I felt, I couldn't stop the nerves from overwhelming me. A receptionist guided me back to the inner office where a beautiful woman sat behind an L-shaped desk guarding access to the big boss's office.

Before I could issue a greeting, a booming voice sounded from within the open double doors. "My sista, my sista!" A blur of movement happened before large arms swooped me off the ground against the solid chest of a man who looked nothing like my brother despite his term of affection for me.

"Christ! Tavian, let me down!" I groaned as his arms squeezed even tighter. He was the only person I let do this to me, but only because I often retaliated the same way.

"I've missed my Gray," he proclaimed, swinging us once more before finally letting my feet touch the ground again. My hand lashed out and smacked the back of his head. He snickered and rubbed a hand over the short stubble he was now sporting. When I'd first met him, he was working the full-out 70's afro until his teammates and I finally got to him. "Took your ass long enough to get here."

"I brought the rest of me along, too, kinda slowed my ass down," I retorted and received a bellowing laugh from my old friend. It'd been three years since I'd last seen him. We called and emailed twice a month, but it was always good to be in the same location with him. We enjoyed a brother-sister relationship that I wished I had with my own brother. It helped that Tavian and I had been thrown together throughout our college careers as the stars of our respective teams. We'd had to show our smiling faces together so often I was surprised the college didn't ask us to get married just to cut down on the number of coordinating phone calls.

"You're old," I proclaimed, noticing a dusting of grey on his black sideburns and slight rounding of his handsome face. I always liked to remind him that he was one year older than me, a veritable granddad at forty-one now. It helped that I had great genes, too. My dark brown hair wouldn't go white until my sixties if I followed my mom's lead.

"I'm distinguished," he smugly informed me, mischief dancing in his nearly black eyes. "You're still sickeningly in shape. I'm rescinding my offer for dinner. My wife takes one look at you and she'll have my ass out running every morning to get back into basketball form."

I walked around his tall, still athletic body and stared at his ass. "It is a little saggy, babe."

"Bitch!"

"Asshole!"

He grabbed me for another hug and for the first time I noticed the woman, who must be his assistant, intently watching our exchange with a delighted smile. Her black curls jiggled along her shoulders as she tried to contain her laughter.

"Hi," I said to her, pulling away from the only friend who often made me forget we weren't alone. "I'm Graysen Viola."

"I know," her smoky voice had a calming effect on both of us. "It's a pleasure to meet you."

"Gray, meet Kesara Luz, the best ever executive assistant," Tavian informed me without a hint of sarcasm. He often tossed out easy compliments, but I could tell he thought very highly of Ms. Kesara.

"One that needs to remind you of appropriate conduct with staff, obviously," she chastised gently. I laughed and slapped the back of my hand against his chest. Getting Tavian in trouble with his assistant would be an added bonus to taking this job.

"She loves it, loves my hands all over her, don't ya, Gray?"

"Be still my heart," I deadpanned.

"You ready to sign that contract?" He yanked on my arm to drag me into his office.

"Tave!" I exclaimed, finding myself leaving my feet again with the force of his tug. "You know damn well I'm not ready. You wanted me here. I dropped everything to come. I'm not rash, nor will I sign a contract without checking out all the details."

His expression turned pleading. "C'mon, be my savior on this one. You know it's why you flew across the country. You know you want this job."

I did want it, and he knew it, which was why I'd traveled this close to the start of the basketball season. Not a good move for my current coaching post. It didn't matter that Tavian and I had discussed my working here from the moment he snagged the Athletic Director slot three years ago. It seemed too good to be true that the legendary but still young fifties coach would ever retire, especially when her team was so highly ranked. But none of that made me rash. "It's temping, which is why I'm here. But I'm not making a move until I see everything I need to see."

"You had to get permission to visit us." He flashed a knowing grin that begged to be slapped off his face. "They can't like that. They have to know you're considering it. You don't want to go back to hostility like that, do you? Not when you'll have nothing but love here. Jacinda and the kids are ecstatic about your move. Don't make me tell your nieces that you're not actually going to be living here."

"Oh, that's just unfair, jerk." But I couldn't help smiling as I thought of his kids. He insisted they call me Aunt Gray, and I'd always liked the sound of it.

"I play every card I'm given." His eyebrows fluttered as a familiar smirk played across his face. "What will it take?"

"I want to check out the facilities, look at the offices, talk to you about transportation and recruiting budgets, meet the assistant coaches and look at the team. After all that, you'll tell me how much I'm going to make and whether or not I'll be able to buy a condo as nice as the one as I have in DC or if I'll be renting a room alongside some of the students who attend this campus."

"It'll be enough. Don't worry about that. Let's get you that tour." His eyes flicked over my shoulder. "Kesara, will you show Gray anything she wants to see and take her by the arena to introduce her to the team?" His request was startling. I would have thought he'd be dying to show me around. When he looked back at me, he said, "I've got a meeting with the university president, otherwise I'd show you around. Forgive me?"

I smiled at the one friend who never had to worry about forgiveness with me. "No problem. If Kesara doesn't mind, that would be great."

"Kesara doesn't mind," the soothing voice told us from behind.

I twirled to face her. She was dressed in a linen jacket, copper silk blouse, and dark tan trousers that looked made just for her. Maybe a few inches over five feet, both Tavian and I towered over her at six-eight and six-three. I could tell our size didn't intimidate her one bit and liked that instantly about her. It was a rare person who didn't comment on my height or look at me like I was a freak.

"I appreciate it," I told her, noticing her eyes flick along my length before giving me a conspiratorial glance. Perhaps she knew if I took this job, she'd have an accomplice in making her boss's life hell each day.

"Not at all," she said to me. "Anything you need for your meeting, *jefe*?"

"Nope. Head back here when you're done. We'll both convince her to sign."

She smiled, the action stretching her lips into a soft curve and taking away the focus from her dark brown eyes. She had a glorious light caramel skin tone that indicated a Latina heritage. Striking to say the least. If I hadn't known that Tavian was happily married, I'd worry that Kesara was exactly his type. Not exactly the best move to make for an athletic director who was still establishing himself.

"All set?" she asked me before leading the way out of the office and starting the tour.

The next half hour took us all over the athletic department, down to the training room, over to the arena, the locker rooms, the media and viewing rooms, and finally to the practice courts. I felt my anticipation building as I thought about taking this position. I was ninety percent sure I'd take it when I asked my current university for permission to interview for this coaching position, but after the tour, I was at the signing stage. The facilities and opportunities were even better than Tavian had promised.

"Let's take a look at your team." Kesara reached for the door of the practice courts.

We pushed through into the gym. Two steps inside, I came to a halt. The sounds of the gym were always the same no matter how fancy the facility. Balls bouncing, sneakers screeching, muffled grunts of exertion, plays being called, shouts of encouragement, and the chatter of distraction. It was the same everywhere. Only this time, when I took in all the sights and sounds, one thing was different. Instead of the team I was expecting—the one ranked number five last year, the one with three seniors who would be drafted into the WNBA, the one with the most promising incoming freshman class—I was looking at the team that had been cited for thirteen NCAA violations, the one that had lost most of its first string and top recruits to transfers, the one that had three fairly good players on academic probation.

The one that was entirely comprised of men.

I was going to kill Tavian.

CHAPTER 2

As the team continued its shoot around, I reeled from the sight and tried to flip through what I remembered of the official offering letter Tavian had sent to me.

"Are you okay, Coach?" Kesara looked up at me, honest concern pulling at her beautiful features. Her hand came up to rest on my back, patting lightly.

"Gender neutral," I muttered, barely able to make sense to myself much less someone else.

"What?"

"He kept the letter gender neutral."

"What letter?" She gave me her full attention.

I shook my head to dust off the confusion. "I thought he'd done it because he knew how much I hated it when our college always called his team the Tar Heels and mine the Lady Tar Heels."

"Okay?" She looked like she was trying to understand but also slightly uneasy at being in the presence of what she was now thinking might be someone one taco shy of a fiesta platter.

I shifted my dazed glance from the athletes with mismatched chromosomes to Kesara. "Tavian's letter offering me the position of head coach. I'd thought he was just respecting my pet peeve from college."

Dawning sparked in her eyes. "You didn't know it was the men's basketball team?"

"Nope, and he knew I wouldn't because he knew I wouldn't want it if I did."

"Bastard!" she whispered for me, nothing malicious about it. "Evil, but the genius kind." A slow grin inched across her face, telling me how much she respected her boss. "He really wanted you here. Guess he figured out the best way to do it."

"Evil bastard," I agreed, mine a little more malicious.

"I've got a cousin most likely headed back to prison for life on the Three Strikes rule, but I could get him to take Tavian out before he goes back in." Her eyebrows scrunched up into long curly bangs. The grin turned mischievous, making me wonder if she was telling the truth, at least about the cousin headed back to prison, not having Tavian killed. "I now realize why he scheduled that meeting when he was so excited about you being here. I would have thought he'd fall all over himself introducing you to the team."

"Oh, he'll do some falling."

"At least you're not shooting the messenger." She turned an appreciative look my way.

"The gun report would be too loud indoors. I'll wait till we get back outside."

For a second, her grin dropped before her eyes pinged back to mine and a wonderful sounding laugh spilled from her lips. "I'm going to like you, Coach."

"Don't call me that, please. At least not until I've signed the contract, which I'm seriously doubting right now."

The grin dropped completely this time. Back into professional mode. "This program needs you, Ms. Viola. You bring respect. You bring a winning record. You bring legitimacy. This university needs you."

Push all my little buttons, will you? Known her for all of thirty minutes, and she had my number already. "Please call me Graysen. If I do sign, I'll need someone to keep my feet on the ground. Will you do that for me? I can't trust Tavian to do it anymore."

"Graysen," she tested my name on her lips. It sounded fine coming from her. Very fine.

"I'll also need a second for when I challenge Tavian to a duel. You up for it?" I joked.

She looked down, starting at my toes and moving all the way up to my eyes. Heat bloomed in the wake of her gaze as she sized me up. "Usually I'm the one trying to take him down. It'll be nice to let someone else take on that role."

I took my time looking over the petite creature beside me. I could almost picture my six-eight buddy being backed into a corner by this spitfire. It made me laugh, but only because I knew just how overmatched Tavian would be.

I decided to skip meeting the team just then, wanting to get back to see what the hell Tavian had been thinking. Kesara didn't have a problem cutting our tour short, and by the skip in her step, I thought she might be a little giddy about the prospect of seeing me lay into her boss.

By the time we got back to his office, I'd simmered down on the anger, but the apprehension had set in. This was too unbelievable. He knew damn well that I'd risked my other job to fly out here for this interview. In fact, I would be very lucky if they renewed my contract at the end of the season. Nothing short of winning a NCAA title would get them to re-up with someone who was looking at greener pastures. Unfortunately, my current team wouldn't be enough to get me past the second round this year. I was pretty damn screwed, and my good friend Tavian had taken advantage of that.

His hands shot up in the air above his big body the second Kesara and I entered his outer office. "Come in here before you start yelling." I nodded thanks to Kesara before following him inside. He shut the door and flicked his fingers back to his palms several times. "Lemme have it."

"I honestly want to kill you," I started, my voice low and menacing. "Not quickly. I want to torture you, slowly and painfully, then kill you. I want to dismember you once you're dead, maybe while I'm killing you. There will be no trace left of you. You'll disappear like some magician's assistant without the ability to be brought back."

"Now, Gray, you know how Jacinda would react if I didn't come home tonight."

I scoffed. "I'd feel bad for three whole seconds."

"You don't mean that, especially since you'd be the one that she'd lean on until well after the funeral, and I know how you hate all that emotional stuff."

Dammit, he was right. His wife would start to cry, depressed that she'd have to go through life alone now, and then there were the kids, their sweet little faces all teary and sad.

Okay, new plan, I'll just maim him.

* * *

"Grayson, get your skinny white ass over here, lady," Tavian's wife, Jacinda, scolded as she rushed toward me when I stepped out of her husband's car.

"Do you all have a family obsession with asses or something?" I asked Tavian over her shoulder as she squeezed me to her.

"Only yours, " he shot back then turned to his wife. "Where's my sugar, Boo?"

"Don't make me smack you, Stilts." She glared up at him after releasing me. She'd changed her hair since the last time I saw her, going natural. Tight, springy black curls wound out from her head, adding volume around her oval, toffee brown face. The effect was stunning, beauty on top of her already beautiful appearance.

"What did I do?" Tavian's astonished look was almost worth the shady way he'd lured me out here.

"No one ever warned me that men were such morons before I decided to marry one," she informed me, completely ignoring him. Her eyes twinkled in the sunshine, clearly happy to see me. "Why are they constantly surprised when we know everything that happens to and around them?"

"And they can't remember what they said an hour ago much less during the last argument," I inserted.

"You know," Tavian spoke up from behind us as we walked up to the house, "I was thinking having my best bud out here would be a good thing. Instead it looks like I'm going to be bashed every time you two get together."

"Damn straight, skippy," Jacinda gestured me inside and squared off against him. "Do you honestly think Kesara wouldn't tell me what you did to my girl here?"

"She works for me, that little traitor!" Tavian crossed his arms over his chest.

"She knows how to keep her job. Stay on my good side and she'll be your executive assistant for life. She's a smart one. You, not so much."

I laughed, envying their relationship. Part friendship, part partnership, part smoldering love affair.

"What were you thinking, lying to Gray like that?" Jacinda lost her mirth.

"I didn't lie."

"What was it, fiction?" I challenged his petulant expression.

"Men!" she huffed and spun around to head into the kitchen. "We're having dinner where you're going to tell me how you've been. Then once I put the kids down, you're going to tell me how much you want my husband dead."

I laughed again. I'd really missed her. I was so happy that my friend had married such a great person. One who miraculously didn't have a problem with her husband having a female best friend. She'd never once been resentful or fearful of it. Of course she probably recognized that I'd been so focused on my basketball I never had time for romance. Or she could just be a really secure person.

"How much trouble did his idiotic move put you in?"

"Enough," I admitted seriously for the first time and noticed Tavian's head drop. Yeah, bastard knew what he'd done to me. He should feel guilty about it. "I won't lose my job this year, but I won't be invited to stay next year."

"Damn you, Tave!" Jacinda swore through gritted teeth when we repositioned ourselves at the kitchen counter. "This is how you treat your best friend?"

"She's the best damn coach I know, Jaci. You know I'm barely hanging onto my job now." His was a defeated tone. I almost felt guilty for being so mad at him. When the violations had come down last spring, he'd called to ask my advice on what I thought my options were. I'd guessed at the time that the university was looking to fire him along with the head coach. "Yeah, I was mostly thinking of saving my hide, but Gray's the best. It doesn't matter that it's the guy's team."

"Yes, it does!" we both retorted.

"Why? Men coach women's teams all the time. Why not the other way?"

Had to love a guy who thought there wasn't anything different about it. But hell, he knew exactly all the problems that would come with this. He had to. He was also very good at his job.

"Shall we list them?" Jacinda looked at me to start.

"As the first female coach of a NCAA Division I men's basketball team, I'll be the must see carnival side show at every game."

"She's right, and the spotlight will follow her everywhere, waiting for her to fail."

Damn right. "The team is already in ruins having so many transfers and lost recruits. You're setting me up to fail."

His head started shaking. "There are some decent players left. With your training regimen, they'll be more fit than any team they face."

"That's not enough at this level, and you know it." I swallowed my sigh.

"As if everyone wasn't going to be looking at this program with a home CSI kit after the stuff that asshole coach pulled before," Jacinda muttered.

"I can't do this, Tave, you have to know that. I never liked being recognized when I played professionally, but that's going to be nothing compared to this. If I fail, I may never get another coaching job. Not to mention how my failure would justify every man who says that women can't coach men. This isn't the team to do this with, and I'm not the coach."

He pushed off the kitchen stool to place his hands on my shoulders. "Even if you weren't the best coach I know, the bar is set so low for this team that a win would make the next coach look like a miracle worker. I could play it safe and give it to an assistant coach, but they aren't good enough to lead this team. Only you are. Someone has to stand above all the past mess. Someone has to outshine it." He paused, staring intently at me. "I have thought about it from your end. I have, and you are the coach, Gray. You're the one."

Dammit, he knew me so well. It wasn't like I hadn't thought of coaching a men's team before. I'd certainly had other offers, but men's teams were such a different breed from women's teams. I wasn't really sure I would like that breed. I could handle them, but liking them was also a must for my coaching success.

"Now I want to kill him," Jaci half-joked. "Really, Stilts, you're guilting her into this. Run over to Bonnie's and pick up the girls. We'll have a nice family night to take Gray's mind off your manipulation."

I liked her so much. We'd been friends since the moment he introduced us, but I had always thought of her as his girlfriend, then his wife. If I planned to do this, I'd have to start thinking of her as my friend, too.

CHAPTER 3

"No luggage. That's a good sign," Kesara commented mildly as I strode into Tavian's office area the next day.

"No baseball bat, either, that's the best sign," I quipped back.

"I always keep a spare for when he starts acting up. Shall I grab it?" Her brown eyes twinkled in amusement.

Tavian's door opening interrupted my chuckle. "Gray! Perfect, right on time. Come on, there's someone here who wants to say hi."

This was a surprise. He hadn't mentioned having to meet anyone last night at dinner. I hoped it wasn't one of the guys on the team. I wasn't ready for that.

I followed him inside and froze in the doorway. Rising from the couch was the only woman who'd ever made me speechless. Darby Evan, former NCAA champion and one-time captain of the U.S. women's volleyball team, reached to nearly my height when she stood, flashing a brilliant smile that lit up the whole room. Hell, the whole campus for that matter. What was she doing here?

I'd first noticed her during the NCAA championship game on television. She was downright striking, all pun intended. Superior to all of her teammates and opponents in skill, she'd catch anyone's eye. But she was gorgeous, too. Dark red hair that people seemed to crave these days, light blue eyes, a blend of sharp and delicate features on a face that could force anyone to take notice. Her tall, sinewy body was the perfect form for volleyball or basketball or any sport really.

We'd met the summer after I'd graduated. I was standing outside the Olympic arena, awaiting the parade of athletes for the opening ceremony. Her team came over to introduce themselves to mine. I barely managed to say anything to her that night but had plenty of time to chat later when her team joined us for meals, trips to other sporting venues at the Games, and sightseeing throughout the host city. We figured it was because they were all tall like us, and tall women got stared at. Being in a group made it less uncomfortable. I was surprised I hadn't made a complete fool of myself, but she'd always been so gregarious and seemed interested in everything I or any of my teammates had to say.

Having been a really late bloomer, I hadn't put it together at the time, but I finally figured out I was more than just a little star struck with her. She wasn't just another athlete I admired. She was someone who piqued my interest. I'd admitted that to Tavian, and only Tavian, and here he was throwing it in my face. I wondered if he'd lined up the two men on the track and swim teams that I'd also found attractive at the time as well. *Bastard!*

"Graysen, it's wonderful to see you again. I'm ecstatic that you'll be joining us here," she bubbled.

"Darby?" I was so stunned I could barely blink, not bothering to comprehend what she was saying. Especially since she'd closed the distance between us and grabbed me in a hug. A wonderful hug. So unlike Tavian's hug. He didn't have curves like this. *Oh yeah, wow, nice curves.* "I didn't expect to see you."

She laughed, the breath reaching my cheek as she pulled out of the hug. "Obviously, but I hope it's a good surprise. Tavian told me he was going to recruit you to fill the open coaching spot, and we both thought it would be a good idea to surprise you."

"Yes, well," I managed to recover, taking a full step out of the circle of her arms. I was a functioning adult now, I should act like it. "I didn't realize you were on staff here."

"Assistant coach last year, head coach this year. Looks like we'll be starting off our head coaching careers at Merritt together."

I returned the brilliant smile she flashed, ignoring the fact that I'd been a head coach for six years at another university. That didn't make the warm feelings she was invoking any less yummy. "Congratulations, Darby. The university has gained a talent with you."

She squeezed my shoulder, eyebrows fluttering. "Same with you, missy."

Reason seeped into my clouded brain. "Actually, I haven't signed on yet."

"But she's going to, right, Gray?"

The deep timbre of his voice shocked me out of the haze of crushy feelings I kept experiencing in Darby's presence. "Tave," I admonished in my most sincere voice. He always knew I wasn't kidding when I used this tone.

"Oooh, I always loved how you guys could have entire conversations with only one word." Darby swung her severe bob from Tavian to me and back again. It was one of those fashionable cuts, the latest in styles that would probably be out of style in three months. I had no doubt that she would change it the instant it ran its course. She was always trendy like that.

"She'll come around, even if I have to keep her locked up to do it," Tavian cajoled, grabbing me against him. This time I appreciated the stability.

"We're supposed to be ironing that out before I get on a plane today." My tone dropped all mirth, ready to get this done with.

"That's my cue." Darby smiled again. I wanted to be able to stare at those supple lips for the next hour instead of talking to Tavian. "As soon as you get settled, give my office a call, Graysen. We'll have dinner and catch up. It's going to be so great having you on campus." She practically floated out the door, leaving Tavian and me alone.

Five seconds after the door closed, I lit into him, "You living bastard! How could you not tell me I was going to see her today?"

"Damn, Gray, you still got a thing for her?" He jostled my shoulder, nudging me back a step. A teasing grin begged to be smacked off his face. "I was hoping that girl crush of yours would still hold a little influence. Enough to make you sign?"

"I don't have a girl crush on her." *Liar.* Okay, maybe I did, but he didn't need confirmation. "I'm also rethinking my desire to sign with you. How could you pull something like that? You know I hate surprises."

"It was her idea. Honest." His big hands, the ones that could catch any pass from his teammates, spread wide in front of his chest. He pursed his lips, trying to hold in a smile. "I always told you that she wants herself some Gray loving."

He hadn't just told me; he'd teased me relentlessly all throughout the Games and for a few years after. "Again, shut up. Neither one of us has a thing for the other. She's just a really outgoing person. I always thought she had a thing for you."

"Not even," he dismissed without any consideration. "She's all about the girlie love. The last coach confirmed it for me, like I didn't already suspect. Is it the same for you?"

I brushed a hand through the air. "We're not going there. I can't trust you with anything anymore."

"Come on, you can tell me. I'm your bud. You never talk about your love life with me. I finally get you to admit to a little infatuation with not one but three people, and that's all I've ever gotten out of you." He almost looked hurt, like he'd always wanted to have deep emotional discussions about significant others with me.

"That's all it was. I told you then and I'm telling you now, there's nothing there." There wasn't. She hadn't been any nicer to me than she had to my teammates. "I thought Darby was beautiful, just like I think you're handsome. I never wanted to sleep with either of you. Or that swimmer or sprinter, either."

"Sure you did," he taunted. "You could never resist me. You think I'm a hot stud muffin. So much hotter than that track and field dweeb, and swimmers are freaks."

I laughed at that. He'd never lacked for confidence. "I'm not the one who put money into a pool to see if I could bed someone. That was you, mister." I reminded him of the bet that went around our campus during my freshman year.

"The only reason I did that was so that we could split the pot."

"Yeah, that was fun." I'd let him do it because it was the only way I could think of to get rid of that stupid bet. As an added bonus, all the losers who'd tried to hit on me stopped. Once word circulated that Tavian had "won" the pool, almost no one was brave enough to approach me. Of course that just added to the continued state of my disinterest in all things sexual. "But you still wanted me."

He grinned that evil grin of his. "It might have been fun."

"But not happening."

He winked then agreed, "Not happening." And not just because he was married.

CHAPTER 4

Three weeks later, I approached the arena nervously. After dropping my bags off at my temporary apartment, I'd hastened to the gym. I wanted to see the assistant coaches in action during the skills session before I spoke with each of them. I'd taken over another team once before, but I didn't anticipate the same kind of reception here.

The viewing area gave me great insight into how the team functioned. Everyone was here, shattering the rule on maximum players allowed prior to the start of official practices. They were also supposed to be working on skills; instead it was a full-on scrimmage. No wonder they'd gotten into trouble with the NCAA. Terrific. The last thing I wanted to do at a first meeting was scold them.

I hustled back to my office where I'd be meeting with the coaches. The interior was swanky and could use an interior decorator to make it seem less cavernous. I killed the five minutes before the meeting by rearranging the workspaces for most efficient use of natural light. Five minutes turned into ten, then fifteen.

"Graysen?" the voice of my first assistant coach spoke from the doorway.

I waited for him to apologize for being late. He didn't, just strode forward and dropped into the guest chair without asking. "It's nice to meet you, Peter. I imagine this is tough for you." I thought it was best to tackle the hardest subject first. "Tavian tells me you've been managing well enough as the interim coach."

"Yeah, well," he said, or sulked, rather. He hadn't picked up on the fact that I'd said "well enough" rather than "great" because it had been anything but great. None of the student-athletes on academic probation had improved their GPA. All of the freshmen had been ignored during their impromptu scrimmage, and not to belabor the point, but the scrimmage was a violation.

"You had to know that Tavian couldn't give you the team, though." I waited for him to acknowledge that. Unfortunately, he continued to glower at me. "You were the first assistant coach when all the violations occurred. The NCAA wouldn't like rewarding that behavior."

"It wasn't my fault!"

"I'm not saying it was," I stated, even though it was partly his fault. "But from what I saw a few minutes ago, this can never be your team."

He pursed his lips in a near pout. "What's that supposed to mean?"

"You were violating NCAA rules. The same kind of things they found fault with the last coach was going on in that gymnasium not twenty minutes ago."

"What are you talking about?"

Was he really that much of an idiot? "It's three weeks before official practices are allowed to start, and if you don't know that after," I paused and glanced down at his CV, "fifteen years as an assistant coach, then you're not qualified to be on my staff." I knew it was a harsh line to take, but for someone who should be kissing my ass to keep his job, he wasn't showing any humility. I knew I could work with him, but only because I could work with anyone.

"You need me." He glanced around, eyeing my office as if he would be taking it over in a week. "You really think they're going to listen to a woman? I don't know what Tavian was thinking, but, sweetheart, this is a lot different from what you're used to with girls."

I tilted forward in my seat. "First, I've never coached girls. They were women as much as the players on this team are men. Second, athletes are athletes, and since I've been both an athlete and a coach, I'm more qualified than you to lead them. And third, if you ever call me 'sweetheart' again, I'll make you run laps with the team." Since my delivery had been unemotional, he wasn't sure how to respond. I cut him off before he could come up with something. "I do know what I'm getting into. I also know that the team is used to you. If we can work through the expectations, I'd like you to stay on."

He sighed, bothered by a lot of things, I'd guess. "I get that you're trying to flaunt your power over me, but let me do what I do best, and we'll have a winning team again." The seemingly permanent smirk flashed brighter.

"The best team you've ever been a part of was one-and-done in March. I've played on three championship and two gold medal teams. I've been an assistant coach on two championship teams and coached one myself. The worst any of my teams have done is the round of sixteen. So, we'll be following my formula not yours because, whether you like it or not, I'm the head coach."

"This is bull. I'm talking to Tavian." He started to rise out of his seat.

"You walk out that door without trying to resolve these issues with me," I stopped his advance, "I'll assume you are resigning."

"We'll see what Tavian says about that!" he barked and stepped into the hall.

I got up and followed. Once outside, I signaled to the security guard I'd put on alert. "This man has just resigned his post. Please escort him to the athletic director's office where he'll be told that my decision is final."

Peter stopped his retreat and turned to stare at me. The look on his face was a mixture of humiliation and rage, but there was disbelief as well. "You can't do that!"

"I gave you a choice. If you need Tavian to validate my decision, then waste your time storming over there. You'll be right back here in ten minutes cleaning out your office." I didn't wait for a retort, retreating back inside.

Not five minutes passed before the phone rang. "Good afternoon, Piranhas Basketball, this is Graysen."

"Damn, Gray," Tavian's voice came over the line. "The dude didn't even work for you for a day, and you're firing his ass."

"I fired the rest of him, too."

He couldn't help but laugh. "He was seething. What did he say to you?"

"It wasn't just what he said. He was running a scrimmage when I stopped by the gym earlier." Silence came from his end. "What month is it?"

"Sept—oh, damn, that moron. No wonder they got into so much trouble. I should have fired him with the first guy."

"Probably, but I gave him the option of staying on. I knew that anyone you named as interim coach would have expectations of being named head coach unless a superstar was brought in." I felt my pulse finally slow down from the adrenalin surge of confronting that idiot.

"You are a superstar."

I snorted a laugh. "Stop kissing my ass. He was given ample opportunity to stay. I laid out my expectations, and he couldn't accept them."

"Yeah, but your first day?" He sounded a little worried. "This isn't going to look good. We should be ready for a lawsuit."

"Didn't I mention that I recorded the interview? One that had him stating that women weren't qualified to coach men and admitting to violating NCAA rules. I'll send over the file right away." I'd positioned my webcam to record him, knowing it might get a little dicey.

That rumbling laughter sounded again. "You're the best, Gray."

"That's why you brought me here." I hung up just as the other two assistant coaches showed up in my doorway. "Please come in." I stood and walked over to greet them. Both men seemed surprised that they were shorter than me. One African American, one white, both nervous. Good, I wanted them on their heels until we worked out a system. "I'm Graysen Viola."

"Damon Kenner," the taller of the two spoke up first. His head was shaved, the dark brown skin shiny in the sunlight from my window. A neatly trimmed goatee gave him an aged look that I guessed he was purposefully trying to achieve. He looked in his mid-thirties, but I knew from his CV that he was only in his late twenties.

"Bill Jensen," the one who looked like he had a bit of Scandinavian in his family tree spoke up.

"Welcome, gentlemen. Please have a seat." I headed back to my chair. "I realize this has been a stressful time for you. Let me start by assuring you that I have no intention of asking you to resign." Both sets of shoulders facing me sagged slightly. "Peter and I, however, could not come to an agreement on our coaching methodologies, so he has chosen to leave." Or get fired, but I didn't want to scare these two.

"What?" Bill shot wide eyes from me to Damon.

"Peter didn't like that we'd be following my game plan and chose to leave. Do either of you have a problem with that?"

They glanced at each other before saying, "No."

I studied them for a minute. A smile crept onto my face. "I'm not going to pretend this transition will be easy for us, but I don't want a duo of yes-men on my staff. If you disagree with a coaching method, you'll discuss it with me. I've always trusted my staff to do their work. I expect the same from both of you, even if I didn't handpick you two."

Damon bit first, an easy smile slipping onto his lips. "Sounds good, Graysen."

"Better than what we've been used to," Bill added.

"As far as Peter goes," Damon continued with that easy smile, "my mom told me if you can't say anything nice about someone, don't say anything at all. So I'm not going to say anything about him being gone."

We all laughed at that, and I felt a huge weight being lifted off my frame. I was afraid I'd need to hire three assistant coaches after today. Looks like that wouldn't be necessary.

CHAPTER 5

"You haven't even settled in and we're down one asshole around here. Nice job."

I swiveled my chair around from the television screen where I'd been watching game tapes to face the doorway. Darby came into view as soon as I grasped the desk to stop the complete circle. She leaned casually against the doorframe, smiling at me. Practice sweats with the college logo molded to her lithe frame.

"Hi," I managed to get out through the swirl of alternative comments that peppered my brain.

"You really fired Peter?"

Oh, right, now her odd greeting made sense. "He resigned."

Her smile widened as she sauntered inside and dropped into the chair facing me. I wondered if the way she walked was practiced because it looked like she expected to be the center of attention with her movements. "You fired him. Again, I say, nice job. Peter was even more of a pompous ass than the football coach."

I blanched, bucking back into my chair, hoping the football coach wasn't walking our floor right now. Hearing someone bash him from inside my office probably wouldn't start us off on the right note. "We didn't see eye to eye on coaching."

"What'd he say?" She leaned forward and slid her chin onto a propped up palm.

My eyebrows rose on their own. I wasn't sure if she was just making conversation or looking for gossip. "You know, I'd rather keep it at we weren't a good coaching fit."

She nodded, the edges of her dark red hair sweeping along her jaw. "All right, but I'll get you to give it up over dinner this week."

I blinked then felt my heart thump. "Dinner?"

"Don't tell me you forgot my invitation?" She tried to look horrified but her smile gave her away.

I remembered. I just didn't think it was an actual invitation. I thought she meant she'd bring her bag lunch into my office one day, and we'd reminisce about the Olympics for a half hour. "Oh, that's so nice. Maybe we can grab lunch next week once I have my routine down? I know you must be busy with your game schedule."

Her brow furrowed for a moment. "You don't want to go out to dinner with me?"

"No, I do," I rushed to assure her before my head could get involved enough to scream that I had no idea what I was doing.

"Good, so, if this week is too much, then next week. I don't have a game on Thursday. Tell me where you're staying, and I'll pick you up."

She meant this as a casual dinner, right? Was it okay to ask your colleague out for anything other than a casual dinner? "I'll be working late every day until our first game. Why don't we leave from here?"

Her lips parted as if to object, but then she smiled. "Sure. I'll stop by when practice is over, and we can decide when to leave." Darby stood slowly and placed her hands on my desk, leaning forward for her parting words. "See you around campus, Gray."

That sounded dangerously flirtatious, but I was obviously reading into it. She'd always been gregarious and friendly. It didn't matter how much my stomach's summersaults convinced me it might be something more. Not that I had experience with something more. The problem with being so focused on something you're good at was that everything else tended to be pushed aside. I'd be classified as a lost cause if it weren't for the drunken thirty-seconds in my prom date's car before he took me home. Neither of us had known what we were doing, but at least he'd had a good time. The same couldn't be said for me, which was why I hadn't made any real effort to explore my sexuality further. As it stood now, I was merely pathetic when it came to relationship experience.

"Ready, Coach?" Tavian's voice sounded from the now empty doorway. He'd come to collect me for my first team meeting.

I smiled, happy to have something else to think about. I joined him as we made our way from the athletic offices over to the basketball facility. Some of the players were just entering the viewing room when we stepped off the elevator. A sudden bout of nerves assaulted me. I hadn't been this nervous since my first assistant coaching gig.

"Hey, Tavian, Graysen." Bill met us at the door. Damon reached out and shook our hands instead of voicing a greeting.

"Thought I'd introduce Gray," Tavian informed them.

Twelve tentative faces greeted us as we took post at the front. Their expressions ranged from interested to confused. Whispers broke out across the room, but only one was loud enough for me to recognize my name. That was a surprise. Even as an analyst on ESPN, I didn't expect them to know me. I'd only ever covered women's basketball games.

"All right, settle down," Tavian began. "As you know, we've had an interim coach filling in until I could hire the right person. I've been conducting a nationwide search, as well as interviewing your current coaching staff to fill the position."

"Where's Coach R?" Frank, the first string center, asked. His tall, muscular frame barely fit into the chair.

"As of this afternoon, Peter Robinson is no longer employed by the university."

"What?!" someone toward the back uttered in shock.

"Coach Bill it is, then!" Two of the guards high-fived.

"If you'll settle down, I'll answer all your questions." Tavian glared them into submission. "Let me first say that this coaching decision was not made lightly. I had a lot of potentially excellent candidates, but I wanted and waited for the best. I'd like you to meet Graysen Viola." His hand swept toward me, not that he needed to point out the only woman in the room. "She comes to us from George Washington University where she's been head coach for six years and led her team to a championship during her tenure. Some of you may recognize her from her time in the WNBA or as an analyst with ESPN. She and I played together at North Carolina and in the Olympics. We were very fortunate to pick up this caliber of coach, and I know you'll all benefit from her tutelage. Please help me welcome her to the team." He clapped his hands together, inciting applause from Bill and Damon, but the team just stared at him.

I placed my hand on his shoulder to get him to stop. "Thank you, Tavian. Hello, team."

The wait seemed interminable before one kid, Nate Jameson, if I remembered from the files I'd read, offered, "Hi, Coach." He received a jab to the side from the guy next to him.

"Perfect opportunity for our first lesson in teamwork. Let's try that again." I felt a little wicked having this much fun at their expense. "Hello, team." This time a few of them responded in kind while others mumbled around their shock. "I know this is a surprise, but you'll have plenty of time for the shock to wear off. For now, I want to say how happy I am to be given the honor of coaching you all. You're a fine team, and we're going to work together to make you great. I've seen a lot of game tape on you all, and with Bill and Damon's help, I think we're not that far from great right now."

"Are we being Punk'd?" Wendell, the power forward, asked to a round of laughter.

Tavian took a step toward him, but I tapped his arm to signal that I had this. My gaze went back to the new star of the team now that the rest of the starting five had left or graduated. "You are not. No video cameras, no Ashton Kutcher, no joke. I've been brought in to help repair the damage that's been done to this team and the reputation of this university. I won't tell you it's going to be easy, but I am your coach."

"A woman?" he persisted, patting down his stylish short dreads. The movements were deliberate, designed to make me notice how good looking he was. No doubt he used it on every woman he met.

"And who says college athletes don't learn anything?" I let a little snide slip into my tone to warn them I wouldn't take any attitude. "Yes, I'm a woman, and you're a man. I'm a coach, and you're a player. If you want to play on this team, then I'm the coach." My eyes roamed over the rest of the players. "It's time to move past the basics, guys."

Wendell looked like he was going to smart off again when Bill stepped forward. "We've already had one meeting with Coach Viola. Some things are going to change, but after last year, we know we need it. She has a winning record, both as a player and a coach. We'll all learn a great deal from her."

"Thank you, Bill," I said, surprised by his commanding support. "All right, let's get started." Bill and Damon jumped in to help me hand out my standard rulebook. "Over the next few weeks, we'll go through what's going to be expected of you on the court. For now, I want to get the housekeeping issues out of the way. First rule: you go to every class. You complete your assignments, and you take your tests. If you need tutors, I'll arrange for them. It will be your work that gets turned in. I'll check in with your professors weekly on attendance, and they'll be watching to make certain that you are the ones taking your tests."

"Oh, come on! I'm here to ball." Frank slammed his hand down on the desk.

"You aren't athletes," I told them calmly. "You're student-athletes. You're here on a scholarship to college. If you didn't expect to attend classes, you should have tried the European leagues instead of the college route."

"You can't make me go," he insisted.

Little punk. I forced a smile. "One thing you'll learn from me is that every action has a consequence. I expect my athletes to be students. If you choose not to go to class, you don't start. If you do it again, you sit out a game. A third time means you don't dress for the game. Four, and you're off the team. You will fulfill your commitment to this university as student-athletes, and the new GPA requirement is 2.6."

"This is such bull!" Wendell shouted.

"Your coach is talking, son, listen or leave," Tavian warned in that authoritative voice he'd managed to acquire after becoming an athletic director. "And I know her well enough to know that if you leave now you won't be allowed back." He did know me well. I took a very hard line with my players the first time we met as a team. They had to know that I wouldn't be manipulated, but they'd soon learn that no one else on campus would care more about them than I would.

"Here's the way this is going to work," I started, waiting until I had every pair of eyes on me. "You've got till Monday to get used to the rules and the way I coach. If you're still with us on Monday, any violations have consequences. If you decide you don't want to be on the team, feel free to visit me in my office. I can't make you play for me, but I can promise you my dedication and expertise. I know what it takes to win, and I think we have all the pieces in this room."

That seemed to quell the thunder for a bit. None of them seemed happy, but I knew it was mostly borne of not having a rigid system in place before. They'd get used to mine, or this would be one hell of a long season.

* * *

This time when I entered the gym, I was prepared to be the coach. Four players and two coaches were shooting around. I walked over to the coaches to let them in on the practice plan. "We're recording baselines today. We'll work different stations after running lines."

They nodded then Bill blew his whistle and ordered, "Hit the line, guys." A collective groan sounded, but they all took their places on the line.

After the first group had cycled through my various cross-training drills to make them better all-around athletes, I looked over at my assistant coaches. "Everyone seem on their toes?" I'd been most impressed with the kid I was now calling Dash to match his extraordinary speed. The other three were mediocre at best.

"First day jitters and they've certainly never spent a practice day like that," Bill explained as he chased down the last of the tennis balls I'd used to blend both squat slides with hand-eye coordination.

"Frank's got a chip, but he liked the tennis," Damon offered. "They'll come around. I think you can tell by yesterday's meeting who will give you the most trouble."

"Don't take it personally. They'd give any new coach hell," Bill assured me.

"Sure they would," I agreed sarcastically. "No need to sugarcoat it for me. They don't think a woman can coach them. It doesn't matter that men coach women in every sport. This won't be any different...except we'll be under scrutiny the entire time and everyone will expect me to fail. So really, the guys on the team will be the least of my worries."

Damon appreciated my sarcasm, but Bill looked a little uneasy. He didn't know me well enough to figure out when I was kidding, but we'd work on that.

"Where are the guys?" Wendell asked in a booming voice when he entered the gym.

"Skills sessions are with four players," I informed him.

He would be my biggest challenge, even if he weren't a sexist punk. The fact that he was the best player, someone that was looked at by the NBA last year but passed over for another year, would be the biggest challenge to overcome. Or biggest ego, I should say.

"We were scrimmaging yesterday. I ain't wasting time on skills when we've got to get this team ready." Wendell stalked toward the ball rack.

"Your assistant coach was violating NCAA rules yesterday. 'Ain't' isn't a word. You're in college; I expect you to utilize the proper English that you're learning. And I'm the one who will get this team ready." My unemotional retort pulled him up short of the ball rack. "Stretch out, warm up for five minutes, then you're all on the baseline for suicides." I didn't wait for his sure snarky reply. "Or sit this session, your choice. But if you don't practice, you don't play. It's as simple as that."

"Whatever," he scoffed and took a seat next to his buddy where they proceeded to stretch out. I had a feeling I would like hitting tennis balls at little harder at him than would be considered professional.

CHAPTER 6

Loaded lunch tray in hand, I glanced up at the sound of my name being called. "Hi, Kesara. What are you doing on this side of campus?"

She ducked her head with a sheepish grin. "The café in our building is usually filled with people who want things from Tavian. I prefer eating here when I have time."

"If I promise I won't ask you for anything from Tavian, may I sit with you?"

"Please do." She beamed, her smile inviting me as much as her words.

I plunked the tray down and took a seat. "Thank you for setting up those professor conferences. It would have taken me weeks to get around to seeing them all, but you managed to get them lined up for only two days."

"How's that going?"

"I don't think I should tell you about some of their reactions. It'll just make your boss's job more complicated."

Her brow furrowed as worry slinked into her eyes. "Is it something he should be worried about?"

"No, sorry, I should have said that what I expect from my players appears to be quite different that what most professors were willing to do for the athletes. I won't have my players slip through the cracks, even if a lot of them just hope to leave early for the NBA."

She smiled, slow and genuine. "I knew you'd be different." The words were spoken as if part of an inner dialogue that no one should overhear. "Is there anything else you need?"

"I think I promised not to ask for anything when I sat down."

"I meant from me, not Tavian. You don't need to get on my good side to ask him for whatever you want."

I felt the seriousness in her lighthearted remark. The other coaches must try to manipulate her to get in front of her boss. It couldn't be an easy job to hold. "If you can point me in the right direction to list a work-study job for a team manager and where I might find some tutors who are not cute girls willing to do anything to help one of the basketball players, I'd appreciate it."

"I can set that up for you."

"No." I reached to grasp her arm and was immediately overloaded with the sensation of warmth and softness. "I just need to know where the work-study office is and how I go about finding tutors for each of the classes."

"Graysen," she started, glancing up from where my hand still touched her arm. "You've been thrown practically mid-season into a job that you didn't realize you were taking. This will take me twenty minutes to do. Please let me help you."

"I've got twenty minutes," I assured her.

"You don't like asking for things." Her smile was all-knowing, and if she weren't such a nice woman, I'd label it infuriating. "I've noticed that about you. Tavian asks me daily to help him find the wallet that's been in his jacket pocket ever since I've known him. You show effusive gratitude for a schedule that I pulled off a computer and a few phone calls to get you meeting times. You, my dear, are probably too independent for this job you've taken."

If she weren't dead right, I'd probably be bristling right now. Plus, she had a teasing smile that made me think I'd known her for years. "Twenty minutes?"

"Less if you've got the job description ready."

I shook my head, giving in. "You could probably handle my job better than I can."

"Not a chance, but more importantly, I don't want it. I like my job and my boss. That's all I need or want from work."

I liked that she'd said that. It wasn't because I was Tavian's best friend and she hoped I'd report back to him. She took pride in her job, ratcheting my respect for her into the stratosphere. "Okay, thank you for the offer. If I beat you to the cafeteria line here next week and any week thereafter, will you let me buy your lunch?"

She shook her head, smiling. "Only until you realize that paybacks aren't necessary."

I blinked a few times. "Sure they are. You're taking time out of your workday to help me. That's not part of your job description."

"Friends don't need payback, Graysen." Her eyes showed her sincerity. "And I hope to become your friend."

The way she said it made me think that she didn't take friendship lightly. So many people these days just throw that word about like it applied to absolutely everyone they've met. Few people seemed to hold friendship as sacred as I did. Seems like I've just found one of the rare ones. "I'd like that, too."

* * *

A sea of mixed expressions met me as I walked back into the viewing room. I'd won over at least three of them, possibly four. They'd liked the tennis yesterday and the football tosses today, but I was about to lose some of them again.

"Jeez! Didn't we just have a team meeting?" I think it was Frank who'd spoken up. I wasn't good with their voices yet.

"We're all still getting to know one another, so we'll be having plenty of these over the next few weeks." That seemed to quiet everyone down. They'd seen me in action at two practices. I'd had to snap at one or two players in every session, so they knew I meant business. "First, I'd like to say how pleased I was by the skills sessions today. You all showed great athleticism. It's definitely something we're going to build on for this season." I let them soak up the compliment. "I'm also sure you know that this isn't the team from last year. We've got one senior and lost all but two juniors. None of the sophomores had any playing time in their freshman year. That means we're going to have to work as a team to win. I know that's a novel concept in men's basketball, but, hey, it's a proven technique." That probably wasn't called for, but I was getting sick of their attitude.

"What's that supposed to mean?" one of the small forwards grumped.

"It means that men's college ball and the NBA have shifted from teamwork to one-on-one matchups. That won't work for our team. We're going to stick with the basics. We work as a team; we win as a team. It's always worked with my teams."

Laughter sounded from more than a couple of players before Wendell scoffed, "Yeah, but women's ball, I mean, come on."

"Come on, what, Wendell?" I asked devoid of any humor.

"Women aren't as athletic as men so teamwork is all they have." He said it so simply, like I was a moron for not understanding this common truth. Enough heads nodded along with him that I knew I had to address this directly.

"What's your definition of athletic?" I posed, reining in my ire.

"Well, you know, y'all can't dunk."

Typical. "I see. So, your definition of athleticism is how high someone can jump?"

"Not only that," another chimed in. "Women don't have an inside game. It's all jump shots and no offensive rebounds."

"This is very interesting." It wasn't, but I turned and picked up a marker to write the words Dunk and Inside Game on the whiteboard. "Anyone else?" They started yelling out suggestions, and I wrote them all down no matter how stupid or sexist the suggestion. "So, what I'm getting is that if I bring in the women's high jumper, the women's 100 meter sprinter, the women's rugby and softball stars, watch them all whip your asses at their particular specialty, you'll stop thinking that men are more athletic than women?" Several of them scoffed while most of the others sunk into their chairs and crossed their arms. Or should I just invite any of the thirty or so women in the WNBA and college ranks who dunk to prove you wrong?"

"I know one or two can dunk, but it's not part of your game. And you won't find a woman more athletic than me," Wendell insisted.

"Knowledge is power. I've always believed that." I smiled serenely at him. "I know how fast you run, how high you jump, how far you throw, how well you catch, and how many sports you played in high school. You don't know any of those things about me. That means that if we were to play one-on-one, I'm the only one who knows for sure who'd win. You think you know, but that's an assumption. I actually know." A cough sounded from the back of the room. I zeroed in on Nate and something in his expression told me he agreed with me.

"Let's go right now." He started to stand, all bluster and arrogance.

"We're not playing, Wendell. I don't need to prove myself, and if you're wrong about your assumption, you'll probably be humiliated. Not for the reason you think—that I'm a woman and you're a man—but because I'm more than a decade older than you, haven't played competitively for eight years, and you've got four inches on me which gives you a half a step to react to anything I do. Those reasons should be the source of your humiliation if you lost."

"I don't have to be worried about being humiliated."

"You haven't even given a thought to how you'd feel if I won, have you?" My question made him stall. "That if we played to ten right now, I could win by six. That if I beat you by even one, you'd be humiliated. Are you prepared for that?"

"I won't lose."

Now I just wanted to smack him. Cocky was one thing; stupid was something entirely different. "I'm nowhere near the best female player there is, but I'm guessing you've never seen me play. Has anyone?" I looked out and saw two hands rise, one was Nate's. "In your opinion, is there any chance that I might actually beat Wendell?"

"Yes," Nate said while the other said, "Maybe."

"Two of your teammates think it's possible that I could edge you out. Since you've never seen me play, you might want to listen to the two guys who have." I held up a hand to stop him from continuing. "Nevertheless, we won't be playing because you're not ready to accept the consequences if you lose. If at some point during the season I think you've matured enough, we'll play. For now, we're concentrating on turning this group of men into a team."

"We were a good enough team last year," Ollie stated.

"Really?" I looked at him, challenging. "My team was in the Final Four last year. How'd your team do?" They'd only made it to the first round, even with all the superstars they no longer had, and their stunned looks told me they all realized that I'd just put them in their place.

"We're going to learn to work together in everything. I don't care if you can't stand each other; we keep our differences in the family. No one but us will know if you don't get along. And if you don't, you'll find out that I have the annoying habit of making you spend more time with the person you don't get along with. So, look around the room, fellas, these are your new brothers. You may fight with them, they can annoy you, but in the end, you're stuck with them, so you'd better find a way to get along or it's going to be a really long winter."

I signaled to Bill and Damon to hand out the playbooks. "Start learning these plays, guys. We'll be doing a walk through on the first official practice," Damon told them.

"If you don't know them backwards and forwards, you're running," Bill added, winking at me. He'd figured out after two days how serious I was about fitness. They'd also been very pleased that I'd asked them both for a few plays to include so they could feel ownership right away.

"One last thing, the best way to improve on all your baselines is to train on your own or with your teammates. The hour skills session a day isn't going to meet my goals. Weight training, endurance training, running, and swimming is highly recommended. Any questions?" I cut them off before they could ask anything. They didn't know enough to ask anything right now. "Weight room is down the hall, fellas."

CHAPTER 7

Even though I suspected it, I was still a little surprised when everyone showed up on Monday. As much grumbling as they'd been doing—the little babies—I didn't think any of them had the courage to stand by their grumbles and quit. It wasn't perfect, though. Wendell had missed two of his classes today, and my shooting guard, Ollie, and small forward, Jeff, had left one of their classes early. Pushing boundaries. They were about to find out that my boundaries were reinforced by electric fencing.

All three of them sat in my office, two looked smug, but the other had a touch of guilt ruining the homogenous scene. "What was your understanding about class attendance?"

"We have to go," Ollie answered.

"Do you have to stay?"

"Uhh," he hesitated.

" 'Yes' is the answer you're looking for," I informed him then turned to Wendell. "And your understanding?"

"After today, you'd be making us go to all our classes."

Actually I'd said the rules would start today, but I could see how that could be misinterpreted. "All right." I considered my options. "From now on, you will attend every class from start to finish. You will not be late or try to leave early. You will complete every assignment and take every test. You will participate if asked. All of your professors are reporting back to me, which is why we're in here today." Little punks hadn't expected to get caught. "Just so we're all clear, what happens starting tomorrow if you leave early or don't go to class?"

"We don't start," Jeff offered as his buddy, Wendell, snorted.

I wanted to pound the arrogant smugness out of him. "I don't care how good you are. You won't start if you miss a class." I waited until I thought he got it. "If today had counted, and be very glad I'm letting it slide based on a misunderstanding, you'd sit the bench the entire game based on the two classes you missed. Don't do that to your team, Wendell."

"Whatever," he sighed.

If he'd been a sassy woman, I'm sure he'd have formed a "W" with his fingers. This was a pet peeve of mine, heightened over the seasons of dealing with college kids. "That's not a response."

He glared at me but finally submitted. "Yeah, I get it."

I could tell he barely managed to keep the word "bitch" out of the sentence. "Great, head out to tutoring and see you all tomorrow at skills."

"We playing football again?" Jeff asked as they stood.

"Sculling."

"Seriously?" He turned back with wide excited eyes.

"You'll love it, and it's great exercise." Both physically and in teamwork. It was going to be fun seeing these big men trying to coordinate their oar strokes.

Before he could react, Wendell, pulled him from the office. Wendell was going to be a problem. One I hoped I could conquer before games started.

The good feeling I had about getting through to them ended by noon the next day. All but two of them had skipped their classes. Damn that Wendell. I should probably take the good out of this. He'd managed to organize a boycott. That showed leadership, didn't it?

Assembled in the viewing room once again, half of them carried a proud smile, the other half looked sick to their stomachs. "Hello, team."

"Hi, Coach," a few of them offered. I was too angry to make them try it again.

"Dash and Nate were the only ones that went to class today, so you two will have the regularly planned skills session. The rest of you will be running all hour. For every lap you walk, two more will be added to the usual amount at tomorrow's practice. As for the first game—"

"Can't not start us all," Wendell interrupted from the back row.

"Actually I've got three choices. One," I held up a finger to emphasize my point. "I can impose the suspension on half of you, and the other half will be suspended for the next game. Two, I can hold walk-on tryouts for the rest of this week and pick up a few players for the first game. Or three, I can forfeit the first game because I've only got two players who can start." That one hit home. Their little eyes bugged out. It didn't matter the stand they were trying to take. None of them wanted to lose and certainly not without a fight.

"Why would you do that?" Ollie called out.

"What, forfeit a game?" I asked innocently. "Do you know how important the first three minutes of every game is? If I don't have my starters, we could easily slip into a hole that we can't get out of. I might as well forfeit. So let me ask you, why would you skip a class when you knew damn well that I wouldn't start you?"

"I never start, what's it matter?" The response came from my third string power forward, Anthony.

I laughed at his naiveté. "When I said you don't start, that means that you miss the first three minutes of your usual game time. If all you get is three minutes, then you've lost it."

He shot a death glare at Wendell. As if I didn't already know the ring leader, I now had proof. What I really respected was that neither Dash nor Nate were whining about the consequences of Wendell's actions. If I chose to forfeit, they'd live with my decision.

"There's a fourth option, and it's only for you, Wendell. I know you organized this, so if you step up and take responsibility, you'll sit the first game and none of your teammates will have the penalty. So, what's it going to be?"

"Do it, man," Victor, who was Frank's backup, urged.

"She's bluffing," Wendell sneered.

"Step up, genius," Dash whispered.

"What's your decision, Wendell?" I posed.

"Nope."

Smug asshole, and now with the groans from the crowd, I thought he'd lost a little of their faith. "Fine. Dash, Nate, you're my starting team. I'll rotate suspensions so that we can have enough to start for the first game. I hope you all realize that these penalties are cumulative. Next time you miss a class, you'll sit a game. Two more after that, and you're off the team."

"Aw, damn, Wendell, what the hell?" Ollie shouted, and several other members came up with similar expressions of frustration. How could they think that the penalties would start over after every game? Either men communicated very differently than women or these guys were complete morons.

"Seems like you fell on your face with this stunt, Wendell. Since your team now understands the full consequences of the actions you goaded them into, I'll give you till tomorrow's skills session to accept my deal. You sit out the first game, and it wipes out the first offense for everyone, including you. You're a team, guys, talk to him." I made eye contact with each of them. "Try this again, and I'll hold walk-on tryouts. I won't have any qualms about starting them and cutting some of you if they're passable. Do I make myself clear?" Nods and mumbled agreement met me. God, they were like little toddlers throwing a tantrum because I wouldn't put soda in their sippy cups. "Fine. For those of you in Professor Chang's English Lit class, you've got a paper due tomorrow. We'll be breaking up the usual skills groups so that you six can stay and work with your tutor. Dash, you're working with Damon on stations, Jeff, Ollie, and Wendell, you three are up first for an hour of running. Get to it."

I really wanted to shake them senseless for their stupidity and putting the team in jeopardy. Arrogant young men, this was one of the main reasons I'd never wanted to coach them. I honestly never would have thought it would go this far, though.

CHAPTER 8

Travel plans for the second week of games took over the center of my desk. Jason, the new team manager, had double checked reservations at the hotels and bookings with buses as well as our practice times on away courts. I was really liking this kid.

The rest of the week's sessions had gone well, not one peep out of the idiots who thought they were smarter than me, especially since I had them running for nearly two whole days. Kinda hard to complain when you're so tired you can't even move your lips. And surprise of the century, Wendell stepped up and took the penalty for a whole game. Got to love peer pressure.

"Hi there, gorgeous, you ready?" Darby stood in my doorway again. Or a more dressed up, made up, beautiful version of Darby.

Wow, that dress looked, well, wow. I'd been so nervous about this dinner at the start of the week until this blow up with Wendell and the team that I'd not had time to be nervous since then. I hadn't completely forgotten as was evidenced by the fact that I had on street clothes. Not as nice as hers, but better than the exercise clothes I usually wore for practice.

"Hi, you look nice." I greeted. "Are we going someplace fancy? I'm afraid I didn't dress for that."

She slinked toward me, or it looked like she slinked because when she moved, it was fluid, like a panther stalking its prey. "You look scrumptious."

Scrumptious? Was that a compliment? I was usually pretty good at making friends, but she threw me off kilter, always had. "Thanks. I was just finishing up. Where to for dinner? I'm still feeling my way around, so any suggestion you've got is fine with me."

"Easy. I like that in a woman," she joked. Or please, let that be a joke. "There's a nice place at Jack London Square that I thought we'd try."

"I'm still in an apartment near there, so that works out great for me."

"Oh, did you want to follow me over in your car?" Disappointment crossed her face.

"Actually, I ran to work. Haven't had much chance to get in my normal workout with all that's going on."

"You run through downtown Oakland? Are you strapped?" Again, I hoped that was a joke otherwise it might sound racist, or at the very least, classist.

"Every city has good parts and bad, and it's not even two miles. I've been on the track in between appointments and skills sessions."

"Not a gym rat, huh?" She reached over and squeezed my bicep. "I take that back. Still as buff as you were when we first met. Damn, lady, how much time do you spend working out?" Her hand was now rubbing the length of my arm. Tingles moved with the fingertips and that fuzzy haze began again.

"Not much." Which was the truth. I spent time doing the things I liked, usually involving physical activity that helped keep up the form. I was nowhere near as ripped as I'd been when I played professionally, but I still had good muscle tone. Darby had always been slimmer than I was, sinewy to my athletic. It worked for her but would have gotten my pushed around on court.

"C'mon, I'll drive." She pulled on my arm to get us going but thankfully dropped it once I was in motion. I couldn't think clearly when she touched me, well, when anyone I didn't know very well touched me, but her especially.

When we'd settled around a table at the restaurant, I was glad I'd worn my best slacks and blouse. This was a nice place. She fit right in with her halter dress. On the way over, we'd reminisced a bit about our first meeting. She was easy to talk to, still had that effervescence about herself, a fun person to be around.

"How do you like Oakland? Quite a change from Washington?"

"I spent a lot of time here when I played ball, so I'm used to the area."

"Oh, that's right, you used to play in Sacramento, didn't you?" Something in her tone didn't sound genuine. Either she already knew that and was being polite or she didn't really care, but that was probably my nerves playing into the assessment. "Must be weird coming back. Are you being recognized all over the place?"

I chuckled at her enthusiasm. "No, thankfully. Once you're done with the WNBA, you're pretty much done. More people recognized me from the coaching gig."

"You were so successful I can see why." She glanced around, perhaps looking to see if anyone was ready to pounce on me right now. When she turned back she seemed a little disappointed that several people hadn't materialized at the table to ask for my autograph. I hadn't had that happen in years, so I hope she'd be fine with that never happening.

"I saw that your team did well the other night."

"Did you go?"

"No, sorry, but I'm definitely going to make it to a game before your season ends. They look good."

"They are, and you'd better make it to more than one."

I laughed at her forceful tone. She was kidding but not by much. "More than one, for sure."

"Do you miss Washington? Leaving anyone special behind?" Her blue eyes sparkled.

"I used to be okay with living in three different cities while I played because of the offseason coaching or the overseas leagues, but ever since I retired, I've really taken to living in one place. Washington was great, but it's nice to be back on the west coast."

"You must miss your friends? Boyfriend? Girlfriend? Both?"

Both? Yeah, I'm a hussy like that. "I do miss my friends. I had a great coaching staff working with me. Kristine, James, and Rebecca were close friends by the time I left. They were pretty angry that I made this move, but since Kristine is now the head coach, they'll get over it."

She laughed softly, the sound rolling over the table in featherlike waves. "You managed not to answer the question I wanted you most to answer." She smiled broadly at my furrowed brow. "Boyfriend or, please let it be, girlfriend?"

My mouth nudged ajar. Something about her question didn't seem like idle curiosity. And certainly not the way she asked if I had a girlfriend.

"C'mon. You're among friends. I've always had a vibe about you."

"Vibe?"

"You know, a gay vibe." The statement came out with certainty. I didn't have time to be startled. "You can tell me, Gray. I'm sure you know I'm a lesbian, and you have to know I'm interested in you."

Holy...

"You're my fantasy woman, have been for decades since I first met you. So, spill, tell me you're going to make my fantasy come true."

...Hell. I was someone's fantasy? Hers? This beautiful woman whom everyone liked and so many lusted after? Did the world turn upside down as soon as I crossed into the Pacific Time Zone? "Fantasy?" I managed with a dry mouth.

"I'm coming on too strong, aren't I?" A touch of worry marred her expression. "My sisters always tell me that I need to tone it down, but I can't help it with you. After all these years, I finally have you in the same city and permanently. So, I'm putting it all out there tonight. I didn't want there to be any confusion about what I want."

"What you want?" *GAH! Could I please stop repeating everything she said?*

"You."

One word, sounds like sue, only less litigious. She wants me. Damn, that even sounds weird just thinking it. Why would she want me? I'm not a person who brings out wanting in people, or I never have been, or I've been oblivious to it my whole adult life.

Jeez, I mean, this was only my eighth date, if this was a date. And I know, eight dates, right? But, like I said, when you're really good at something, other things fall by the way side. My love life foremost among them. Since I'm pretty convinced I was born without a sex drive, I hadn't ever felt like I'd missed much. Why date when I felt nothing? Okay, this time, maybe I didn't feel nothing, maybe this time was a little different, and it wasn't because she was a woman when the others had been men. This time was different because it was Darby. Was she my fantasy woman, too? Honestly, no, but only because I didn't have fantasies of that nature. I must be broken. Everyone else had fantasies, right? Why didn't I? Maybe I just needed to think about it. I could try to fantasize about her. Hmm, that might work.

"Gray?"

Try later. "Huh?"

"Shocked?" She smiled understandingly, and my, was it a beautiful smile. "I wanted to be upfront about this. I want more than just friendship from you, have for a long time."

"This is...I mean, that's very flattering."

"Oh, God." A panicked look came over her face. "You're not going to say that you're flattered but it's not me it's you, are you? Just lie to me and say you've got a boyfriend. I can handle unavailable but don't crush my ego by telling me you're the biggest lesbian on the planet, but I do nothing for you."

My head shook, trying to snap all the whirling thoughts to attention. "I don't know what to say."

"That's better than turning the tables over and racing from the restaurant, I guess." She reached across and grasped my hand. The touch felt comforting. "Just tell me I have a chance?"

"I haven't thought about dating in a while." If she knew how long of a while it might put a stop to this before it had a chance to get started. "You've thrown me for a loop. I'm still trying to catch up."

The smile that surfaced on her face brought out sparkles in her blue eyes and added definition to her sleek cheekbones. "I'm still in the running, then. Good. Enough pressure for tonight, we'll save that for our second date."

Second date? In way over my head here, but it felt pretty good.

CHAPTER 9

In every season, the most exciting day for me was the first day of official practice. This year was no different. I learned so much from the first full practice.

Not surprisingly, Dash was the first into the gym from the locker room. I'd gotten into coaching for kids like this one.

"First day, Coach!" Exhilaration danced in his brown eyes. He'd shaved his head sometime yesterday, the look a startling but attractive change. I was betting that he wouldn't shave it again unless we lost a game.

"You bet, Dash." I bumped his fist as he jogged by, turning back when I heard the rest of the squad wonder through the door. I blew my whistle and called out, "Killers, let's go."

Groans echoed in the gym when they realized they weren't going to get out of our usual starting drill. The whistle blew again and for the first time, I saw all twelve players race to the free throw line then swivel and come back. Dash and Nate were competing on fastest time. Wendell was huffing pretty hard, too. Jeff had some heft and lumbered along. Frank and Anthony weren't too fast either.

"Damn, those are a bitch." Jeff bent over to grab his shorts cuffs while sucking in air after the set was done.

I walked right up to him, making him stand in surprise. "Before I make you run laps, I'm going to tell you why."

"What'd I do?" He managed to channel a petulant pre-teen near screech.

"What's a bitch?"

His eyes popped wide. "Not you, Coach. I didn't say you!" he pleaded.

While I appreciated his panic, everyone needed this lesson. "I know you didn't. I asked you to repeat what you said."

"Oh." The relief slouched his frame. "I was saying that those wind sprints were tough."

"They are tough, but you said they were a bitch. Why are they a bitch?"

"Because they're tough. The worst thing we have to do."

"Why aren't they an asshole or a bastard? Why a bitch?" He flicked his eyes away, pleading with the other coaches. "I'll tell you why. It's somehow acceptable to associate a word that is often a derogatory term for women with horrible things. You're helping to demonize women by using this word interchangeably with unpleasant occurrences in everyday life."

"I didn't mean any offense."

The gym had gone quiet. Nearly everyone looked at me like they would their moody sister when they assumed all of her anger had to do with PMS.

Without emotion, I explained, "I know you didn't. I'm telling you that it's offensive whether you meant it or not. And I'm telling every person here, I do not tolerate sexist, racist, homophobic, xenophobic, or any other bigoted remarks to be made during practice, on road trips, or during games. I'd prefer you don't use them ever, but I can't police your comments when you're not on team time. I also won't allow you to disparage any of your teammates. And while we're on the topic, no swearing during games."

"What?" three of the biggest potty mouths screeched.

"Swear words can get you technicals. You swear, you sit the bench. Bigoted remarks trigger laps in practice, so get moving Jeff, ten laps."

"Shit," he swore as he started into a trot.

"So glad you got my point," I called after him and turned back to the team. "Let's do a walk through of every play first. Take your spots. Hustle up."

That started the rest of our first official practice. By the end, they were so tired I almost let them off on wind sprints. Almost, but they needed to hurt this first week so they could build up endurance.

"Intense, Graysen," Bill commented as we were racking the balls.

"They limped out of here," Damon put in.

"Too much?" I asked.

"Well..." Bill looked like he wanted to say yes.

"They've never worked that hard," Damon offered.

"I realize that, but we've spoken about this. The team's skill level isn't good enough to compete with the schedule they've got this year. Are we still agreed on that?"

"Yes." They both nodded.

"Then the only way to compete is through fitness. Right now, they aren't in the kind of shape they need to be in to outplay their opponents."

"Makes sense," Damon agreed. Bill just nodded, but I could tell he was still a little reticent about it.

"At the risk of alienating you two, it may be because I didn't recruit these guys, but I'm wondering if it's all male athletes or just this team that complains constantly. The women I've had on my teams run laps for the griping these guys do. My women start with five sets of wind sprints during the first week of practice. These guys did three and they whined like I was making them dig ditches in ninety degree heat for two hours." They looked amazed by my revelation. I'd known that women's teams trained differently than the men's, but I guess I didn't realize to what extent. "I get that you're worried because they aren't used to this kind of workout. They'll be coming to you to vent, but they're not in shape. Other teams could embarrass them right now."

"Five?" Damon managed through his shock.

"Yep, and when one of my female players says that wind sprints are a 'bitch,' she does twenty laps. Ten for the sexist remark and ten because she should know better." That got a smile out of both of them. I could tell they'd been worried that I lived on some man-hating island of feminists who thought all men should be eradicated. Right now, I only wanted a couple of men eradicated, but I hoped that by the time the games started, I'd win those guys over, too. Damon nodded and raised his hand up for a high five. I did the same to Bill and watched as they took the ball rack back to the equipment room.

As I was throwing on my sweat jacket, the gym's doors opened and the women's volleyball team entered. They had a game tonight, one I hadn't planned on attending until I figured out what to do about Darby. I thought about dashing through the door to the women's locker rooms and out the back exit, but it was too late.

"Graysen!" Darby called out as she followed her team inside. Her three assistant coaches turned in surprise at her excited exclamation. She scooted past her team and approached me. Her arm came around my shoulders, pulling me against her. "Ladies, come meet the new men's basketball coach, an old friend of mine, Graysen Viola."

"Way to go," one of them spoke up while another was saying, "Cool."

Several other greetings called out, but I only noticed that Darby still had her arm around me. Even four days later, I still didn't know how to handle the swirl of feelings at hearing her intentions toward me. No one had ever voiced that she or he wanted me. They might have made overtures when I was out with my teammates, but I'd brush them off because they were usually strangers. If I'd known them, I would have brushed them off because I wasn't interested. That didn't apply with Darby. I'd taken notice of her years ago, and I couldn't just walk away from that because she was moving too fast for me.

"Hi, ladies. Good job with your game last week. Are you going to win tonight?"

"You bet!" all of them said at once. It made me smile. My women's teams had always been like this, too.

"Good answer," I told them and stepped back to break Darby's one-armed shoulder grip. "We were just finishing up. First day, so my timing is a little off. We'll make sure we're done long before you need the court next time."

"Not a problem. My girls won't hesitate to run them out of the gym." Darby's comment elicited a round of laughter.

"I've got a meeting with Tavian, so I'd better run. It was nice to meet you all. Good luck on the game tonight."

"You going to catch it?" Darby asked, her eyes twinkling with a secret.

I stepped closer because I didn't want her team to hear. "It's dinner with his family. They've been having me over once a week. I think it's because I'm free entertainment for their kids."

"Oh, all right, but maybe Thursday's game?"

I mentally went through what I had to do on Thursday. I should be watching game tape, but that was every night now. "Sure, Thursday's game."

"Promise?"

Consternation scrunched my brow. We weren't in elementary school. Saying that I promised something wouldn't make it any more valid than saying I was going to Thursday's game. "I'll be at Thursday's game." When I said I'd do something, I did it. I didn't need to throw in a word to make it more legitimate.

CHAPTER 10

As I took my place in the cashier line, I realized the conversation coming from the table closest to the half wall separation was about me. I recognized the voices of some of my players, and what they were saying I shouldn't be hearing.

"She's a fucking bitch, man. What the hell were they thinking hiring a woman? And she's all making us run because she doesn't think we're good enough. That's BS, man, I could beat her with one hand tied behind my back," what sounded like Wendell spoke up.

"Right, dude, dream on. I've seen her play. She's got some game," another player retorted.

"For a chick, sure. I'll give her that, but she ain't beatin' me. C'mon, you know I'd kick her ass. The only reason she doesn't want to play me is because she knows damn well the second I kick her ass I won't listen to a word she says."

Damn Wendell was an idiot. Did he think that if he'd kicked his old coach's ass, which he actually could have done with that one hand tied behind his back, he wouldn't have had to listen to him either?

"Do you know anything about women's pro ball, Dub?" a new voice asked.

"What? That it's like watching *Hoosiers* without any of the suspense?"

Oh, Wendell's just hilarious. I wished he had the guts to say something like that in practice. I'd make him run for two weeks.

"No, man. Nothing like that. They practice against men who mostly play in European leagues. I've seen her play against men, her teammates, and other women's teams. She's really good."

"So? She played against some half-assed men. Doesn't mean she'd beat me."

"Yes, she would," the voice insisted. "She took on our athletic director one-on-one. She didn't beat him every game, but she beat him enough times. She's that good."

"No way, bro." Another voice piped up.

"Yep, and, dude, you should see how good she is when she goes three-on-three with her teammates. She could beat any team nine times out of ten."

Who was this guy doing all the talking? It sounded like Nate or Victor, but how would either have known I'd played against Tavian? Only players on my former teams had seen me play him. I so wanted to peek around the wall, but I kept my place in line.

"You lie, Nate," Wendell blew him off. "We've got to figure out how to get her fired."

"I'm not listening to your crap anymore. I'd suggest you guys stop listening, too." Nate's no longer mystery voice faded as he pulled back from the table.

"Screw him. I'm working on Bill. I think he's going to come around. How are you guys doing with Damon?" Wendell asked.

"Hard to say. He listens, but he won't commit to saying she needs to go."

I should feel nervous that they were trying to rope Damon and Bill into this, but I didn't feel I needed to be. They had a lot of autonomy, and neither of them was ready to take over the head coaching job.

"I don't know, man, I think we just let it play out. I mean if she's not a good enough coach for us to win, she'll be fired anyway, right?"

"Plus, I'm in better shape than I've ever been in." I recognized Eli's deep voice and smiled at his truth.

"That's because all we ever do is run in practice. Whoever heard of running ten laps because I 'used a term that represents the worst part of American history and should be eradicated from the English language.' I mean, come on!" Wendell's impression of my voice was awful, but he'd gotten the words right. "I'm black, you're black, all but two of us are black. I can call you whatever I want. It's only racist if a white person says it."

"No, it's not," someone else spoke up. I wished I was better at recognizing voices. I was also starting to feel bad for listening in on their conversation, but I couldn't help being stuck in line and them being so damn loud. "You got a T for using the same word in a game last year, just like she said you would."

"Whatever. I still say she's a goddamn bitch."

I finally broke free after paying and headed around the half wall straight for them. The ones facing me all reared back in their seats as they saw me approach. I carried a smile on my face as Wendell swung around and saw me. He had the decency to look worried. "Now that was the correct use of the term, at least as far as you're concerned, Wendell. Though, my greatest hope for you is that you'll finally realize that a woman who disagrees with you isn't automatically a bitch. See you at practice, fellas." I sauntered away from their table toward the windows where I'd spotted Kesara.

"Nice going, dude, we'll be running all practice now," Frank shot at Wendell.

No, they wouldn't, but I'd let them sweat it out until practice. They weren't on court or at an official team event, so I wouldn't hold them accountable for their thoughts or opinions.

Plus, I *was* a bitch to Wendell, but only because he was such an asshole.

"Hey, Graysen, what was that about?" Kesara asked, glancing over my shoulder to where the guys were now getting up to dump their trays.

"Shouldn't you have warned me just how different boys are from girls? I know I couldn't count on Tavian to do it. You should have stepped in and told me to run screaming from this job."

She leaned forward, concern marking her face. "Is it really bad?"

I let out a breath. "No, it just takes some getting used to. They aren't like what I remember from Tavian's team or the players we'd go against in practice."

"I'm sure if you asked Tavian to talk to them, he'd be happy to help."

"No!" I practically screamed and followed up with, "Sorry. It was my choice to take this on. I knew exactly what I was getting into. I can't have a man pull me out of this. They'd expect that, and I won't respect myself for doing it."

"Okay." She nodded, worried but letting the subject drop. "The boss said he showed you some houses on Sunday. Are you thinking of buying in the area?"

"My condo in DC sold last week. I was thinking of staying in an apartment, but it's a good time to buy right now."

"Where are you looking?"

"Tave and Jaci are only showing me places within a five block radius of their house, but I'd rather get something in or near Berkeley." Something about that town spoke both sophistication and comfort. I knew I'd be happy there, even if I only stayed for this season.

"If you need any help house hunting, let me know. My cousin is a real estate agent. He gets great listings all the time."

I liked how she so freely offered help. She was a problem solver. Something I found easy to relate to. A lot of my other friends didn't want solutions. They just wanted to be able to whine. "This isn't the cousin with the three strikes, is it?"

She smiled brightly but a hint of wistfulness toned it down. "No, he's a different worry. Santiago, the agent, is a great guy, very dedicated. He can easily find you something. That is if you want to work with an agent?"

"I always have before, and it'll keep me out of Jaci's clutches. I adore them, but I do not want to be their sitter any night they want some peace and quiet."

She laughed, obviously familiar with their kids. They were very sweet, but lots of energy. Even when I made them run laps, they'd giggle the entire time. And yes, I made them run laps whenever they insulted one another. I knew that by the time they were done with the two circles of the yard, giggling away as I barked out matching orders, they would be back to being best friends. Plus they adored me, so they did anything I said. "We can head over to his office anytime."

"If this is some favor that you have to call in, I can find an agent on my own."

"No," she insisted, reaching out to squeeze my forearm. The touch brought a sense of calm and reassurance. "You're doing me a favor by using him. The housing market has been really slow these days. He'll be delighted to have a new client, and he'll worship me for bringing you to him."

"Okay, if you're sure?"

"Definitely."

* * *

On Thursday night, I watched as Darby scanned the crowd at the game. She looked beautiful in form fitting cream colored slacks and a green blouse in the school's shade. Her blue eyes danced when she spotted the frat boys who'd painted their faces and chests. Frat boys were the same everywhere.

When they introduced her, she did a little circle, acknowledging each section with a wave. She caught sight of me as she finished her turn, waving just to me, and that smile—my goodness. I felt my heart thump erratically in response.

I still hadn't made a decision about what to do with her. I felt like I was being pressured without her saying or doing anything more than expressing her interest in me. I just didn't know if I wanted to take that step. We were colleagues. It would be awkward if it didn't work out, and from what I knew about relationships, they were a complicated mess. Only Tavian had a decent one. Everyone else I knew spent more time bemoaning the relationship than exalting it.

The match started and Darby instantly focused. It was close for two sets. Then the other team pulled ahead and won in four. Her team looked dejected, but Darby gave them some words and by the time they left the floor a few had smiles on their faces. She followed them to the locker room, and I wondered if I should wait or head home. We hadn't made plans to speak after the game, so I started out with the rest of the crowd.

"Ms. Viola?" A young blond woman with a dry erase board in her hand stopped me before I hit the exit door. "Coach wanted me to grab you before you left." She led me over to the team bench.

"Thanks." I prompted her exit then took a seat, wondering what I'd say when Darby came inside, wondering if she'd try to hug me again, wondering if she thought I'd been awkward when she hugged me after dinner. I felt like the whole night had passed in a blur after she'd declared her feelings for me, like I'd been hypnotized and not in complete control of all my faculties.

Suddenly, sitting here, waiting and thinking, didn't have much appeal. I went over to the scorer's table and found the spare game ball. Concentrating instead on bump passes and sets, I managed to keep from worrying myself into dust.

"I should have guessed you could play volleyball, too." Darby's voice made me miss the next bump, the ball shooting off the side of my outstretched arms. She held back a laugh as I managed a lame wave. "Sorry you had to see us lose. My girls are usually better than that."

Gathering my senses, I analyzed it from a coach's perspective. "I saw a lot of talent there."

"They're having trouble closing out matches."

"They're young." I bent to retrieve the ball and caught her watching me intently, or watching a part of me intently. "Mental toughness comes with experience. When they decide no one can beat them, they won't be beaten."

"I should have you come talk to them." She moved toward me and took the ball out of my hands. "I always wanted to see you spike the ball. The way you grabbed those rebounds made me wonder just how hard you could spike a ball from that height."

"I seem to remember you being the killer on your team. I don't think I could hold a candle to your technique."

"Wanna give it a try?" she asked. I looked down at my footwear then shook my head. "C'mon, Gray, this is an easy fantasy to fulfill." She winked and headed over to the middle of the court as I felt my cheeks warm. Wondering if someone could spike a ball wasn't a fantasy, but she managed to put enough innuendo behind the request that I was actually blushing.

"Volleyball's not my sport, Darby."

"One spike, for me?" She batted her eyelashes in a theatrical manner. I was starting to remember how much of a goofball she could be, and I found myself laughing.

I headed over to where she stood, taking a spot three steps to the side and two from the net. I tipped my chin up, indicating she should set the ball. As fluidly as she walked, she placed the ball up onto her palms and flipped her hands sending the ball into a high arc above the net. I took two steps toward her and the net before leaping up as high as I could and swinging my arm into action. The slap of the ball against my fist echoed through the empty gym as the ball rocketed toward the ground on the other side of the net.

"Damn!" Darby shouted. "That was hot. If I didn't know just how good you were at basketball, I'd be ripping you apart for not having played volleyball. If we'd had you on the Olympic team, we would have won gold instead of coming in fifth place."

"I'm nowhere near Olympic caliber, and you know it. Thank you, though, that was fun. Want me to set you?"

"No, I get the assistant coaches into a game every once in a while." She hustled over to grab the ball. "Unless seeing me spike the ball is a fantasy of yours, too?" That wicked smile played on her lips again.

I shook my head and laughed. Yeah, she had always been a lot of fun. I was going to enjoy getting to know her better, whether we stayed friends or followed her wishes for something more. "It was a good game tonight. You handled them well. It's hard to believe this is your first year as a head coach."

"I learned a lot from Leslie over the last few years," she said of the former coach, setting the ball back behind the scorer's table and turning to face me again.

"You love it, though, don't you?"

"It's awesome." She approached and gripped my shoulder. "But I don't need to tell you."

The hand squeezing softly distracted me for a minute. She was wearing perfume, not cloying, but heavy enough to mask the scent of a once partially filled gym. It would take some getting used to, but for that touch and smile, I'd give it my best effort. "I do enjoy it."

"Thank you for coming tonight."

"It was fun, but I'll let you get back to making sure the team finishes up."

She stared at me for a second then stepped forward and wrapped me into a hug. A breath escaped as she settled against me. She felt so good that I didn't even have time to think about what this meant. "Goodnight, Graysen." She released me and smiled.

"Night, Darby." That hazy feeling was back. I felt like I was buzzed without having had a drink. The effect was rather enjoyable.

CHAPTER 11

When we pulled up in front of a row of storefronts, Kesara reached into the back seat and grabbed a steering lock. I couldn't help but smile. This was a Solara, not a Mercedes, but then again, I'd only been living in Oakland for a few weeks. What did I know?

"Stop laughing," she instructed as we got out of the car. "I love this car."

"I can see that." I bit my lip to keep the full smile from forming.

"Okay, Ms. Jester, what do you drive?"

"I don't have a car."

She stopped then staggered, weaving along the sidewalk. "What kind of Californian are you?"

"One from Washington, DC," I replied dryly, trying to keep from laughing at her appalled reaction. "I lived five blocks from campus and the Metro system was excellent."

"What have you been doing for transportation here?"

"I run to work, and BART takes me everywhere else."

"You're seriously not going to get a car?" Her pretty brown eyes stared at me, disbelief and amazement jousting for dominance.

"I haven't given it much thought. I guess it depends on where I end up living."

Kesara shook her head, the black curls brushing the tops of her shoulders. She gave a bothered sigh, the same kind my mother would give me right before the words, "What am I going to do with you?" came out of her mouth. The fact that Kesara's sigh and head shake were borne of amusement made me feel like we'd known each other for years. Other than with Tavian, I'd never felt this at ease with someone so quickly. I always looked forward to seeing her even if it was just to say hello in the hallways at work.

"Let's at least get you a place to live. We can worry about transportation later." She grabbed my arm and led me through one of the doorways.

An empty reception desk took up most of the space in the front room. I didn't have time to study much else about the reception before a voice called out from the back office.

"*Oye, prima, cómo estás?*" A man with thick black hair and a few facial features that matched the woman standing next to me approached, his arms thrown wide.

"*Muy bien, Santi, e tu?*"

"*Fantástico.*" He grabbed her into a bear hug, lifting her off the ground. He wasn't much taller than she was at five-seven, I'd guess, but he was built. His rolled up cuffs showed muscular forearms. I'd learned a long time ago, you do not mess with people who have muscular forearms.

"Graysen Viola, this is my cousin, Santiago Pacheco."

"It's nice to meet you. Thank you for staying late tonight." I shook his hand.

"It's my pleasure. Anything for my favorite cousin." He gripped her around the shoulders, his gaze as fond as hers. "*Ella es muy alta.*" He looked back at her and continued to speak in rapid Spanish. She responded in clipped tones, giving me an apologetic look.

"Yes, I am tall, I did fit in her car, I don't get nosebleeds, but I have bumped my head on tree branches before," I answered his questions to Kesara in order. The shocked expressions on their faces made me laugh. "I played in Spain for four years, and I detest tourists who expect everyone outside the U.S. to speak English."

Santiago laughed loudly. "You're fluent?"

"Only so many ways to say, 'damn, she's tall.' Believe me, I've heard them all."

He looked sheepish but didn't break eye contact. "Let's have a seat and discuss what you're looking for." We followed him into a nicely appointed office and sat facing his desk. "Sara tells me you're from Washington?"

Sara? Must be a family name. It sounded nice with a Spanish pronunciation.

"Relocated, yes."

He proceeded to ask me what I was looking for, where I was looking, and a whole slew of other real estate questions that convinced me he was damn good at his job. He paused when I told him my price range, shooting an arched eyebrow at his cousin. I hoped it was a good arch and not a you-must-be-joking-if-you-think-you-can-buy-anything-with-that-pittance arch.

I summed up my requirements. "Basically, I want a nice area, at least two bedrooms, no paper walls, and can be sold in a year if I lose my job."

"You won't lose your job." Kesara nudged my shoulder with hers.

Santiago frowned again. "Aren't you the head coach? Shouldn't that have longevity?"

"Not when you're responsible for a team that might not win." I swallowed a scoff.

"Isn't the basketball team ranked pretty high?"

"We're not ranked yet. I hope to change that, but we'll see." I'd been using this as my mantra for the past few weeks.

He continued to look confused, but Kesara clarified, "She's the coach for the men's team."

His face opened up with a huge smile. "Get out! Damn, and I liked Tavian's guts before, but this is great. Congratulations."

"Thank you, but we aren't a winning team yet, so let's save the praise for Tavian till later." Or never.

"Will do," he said, getting serious again. He made a few notes on his paper. "Two bedrooms, solid construction, high turnaround area. I can do some research on what you're looking for and line up some appointments by Sunday if that works for you?"

"Don't waste her time with all the worst ones first," Kesara cut in.

His fond smile let me know just how close these two were. She'd called him out in front of a stranger, and he had nothing but fondness for her. "Only the best, *prima*."

"Good." Kesara stood and I followed. "She doesn't have a car, so you'll have to pick her up at her apartment."

His mouth popped open. "There are really people in this state without a car?"

"Your cousin already spanked me on that," I told him, feeling almost as comfortable with him as with Kesara. It probably had to do with how much she obviously adored him. "I don't mind taking BART over here if you want to head out from here."

"He'll come pick you up," Kesara said firmly. She handled him like she handled Tavian with an adorable commanding tone.

After setting a meeting time, Kesara and I headed back out to her car. "Thank you for setting that up."

She paused when she got to my door. "There you go again. All grateful for something that was a phone call on my part and major points with my cousin for me." The glance she gave me was part teasing, part scolding.

"I'm not used to people..." I didn't bother finishing, just opened the door and got in.

"Doing anything for you?" she asked when she slid into her seat. "I would think people would fall all over themselves to do something for a professional athlete."

"They did. I just didn't accept."

"Rare bird. I like that." Starting the car, she turned a beautiful smile my way and repeated, "I like that a lot."

* * *

I was waiting at the curb when Santiago drove up. Last Sunday we looked at six places and a few more after work during the week. I'd narrowed the choices down to the four we were going to look at again today.

The passenger door opened first to reveal Kesara. I felt my heart jump, happy to see her when I'd missed our usual lunch this week. "Hi, what are you doing here?" I nearly sang out to her.

She smiled as her cousin answered for her. "If she's here with us, she doesn't have to be at the family brunch after church."

"I'm making you miss a family gathering?" I stopped mid-stride, turning to Santiago.

"Graysen," Kesara pulled on my attention. "You're not asking him or me to do something out of the ordinary. He's making a commission, and I felt like a change for today."

She had a way of making me forget my worries. That was exactly what I needed to hear in order to stop feeling like I was ruining their weekend. "Okay."

"Plus, Sara can make a decision faster than anyone I've ever seen," Santiago added. "If you liked all four condos, she'll point out the features that will make your decision for you. She's like a house whisperer."

My eyebrows rose as I glanced at Kesara. She wore a lovely blush before turning to encourage us into the car.

After parking next to the first condo complex, we walked maybe five steps down the front path before Kesara stopped. She tilted her head to the side with an intense look.

"Uh-oh," Santiago muttered next to me. "What's up, *prima*?"

"You didn't notice the traffic noise?"

As if she'd planted the suggestion hypnotically, the roar of the traffic from the main thoroughfare one street away assaulted my ears. "We must have been distracted."

"We also saw this place at eight o'clock the other night, so it might not have been as bad then," Santiago added.

"Let's see if it's as bad from inside." She spurred us into motion inside the unit and closed the door. "Yep, it's as bad."

It was pretty loud. I wondered how I hadn't noticed it. This wouldn't do, but I didn't want to say anything that might make Santiago feel bad. Thankfully, Kesara took care of it for me.

"Do you like all the places equally?" She waited for my nod. "Then this one's done."

"Sounds good to me." I was grateful to have someone else's opinion on making this big of a decision. Until she'd knocked this one off the list, I hadn't known how I'd narrow down the choices.

When we got to the next townhouse, Kesara stopped again as soon as we hit the master bedroom. "Nope, baby next door. You don't want any part of that."

Santiago and I just looked at each other. He shrugged as if to say, "Told you so." And we found ourselves moving on to the next condo.

Two steps inside the next place, Kesara asked, "What's that smell?"

Even I noticed the smell right away, although I hadn't the other night when we'd looked at the place. We headed to the balcony and spotted the problem. It overlooked the complex's dumpster. Yeah, that would get smelly as it got fuller each week. Damn, I was glad she was here or I might have chosen this one. I'd been leaning toward it, but not enough to eliminate the other choices.

On the drive over to the fourth and final option, I kept my eyes on the passing scenery. If we eliminated this next house, I hoped Santiago could come up with more to look at next week. "That's a beautiful building," I mentioned as we drove past a characteristic Spanish villa that peppered so many residential areas in this state.

"Stop," Kesara ordered from the backseat.

Santiago slowed to a stop at the curb and glanced in the rearview mirror. "Don't tell me?"

She fluttered her eyebrows further confusing me. "Realty sign."

"Not yesterday when I ran a search. You sure?" He twisted in his seat to look back at the building. "That complex rarely has listings."

"Let's get in there." I was excited by the prospect of seeing something in this beautiful building. The other places all looked the same from the outside, boxy and modern. This one had some character.

"I'll circle and get us closer."

"Does no one walk in California?" I teased, opening the car door.

"Are you from another planet?" Santiago tossed back, but he turned off the engine and the cousins joined me on the sidewalk. I started off at an excited pace, not realizing that I was leaving them in the dust. "Hold your horses, there, Stretch."

Kesara and I actually giggled at his exasperated tone. I hadn't giggled in years, liking how being with these two close family members made me feel so comfortable. I slowed down to a human pace, and we all strolled to the wrought iron gates that surrounded the beautiful building's yard. We got buzzed inside by the realtor.

An opening in the building led to a Spanish style courtyard with flagstone pavers around a big fountain in the center. There were six units surrounding the courtyard. We headed to the one with the realty sign.

"Hey, Santiago," a woman with bleached blond hair called out from the interior. "You in the neighborhood or did you see the listing?"

He went to shake the realtor's hand while Kesara and I started looking around. The bones of the place were just as extraordinary as the classic style of the exterior. Some features were very outdated, but that didn't deter from its charm. As Santiago got the listing info, we looked through every room. Both bathrooms and the kitchen needed help, but with the right crew, they could be updated easily. French doors instead of the back door would add more light throughout. The detached garage faced a back alley, a rare feature for this area. I felt my heart rate increase. I really liked this place. With the right work, I could see myself living here for a long time.

"Verdict?" Santiago approached us with a grin.

I turned to Kesara. Her lips pulled into a wide smile, which said all I needed. "Yes," I said simply.

"Great," Santiago clapped his hands together. "Let's head back to my office, and I'll tell you what else I learned as we write up an offer. I've got Camille holding off advertising for the open house. She owes me for a pocket listing I gave her."

We took one more circle around the house with Santiago in tow. He liked it as much as I did, and as we headed back to his car, he pointed out all the other features. "The estate of the previous owner wants to offload this pretty quickly. I think we can get it for a steal if we act now. Units don't come up for sale often. When they do, there's always a nice profit to be made. I think it fits everything you need, but I don't want to pressure you."

I glanced over my shoulder at Kesara. She smiled back at me. I really liked her smile. She offered it so freely, and I appreciated that about her. "You're not. That's exactly the kind of place I was looking for. Everything feels right about it. I'd like to update the bathrooms and kitchen, which will be a hassle, but with those improvements, I could make a profit even if I left in a year or so."

"Absolutely," Santiago agreed.

"And if you don't know a contractor, we do."

I shot Kesara a knowing look. "Don't tell me, another cousin?"

"Two, Jose and Juan," Santiago supplied.

"You don't have to use them, but they're very good," Kesara added.

"Thank you. I'd love to use them if they have time."

"Let's get you the place first. Then Sara can call the J's."

"Can we get it soon?" I felt eager all of a sudden.

"If they accept your offer, you'll be able to pay cash from the appreciation on your last place, so we'd only have to wait for the inspection. A week or two?"

"Works for me. Thank you, Santiago, you're a great agent."

He swelled with pride. Kesara seemed equally proud to hear me praise her cousin. I liked how close they were almost as much as I liked that they didn't make me feel excluded by their closeness.

CHAPTER 12

The posts and centers were working well together today. I didn't have to worry about the complexity of the plays anymore. They all seemed to get where they needed to be, but that didn't mean they liked it.

"Why aren't there more plays for me?" Ollie asked.

"Because you're a scrapper. I'd rather you be in rebounding position when a shot goes up for the cleanup if necessary."

Tension unknotted from his expression. He liked the idea of making his own plays and liked that I'd recognized that about him. "Yeah, okay."

"Great. Jeff, you're going to get the ball in position, but Eli and I are going to drop in on you. Find the open man." We set up in position. I kept a forearm on Frank, whom I was guarding and Eli smothered Jeff who was trying to get around him. I cut off his baseline, forcing him to pick up his dribble. He tried to push off, but I held steady and stripped the ball from him. "What happened?"

"I didn't expect you to go baseline."

"Why wouldn't you? That's your trademark move, fake high and go baseline. You think other teams won't do the same research I've done on you?"

"Uhh..."

"Yes," I supplied for him. "I told you we'd be doubling you. Victor should have slid over and taken Frank once I shifted to you. That left who open?"

"Me, idiot," Wendell told him.

"Start running, Wendell," I ordered without looking at him.

"What'd I do?"

"You insulted your teammate."

"Shit," he sighed, but that had been the extent of his complaints recently.

Before he started into a trot, a clump of my players started whistling and clapping. I turned to look at the doors of the gym. Darby was walking toward me, and my players were now distracted from practice, standing around acting as if they were on some construction site, whistling and cat calling.

"Knock it off!" I yelled, shooting death glares at my assistant coaches for not having put an immediate stop to their boorish behavior. I trotted over to meet Darby before she stepped onto the court, a playful smile on her lips. She looked like she liked the attention the players were giving her.

"Hi, Gray," she said in a singsong voice. "I didn't mean to interrupt."

Of course she did, but I went with it. I didn't like anyone interrupting my practices, no matter how much I liked seeing her. "What can I do for you?" I walked us a few steps back to avoid any eavesdroppers.

"You haven't been around the offices lately, and I can't seem to get you on the phone. I was hoping you were free tonight."

"Tonight?" I echoed stupidly.

"Yes. Tonight." Her steady gaze revved up my pulse. "You promised me a second date."

Actually, I hadn't, but who was I to argue when she stood this close looking so gorgeous and interested? "Okay," I heard myself say without thinking. Thankfully, I hadn't made plans tonight or I'd be smacking myself.

"Wonderful. How much longer will you be?"

"Probably two hours."

She glanced at her watch and flashed me a sinister grin. "See you in two, Gray. Can't wait." A four fingered wave preceded her saunter to the exit.

The team hadn't gone back to practicing by the time I turned around. They all seemed fixated on Darby's retreating form. It was like they'd never seen a visitor before.

Before I could bark at them for not practicing, I overhead a player on the far side of the court say, "Damn, she's smoking hot. I'd like to show her my skills."

"Hell, yeah, I'd bend her over that ball rack and—"

"Cut it, right now!" I shouted at them. "Gather 'round." They all looked a little shocked at my vehemence but did as I asked. I couldn't tell if I was angry at them for being pigs or for being pigs about Darby. I didn't care, pigs were pigs. "I realize that we're a team here and you should feel relaxed enough to say what you want. But dammit, you better learn the difference between ego stroking locker room commentary, and inappropriate comments made in public especially among mixed company." They stared dumbly at me. "Frank, would you have said what you said if your mother was in hearing range? Or Anthony, would you have wanted someone to speak about your sister like that?" Scowls erupted on their faces. Yeah, they didn't like personalizing crass remarks.

"She's not my sister, and she might like it," Wendell offered, waggling his eyebrows.

I gritted my teeth and let out a long breath through my nose. "How would you like it if I made an unflattering general statement about men? Like if I stood around with my teammates and said, 'Men, they're only good for one thing...and how often do you need to parallel park anyway?' Would that make you feel like I was treating you with respect?"

My comment actually drew laughter. It was pretty funny, but it was disrespectful and objectifying, too. Wendell didn't seem like it bothered him too much. Since it hadn't been on the same scale as the comments about Darby, I could see why, but I'd made my point. "I'm asking each of you to be more conscientious of what you say. At some point, you need to realize that mature adults don't speak that way. And if any of you have to make a living outside of basketball, those kinds of comments could get you fired and sued. College is a learning experience. I hope to teach you more than just basketball."

Heads nodded as I finished up. I was starting to get through to them. It was all about maturity, and I was getting the impression that very few of them had been expected to act their ages before stepping onto my court. "Dash, head over to run plays with the 4's and 5's. Anthony, Frank, and Wendell, come on, we're running." I started toward the sideline, noticing that no one had moved. "I made a sexist comment. It doesn't matter that I was trying to make a point. It was objectifying and sexist. I'm running. Now, let's move out."

I'd never seen Frank move so quickly. They were right with me for the first four laps, then it was down to Wendell and me through eight, step for step. I started to pour it on, sprinting full out for the last two laps. Wendell couldn't keep up. I'd done it on purpose. They hadn't seen me do anything other than play some defense, make some passes, and walk through plays. They needed to know that I was as fit as I was making them be. My three running buddies stared wide eyed at me as I headed back to the key, taking over from a smiling Dash. He winked at me before trotting back to Damon's group.

* * *

"What is this place?" I stared out the window of Darby's car at what looked like a club entrance. Next door, flashbulbs were going off along a red carpet of a theater.

"It's a dance club." Darby smiled and reached out to squeeze my hand. "The kind where we'll fit right in." She fluttered her eyebrows, pumping my fingers. "I wanted to dance with you, and the city provides a lot of places to do that."

I didn't think dancing was a good idea when I still didn't know what I should do about her. She looked hopeful enough to make me give in, though. "Can we find a different place? One that isn't next to a huge crowd?"

"Are you ashamed?" Her voice challenged me even as her expression showed concern.

"I'm going to make national headlines when my season starts. So far, Tavian has managed to keep people from finding out the Graysen Viola he named as a replacement is a woman. Once sportscasters have that information, I'm going to be put on display. I don't want to offer up my private life for examination. I'm not crazy about dancing, but if you want to go, I'd be happy to, somewhere away from all that fanfare next door. Is that an acceptable compromise?"

"I don't think I've ever seen you rattled before. I thought you loved the attention you got while you were playing?" She seemed shocked by that observation.

"Not even close," I replied, my tone more serious than I intended. "I liked playing. That's it. It didn't make me any more special than anyone else on the street."

She let out a laugh, almost disbelieving but shrugged. "Okay. There's another place that I like. Or, we could just skip it and go someplace more private."

More private would be good. Or would it? "Where?"

"My place or yours?" She must have recognized the look of panic that crossed my face. "You're not there yet. That's fine. Dancing or something else? The city has lots of possibilities."

I nodded in agreement. "We used to come down here to a comedy club or a jazz club on the wharf. Some of my teammates liked the art walk along the galleries on Van Ness."

"Hey, you really know San Francisco."

"We liked exploring when we had nights off. I'm more familiar with Sacramento, but we came to the city often enough."

She pulled out into traffic, leaving behind the very visible club entrance. "We'll keep the road trip for another date." She grinned, and I felt the tension drain away. "Seems like maybe tonight isn't the right night for dancing. How about we try a movie instead?"

Not one of the options I'd posed, but it was far better than dancing. I'd never been very good at it, and I doubted it would matter that I wouldn't be towering over this dance partner. I didn't like being noticeable outside the gym. "Sounds good."

As she pulled into the movie theater's parking garage, she grabbed my hand, not allowing me to open the door. "I want you to feel comfortable with me, Gray."

That would be nice, probably not going to happen any time soon, but a nice wish on her part. Before I could form a response, she leaned over the console, inches from my face. My heart started clattering in my chest, wondering what she was doing.

"I have to kiss you." She put an end to my wondering. "Tell me now if that's not okay."

My jaw nudged open. My pulse rate hammered, making me feel dizzy again. I didn't want our first kiss to be in the front seat of her car in an underground parking garage, but my brain wasn't telling my mouth to say anything.

She smiled, satisfied. For a moment, it looked a little smug, but then I felt her breath on my face and watched her eyes zero in on my lips. A moment later, her lips pressed against mine. I sucked in my breath at the softness. I had a lot more experience with kissing than I did with dating or sex, courtesy of the usually bold and slightly drunk fans or acquaintances who surprise attacked me in whatever bar my teammates chose to frequent after a game. None of those kisses felt as good as the soft brush of her lips. When she came back for more, I caught her lower lip, pulling slightly so that it was between mine. She let out a moan as her mouth pressed down with more insistence.

Before I knew it, she was pulling my body against hers, our lips meeting and retreating with urgency. Fire shot through my veins, making me forget about everything else under the intense heat. Her lips on mine, a tongue sliding along my upper lip, her hand moving from my side up toward my—I jerked back, grabbing her hand before it closed over my breast. Breath spilled in gasps until I managed to douse the flames licking at my reason.

"Too much?" Mischief flickered in her gaze. She looked down at my hand still gripping hers. "All right, too much. You don't know how long I've wanted to do that. Fantasized about it for ages."

"Darby." I didn't recognize the husky voice that came out of me. "You've had a lot more time to think about your feelings. Can you be patient with me? I don't want to lead you on, but I'm not like you. It takes me a little longer to decide where to go in a relationship." A lot longer, actually, but only because I'd never had a relationship. I was making this up as I went. But I did know that I wasn't ready to have sex with her, and that kiss had been moving into an R rating.

"I can wait, babe. I have for almost twenty years. A couple more dates won't kill me."

A couple more? Pressure's back on. I had to make a decision, and it wouldn't be easy to do if she kept kissing me like that. But damn, that had been a great kiss.

CHAPTER 13

A melodic five tone ring belonging to my new doorbell interrupted me before I could start some coffee. I'd just spent my first night on a brand new king sized mattress set, listening to the sounds of my new complex. The walls were solid. I couldn't hear the neighbor that shared one wall, but when I'd gone out to get some dinner, I detected some faint music spilling out of the open doorway diagonal from mine. I thought about stopping by to say hello, but I hadn't had a shower after moving boxes and didn't feel like being social.

Now that it was morning, I was betting that my visitor was either Jose or Juan or both. I unlocked the door to see Kesara standing on the doorstep with a smile and two cups of coffee.

"Good morning. Did you enjoy your first night?"

Surprised to see her here, I wasn't too shocked to notice that she hadn't pushed her way inside like most people would have. "Yes, thank you. I didn't expect to see you this morning." I stepped back to let her in.

She handed off a coffee as she came inside. "I wanted to see if I could be your first visitor and make sure my cousins showed up on time."

I laughed at her forceful tone. I was starting to get that she might be a central figure in her family unit. "I'm sure they will, and I'm glad you're my first visitor, seeing as you're the reason

I've got the place. Thanks for the coffee, saved me the effort of making some."

She nodded and looked around, noticing the still full boxes stacked up against one wall, flattened boxes outside the kitchen, and a few more stacked by the back door. "Where's all your furniture?"

I ducked my head, embarrassed that I couldn't offer her a seat. "I sold my condo with the furniture included. I was thinking that it would save on the hassle of moving, but it probably wasn't smart, especially since I don't have time to shop." A smile played on her lips. I thought it might be at my predicament, but then I guessed, "Don't tell me, you've got a cousin —"

"Who's an interior designer? Yes, I do. She's still new in the business, but she's a hard worker and has a great eye. You could take a look at her portfolio and have a chat, but please don't feel obligated to use her. If nothing else, she can give you a few pointers on where to shop."

"That would be so great." Choosing the bed had taken more time than I could afford right now. Having a designer whom I could trust would be a big relief. "I can't believe how talented your family is. I hope they don't mind dropping whatever it is they're doing to help me out."

"Shall we go over this again?" That compelling smile touched her lips again. "You're paying them to do all this help. With the current housing market, you've just helped my family with a realtor's commission, a contracting job, and now an interior designing job. You're the one that's helping them, and I'm grateful that you're so open to using these people that you don't know."

"But you do." That was all that mattered to me, but she continued to look at me amazed. "What?"

She shook her head. "I'm just glad you said that. Not many people would."

Before I could ask what she meant, the doorbell sounded again. She checked her watch and winked. Two solid looking guys stood on my doorstep, nearly identical in appearance except for the parts in their hair and a slight bump on one nose. "Good morning. You're Ms. Viola?"

I opened the door wide and gestured them inside. "Call me Graysen, and who is who?"

Kesara stepped up beside me and pointed at the one with the bump on the bridge of his nose. "This is Juan, and that's Jose. Right on time, guys."

"Hey, cuz," they both said at once. Jose added, "Should have known you'd be here."

"Gonna translate for us, Sara?" Juan asked with a playful smile.

"Don't need to. Graysen speaks Spanish," she announced, pride in her voice.

The tone made me feel pretty good. "But not enough to understand contractor speak."

"*No hay problema.* Take us through what you're thinking for the place," Jose offered.

"Bathrooms and kitchen mostly, but if I could get French doors instead of that back door, and replace the linoleum and carpet with better flooring, that would be great."

"What kind of flooring and what kind of renovation did you have in mind for the bathrooms and kitchen."

"I want to stay true to the building's style, so nothing too modern. I'm assuming some kind of tile would be authentic for flooring?"

They looked at each other with raised brows. "Yes, it would. You don't want the wood floors and stainless surfaces that are so common on those flipping shows?"

"Don't get me wrong, I want modern amenities, but I want to restore where we can, not remodel. The outside of this building is what drew me in. I'd rather stay true to that style."

They both turned and nodded at Kesara, smiles brightening their serious expressions. "We can do that. Let's go take a look at the rooms so we can write up a bid."

With that we started in on the details of the job. They were enthusiastic guys, obviously loved what they did. They had great ideas, and I'd read enough books on renovation that I could tell they would be paying attention to all the details. By the end of the consultation, I knew it didn't matter what their bid was. I'd be signing the contract as soon as they brought it by.

* * *

"How's practice going?" Jacinda asked as we set the table. Dinner at their house had become a weekly event. I'd come to rely on it as my only moment of normalcy among the ever changing landscape of my job, the work on my house, and if I was being completely honest, the semi-relationship with Darby. She was on a road trip right now, so I was a bit more relaxed. I shouldn't be reacting this way, but she had me all twisted up.

"They aren't ready yet for the first game next week. I'm starting to worry."

"Anything Tavian can do to help?"

"You sound like Kesara."

Her eyes widened before a smile replaced the surprise. "Really? She offers his help, too?"

"Only after she's offered to help herself, and I'm pretty sure she only offers Tave's because she knows that we're friends."

"She's great, isn't she?"

I cocked my head, wondering about her tone. There was some meaning that I was missing, but I didn't have time to question her before her daughters were on top of me. "Aunt Gray, Aunt Gray!"

Dameka, the nine-year-old, and Alicia, the eleven-year-old, danced around me, demanding attention. I reached down and grabbed the smaller of the two, who happened to be the eleven-year-old. "Hi, girls, how was music and soccer?" I caught Dameka next and hugged her briefly, calming both as their father joined us.

They went on in excited chatter about their saxophone lesson and soccer practice as we set the table. I liked that Jaci and Tave didn't make them do the same activities. Dameka was the athlete. Alicia the more creative of the two. Their parents encouraged whatever interests they wanted but didn't stack their schedules so much that the kids had no free time.

The doorbell sounded as we were heading in to help Tavian set the food on the table. Jacinda went to answer the door, and I threw a questioning glance at Tavian. He turned and went out to the grill. The quick retreat alarmed me. I told the girls to finish putting the croutons and sunflower seeds on the salad then followed him outside.

"What's up, Tave?"

"Not my idea. I promise you."

"Oh, there you both are." Jacinda interrupted us. An attractive blond man stood at her side. "I want you to meet, Leo, one of the top salespeople at my company. He's in town for the week, and I offered a home cooked meal. Leo, meet my husband, Tavian, and this is our good friend, Graysen."

He stepped outside and shook both of our hands. His eyes widened at Tavian's height and seemed intrigued by mine, which matched his. "It's nice to meet you both. Thank you again for the invitation. It's not often that I get a home cooked meal on the road."

"Where are you from?" Tavian asked.

"Here, actually, but I'm on the road so much, it doesn't feel like home."

"I remember how that felt," Tavian said for both of us. He'd played in the NBA for about a season and a half before shredding his Achilles' heel and ACL. He'd tried for a comeback in the European leagues but the injury had proven career ending. The amount of travel he'd done in those couple of seasons, though, amounted to about the same as my travels with the WNBA, European league, and broadcasting or coaching duties per year.

"Jacinda mentioned you played in the NBA?" Leo asked, following us back inside once we'd collected the chicken.

"Barely, but Gray, here, was in the WNBA for several years."

Leo turned his appraising gaze on me. "That explains the height."

Actually it didn't, but I didn't want to be rude. Jacinda was almost six feet and he wasn't making a mention of her height. "How do you like being a salesperson?" I'd always wondered what motivated salespeople.

"It's exhilarating. Nothing beats a big close," he said as we settled around the table.

The girls looked affronted when they both had to sit on the opposite side of the table from Leo and me. I couldn't blame them. I had the feeling this was going to be a boring dinner, but since he was a friend of Jacinda's the least I could do was be polite to him.

Halfway through the dinner, I was done being polite. Leo had talked pretty much nonstop and not only ignored the girls, but cut them off several times. I found it hard to believe Jacinda liked this pompous jerk. I tried to pay attention to the girls but also acted like I was listening to all of his sales methods and sales achievements and sales conferences. This dude lived sales. I guess I couldn't talk, seeing as I felt like I was living basketball right now.

"I never asked Jacinda, but what do you do, Graysen?"

This question came during dessert. It was the first break in his monologue about the joys of sales. "I coach basketball."

"Really? Like a high school team or something?"

"College."

"Not the college Tavian works at?"

"That's the one." I shot a look at Tavian that said I wished I could roll my eyes.

"That's a good program, isn't it? The women's team is always on the news."

"There are, but Graysen's coaching the men's team," Tavian supplied.

"You're kidding." It was a statement, not a question. As if I already didn't like the guy, I really could have lived without hearing how shocked he was by the prospect of me coaching the men's team.

Jacinda flashed an apologetic look. "He's not, and she's the absolute best coach for them."

"I'm sure," he all but blew her off.

I'd had enough. "Well, this was delicious. Grill master, Tave, you've done it again, and Jacinda, nothing beats your scalloped potatoes. Girls, the salad was the best part. You're both culinary geniuses. How about we finish the evening with another *Harry Potter* chapter? I've been dying to know how Hermione will get Harry and Ron out of the next mess they get into." The girls giggled in delight as I pushed back from the table, freeing them from their own imprisonment. "Leo, it's been so nice meeting you, but we've got a date with three magical teens at a British boarding school. I hope you understand."

He stood to shake my hand, confusion mapping his brow. He looked over at Jacinda as if to ask for help. I wasn't sure what was going on, but I didn't care to stick around to find out. "Yes, nice to meet you. I hope we can do this again sometime."

Sure, let's get together and be bored to tears again soon. "Goodnight." I followed the girls up to their room where we all giggled about how much talking Leo did before settling onto their beds for a chapter of *Harry Potter*. I'd had to promise them that I wouldn't read the stories, so they could read them to me. We've been doing this by phone and in person for years.

"Guess that was a bust," Jacinda commented when I returned to the kitchen after leaving the girls to get ready for bed.

"What was a bust?" I asked. "And wow, do you hang out with that guy just so you don't have to talk?"

Tavian cracked up, but Jacinda elbowed him. "For your information, that was your date tonight."

"What?" I spluttered through my shock.

"I might not have realized just how enthusiastic he was about his job, but you didn't have to sprint from the room."

"What do you mean he was my date?" Was she joking?

"I thought I'd invite some of my colleagues to the next few dinners to see if you clicked with anyone. You've been alone for as long as I've known you, or at least you never mention being with anyone. I wanted you to find someone."

I looked back and forth between the two of them. Part of me appreciated her concern and care, but the other part was completely amazed that she'd even thought about this. Did all couples want you with someone? "That's really kind, Jaci, but..."

"But what? Are you with someone? Did I just screw up?"

She looked worried that she'd offended me. I reached for her and pulled her into a hug. "You didn't screw up. I just didn't realize you were trying to set me up."

"Gray's a little clueless, sweetie, I tried to tell you. I can't count the number of guys on my teams that tried to get her to go out with them and she had no idea they were asking her out," Tavian supplied.

"That's not nice," she scolded him.

"But true, I'm afraid," I admitted. "You'd have to hit me over the head to get me to realize what you were trying to do. And even if I had, that guy was way too self-absorbed."

"He was pretty bad, wasn't he?" She leaned back from our hug. "Well, there are lots of other nice people at work that would be lucky to have a date with you."

"Really nice, but pleases don't set me up." I almost said something about Darby, but since Tavian was our boss and I still didn't know which way was up with her, I kept quiet.

"I just thought it might be nice, but I understand. You'll let me know if you'd like me to introduce you to more people?"

"I will." Just as soon as I figure out if I even want to date.

CHAPTER 14

"*B*uenos días, Jose," I greeted the contractor on my doorstep. Sometimes I left before they arrived, but when I didn't, I noticed that Jose beat Juan to the job every morning. "*Te gustaría un café?*" I gestured to the nearly full coffee pot on the kitchen counter in offering.

"*Ahora no, gracias,*" he declined the offer of coffee for now, lugging in his tool bucket. "Did you see the tile samples in your bathroom?" He was mostly all business. Juan joked around a lot more, but Jose never forgot to switch to English whenever we spoke about the work that needed to get done.

"I did. I liked them all but I'm leaning toward the maroon patterned tiles. That will go with the terra cotta tiles you're going to put on the floor. Don't you think?"

"I think so, but I was going to ask Mirabella when she stops by today. Are you okay with her choice if she likes one of the others better?"

"Do you think she will?" I goaded, hoping to get him to bite with a smile at least. He had such a beautiful smile. Before I could get a response, the doorbell rang. It wasn't Juan because he usually used his key in the morning even if I was here. Instead Mirabella, the interior designing cousin, waited on the doorstep. "We were just talking about you."

"Jose or Juan?" She poked her head inside and got her answer. "Okay, then it was all good."

We laughed at her joke. "I didn't expect you this early."

"I wanted to catch you before you left."

"She's got that dreaded color wheel out, Jose, save me," I appealed to the stoic man. He threw his hands up and disappeared into the master bathroom. "Did you beat him up when you were younger or something?"

"His brother," she deadpanned. The five-five curvy woman probably couldn't even twist those boys' arms, but it was fun imagining her bullying Juan. "Jose was a sweetie. Still is." She slapped the color wheel down on the soon to be demolished kitchen counter. Two furniture books and her sketch pad followed suit. "It's time to get serious about a color palette, Gray. You gotta help me out here." Her brown eyes pleaded with me from behind clunky but fashionable tortoiseshell frames. Straight black bangs edged over the rims, but the rest of her hair was in a long ponytail similar to the one I was wearing. Like her cousin, she was beautiful. Her skin tone was more like the men in the family, darker than Kesara's, and her hair was stick straight, also unlike her cousin's. Some of the men had some wave to their hair, but so far, no one else had Kesara's curls. I started wondering what Kesara's siblings looked like, if they'd be curly beauties, too.

"As long as it's not pink, I'll be fine."

"Not good enough. Don't make me call Sara. You know she's tough enough to drag a decision out of you." She got me to wave my hands in surrender. "Let's start with your favorite color?"

"Don't have one."

"Everyone has one. Ooh, I know, I bet it's green, like your incredible eyes."

I shook my head, not having heard my eyes described that way. "I don't really like green, which is funny seeing as it's one of the school colors."

"You're kidding? Not even the dark jade of your eyes?"

"They're just green, Bella. They only stand out because of my hair," I reasoned, knowing that dark brown hair and green eyes were an unlikely color combination. This I learned from every doctor I'd ever had. Apparently the majority of people with brown hair had brown eyes, but if a recessive trait came in, blue eyes were the result. Since I'd never met anyone else with dark brown hair and green eyes, I suspected they were right.

She must have recognized the finality of my tone. "Just name a color, any color, and don't say black or white."

"Well, I like watching the leaves turn in the fall, so I guess reds and yellows, or that maroon that Jose had for the tile in the bathroom is nice."

"Jose?" she called out. He surfaced from the bathroom carrying the tile, either having heard us or guessing what she'd want. "Oh, that is nice. Are you thinking all the way to the ceiling with these?"

"That's what we were discussing. Still okay with you, Graysen?"

"Whatever you guys think. I can't wait till you have that shower done. It's going to be so nice not having to take a bath in the morning or waiting until I get to my office to shower."

Mirabella herded me onto one of the bar stools that she'd just picked up. "This is what I'm thinking." She proceeded to show me several sketches and swatches for the couch and chairs she had planned. She really was talented. "What do you think, and say something other than, 'It looks good to me.' I've heard that one before."

I laughed at her threatening tone. She and Kesara shared a lot more than just good looks. "Honestly, I don't like the style of the chairs. Can you make them a little more plain? Sleek lines, not rounded fluff? And I'm not afraid of dark colors, so if you want to go bold, go bold."

"Perfect, thanks, Gray. We'll get this place gorgeous and livable in no time."

Considering Juan and Jose had already gotten the French doors in, all the fixtures and cabinets in the master bath done and were a day or two from finishing the tiling, I knew she was speaking the truth. They'd probably finish by the weekend and move on to the guest bathroom on Monday. They were waiting for my first road trip to tackle the kitchen because I wouldn't be able to use it while they were working on it. Probably a month or so and my house would be completely up to date and nearly filled with furniture.

"Thanks, Bella, you're doing a great job. And you're a genius with a hammer and nails, Jose. Say hi to Juan for me."

"You get to work early," Jose observed.

"I run to work then I workout in the gym for a while, grab some juice at the café, and finally sit down at my desk. It'll be almost two hours before I'm settled in to work."

"You run? To Oakland?" he asked.

"It's only six miles. Plus, it's a beautiful day."

"Do you need a ride?" Mirabella asked, shooting a concerned look at Jose.

"No, thanks. I like running. See you both later." I headed outside. It was the last day of practice before our first game, and I wanted to put in a full day.

Sticking to side streets and sidewalks once I hit the main part of Oakland, I was at the campus in about forty-five minutes with all the stoplights. Several honking horns and one very loud driver shouted out encouragement as I made my way. Friendly bunch, these Californians.

"You look so sexy," a low voice said in my ear as I pushed through the athletic department building.

I nearly jumped at the sound, turning to find Darby who'd snuck up beside me. My eyes automatically flicked to her lips, the ones that had almost coaxed me into sex in her front car seat. Well, had me thinking about sex in her front seat, anyway. They were as luscious today as they'd been that night. "Good morning," I managed, forcing my eyes back to hers.

"You ran to work again, or were you running the track?"

"To work. How come you're so early this morning?"

"You didn't respond to my email so I thought I'd catch you before you got entrenched in game tapes."

"Email?" I stopped to turn to her.

"Your personal account, asking if you wanted to go out tonight? Friends of mine are throwing a party, and I wanted to bring you."

Guilt made me grimace. "I haven't had a chance to look at my personal email account in over a week. Sorry about that."

"It's okay. I should have called, but I knew I'd see you today. So, how about it? You'll really like these friends. It'll be a lot of fun."

"I'd love to, but it's my first game tomorrow night. I need to focus."

She did a terrible job of hiding her disappointment. "That's okay. I understand. It's your first game with a new team, and you want to do well. You'll win, won't you?"

No. But I didn't voice that. Positive energy and all. "We have a good chance."

"Well, I'll be there cheering you on. Can I take you out afterward since you're not available tonight?"

"Actually, I've got plans with Tavian, but maybe Sunday?"

Since this was the first time I'd made the suggestion for a date, she let her smile burst through the disappointment of not being able to go out after the game. Relief washed through me, both that she understood my not being available and that I'd just made a decision to see where this romance might go. "Sunday night. I'll make you dinner."

"You won't let me take you out?" I asked playfully, my heart pounding with hope that she'd allow us to take this slowly. Dinner at her place probably wouldn't go along with the pace I preferred.

"That sounds good. You still without a car?"

"I am, but I can meet you at the restaurant?"

"No, I'd love to see your new place. I'll come pick you up."

"Thanks, and thanks for understanding about tonight."

"Good luck if I don't see you before the game tomorrow. I know you'll do great." She looked around the deserted lobby before leaning forward and kissing my cheek. "Mmm, salty, but very sexy." Then she glided down the hallway toward her office, leaving the feel of her lips on my cheek to follow me around all day.

* * *

Shoot around had gone well. The team was energized and excited as they settled into the seats in front of their lockers. I'd drawn several of our opponent's plays on the board to go over for the pregame talk.

"Remember the game tapes. Their star is number twenty-two. He hates being bodied up. Ollie, I want you to make him feel like he's wearing you." They laughed at my description. "Jeff, if Ollie loses sight of this guy, you make sure he sees nothing else but your jersey number. Dash, when they're running their motion offense, your hands are on any pass as you come off the picks. Eli, always have an eye on Dash's man. When he's going to add pressure, you'll need to help cover his slot. Frank, when their point drives inside, he always dishes off to twenty-two. Put your hand in the passing lane, even if you only knock it out of bounds. We want them to have to restart their offense as much as possible."

I looked at Damon who stepped up to the first two plays on the board. "They call these Help-C and L and run them forty percent of the time. If we stop them on the first pass, they fall apart. Guards, make them fall apart."

Bill took up where Damon left off. "We'll press after every made free throw. If we throw up the sign, cross the line and pick them up full court."

"Any questions?" I waited for a moment before continuing. "First game, first chance to make an impression. We can beat this team. I don't care what their rank is or how they look on paper. We know their offense, and they don't know ours. Let's use that to our advantage. We're fit, we're ready, we're a team. Get taped up and dressed and meet me on the floor." I left them to get suited up for the first game.

A half hour later, I was watching my team run layups. The arena was half full, about what they'd averaged for last year's attendance. Three reporters sat at the press tables instead of the full lineup of twelve. Tavian hadn't made a big deal when he'd announced my hiring and managed not to use a pronoun with my gender neutral name. Or maybe my ego was just playing this up. Perhaps no one was interested in a female head coach of a men's team. Wouldn't that be great?

That hope went out the window when the announcer said, "And your new head coach for the Piranhas, Graysen Viola." The spotlight hit me and the crowd, who'd been applauding our players and assistant coaches, sounded liked they all gasped at once. It was probably only a few seconds, but it felt like minutes before the applause started again. I'd managed a modest wave before heading over to shake the hand of the opposing coach. He actually smirked at me as he gripped my hand. Now I really wanted to beat them.

The team started off running the plays, swarming on defense, pressing when necessary, but they got rattled with a few minutes left in the first half. I called a timeout when we fell down by six. They slumped into their seats as only half the bench got up to join me.

I glared at the rest and barked, "Get over here behind me. This is a team, even if you're not playing." I grabbed the whiteboard that Damon was handing me, and scratched out a few X's. "You're missing this pick every time Eli sets it, Jeff. He can't slide over. You've got to run your man into him. Ollie, you've let up on defense. He's getting easy shots now. Change that or Nate takes over. Frank, their point is dribble penetrating and dishing just like I told you he would. It's the only move he's got. Stop it before we get in too big a hole."

"I can't move off my man," Frank protested.

"You won't be. He'll have to pass around you to get to your guy, but he's looking to dish to twenty-two when Ollie drops off him. But Ollie won't be dropping off him anymore, will you?" Ollie shook his head. "Good, let's convert on this set and get a stop on the next." I stuck my hand out. Dash placed his on top before the rest of the team followed suit.

"Defense," the team chanted before dispersing.

By the half we'd managed to pull within three. The team was in better spirits as I went through my usual halftime pep talk. I knew we could outrun the other team, so I wasn't worried about the deficit. If we could stay within six by the last two minutes, we'd win. Anything more and their mental toughness would suffer.

They played pretty closely for another fourteen minutes but started to lose their way toward the end. No amount of timeouts seemed to help. Turnovers and missed defensive assignments dug the team into a twelve point deficit with four minutes to go.

The crowd had begun chanting to put Wendell in, and until now, he'd been smirking from his seat on the bench. "Put me in, Coach. I can win this for us." He came right up behind me as I paced the sideline.

"You're not playing, Wendell, take a seat," I reminded him calmly.

"Are you trying to lose?" he was trying to bait me.

"Sit down," I hissed at him, signaling to Dash for another timeout. "Anthony, you're in for Eli. Remember to help Ollie with his man. That guy is killing us."

"What about Wendell?" Jeff asked as he and the team crowded around me for a twenty second timeout.

"He's not eligible, and you all know why. Anthony, check in. Frank, if you don't get your hand on the next dish off, I'm pulling you for Victor. We're pressing on the next made basket. They're breathing hard right now, fellas, we can outrun them. Our legs are fresher which means they'll be hurting on defense. Let's make up eight in the next two minutes." I put in my hand and got a half hearted, "Defense" in response. I pulled on Dash's arm. "Make them believe we can win. If they see you shoot lights out, they'll hold them off on defense."

"Will do." He hustled back onto the court.

Unfortunately, he wasn't enough. We came to within two with thirty seconds left, but another turnover and Frank didn't stop the pass to their star, who drained a three-pointer. First game of my men's coaching career and we lost by five because my players didn't listen.

The crowd was angry, mostly at me for not putting in Wendell. They weren't booing, but they weren't applauding our effort either. Tavian gave me an encouraging smile and shook my hand, choosing not to hug me for fear of him being accused of favoritism.

When I entered the locker room, I was surprised to see several players stripping off their uniforms. "You've got thirty seconds to put your clothes back on," I said before turning and walking back outside. I gave them forty to make sure. "From now on, you wait until I've given my postgame talk before undressing or hitting the showers." Two of them snorted but sat up straight when I shot them glares. "We're not related or dating, that means clothing isn't optional. Now, tell me how we lost that game?"

They just stared at me. Even Dash didn't have anything to say. He just hung his head. "Would have won if I'd played," Wendell criticized.

"One more word about not taking your penalty, and you'll sit the next game, too," I snapped, sick of his attitude. "You were never going to play tonight. The team knew that and were prepared for it. They lost sight of our defensive strategy. We're going to work on that at the next practice. We had this game in our grasp, and we let it slip away. Are we going to let that happen again?"

"No, Coach," three of them said. I was so disappointed with their play, I didn't bother pressing them all to agree.

"Fine, rest up tomorrow and catch up on your coursework." With that I left the locker room and headed to the press room.

The three reporters I'd spotted at the press table during the game had somehow ballooned to eight by the time I arrived.

The other coach had just left and now it was time for me to face the music.

"Miss Viola, are you really qualified to coach this team?"

Really? Right off the bat like that? I hadn't even sat down. "What's your name?" I asked with more politeness than he deserved.

"Logan Sparks from the *Gazette*."

"Let's start every question with your names so I have a chance to learn them all, please. Now, Mr. Sparks, I'm sure when you have enough time to do some research on me, you'll find the answer to your question. But, I'll tip you off by saying, 'yes'. Oh, and it's Coach or Ms. Viola."

A guy in the second row raised his hand. "Kirk Comstock from the *Trib*. How has the team been adjusting to having you as a coach?"

"Like every other team that's had to deal with a new coach. It's never an easy transition, especially given how the last coach left. We've been working well together, and they're learning my system."

"Does your system include not playing Wendell Chambers?"

"Your name?" I glowered at the snarky inquisitor.

"Jonathon Black, from the *Bee*."

"Mr. Black, I have a system that allows game time for every player. Wendell broke a team rule, so he didn't play tonight. I fully expect him to play in the next game."

"What rule?" he followed up.

"I don't discuss rule violations with people outside of the team."

"You almost had them at the end there, Coach," a woman spoke up when I called on her. "Sally Roberts, *Examiner*. Did your defense center around stopping Michael Cusack?"

The first actual game question and I was proud that it came from a woman. "He's a talented player and virtually unstoppable tonight. When a guy shoots fifty-two percent from the three, it's going to take shutting down the rest of the team or equal numbers from our offense to make up the difference. We fell a little short of that tonight, but we'll make adjustments for the next time we play this team."

The rest of the press conference covered some more details of the game and what our plan was for the next. No more ridiculous questions about whether I was qualified, but I knew what I'd read in the Sunday sports pages when I woke up. I didn't expect them to be kind, not when we could have won. Had we been walloped, I think they'd blame the team not being prepared. With a close loss, it was always the coach's fault. I'd own eighty percent of that, but I couldn't help when the team didn't listen to me. That would have to change if we wanted to win.

CHAPTER 15

Coming to a stop at the curb in front of my townhouse, Santiago turned with a slight groan. He was probably regretting the two hours we'd just spent playing tennis. He'd been the one to suggest it, but I didn't think he expected the level of competition.

"I won't be able to move tomorrow," he groaned. "You thrashed me, *chica*. Promise me you won't tell any of my cousins that I'm a pathetic loser."

I laughed at his dramatic recounting of our match. "You got one game each set."

"You get that when most people say they like to play tennis for fun that they can't actually make the professional tour, right?"

"I hate to break this to you, Santi, but there's no way you could make the ATP tour." And neither could I with the WTA, but I liked his joke.

"You're a riot." He moved to cuff my shoulder but his arm froze mid-stroke. I couldn't smother the laugh that erupted when he realized he was already limited in his motions. A couple years older than me, he just found out that his body tightened up after a workout that used different muscles. "As soon as I can move again, I'm going to be taking lessons so that I can get two games off you the next time we play."

"You're on," I told him and tapped his fist in parting.

Climbing out of the car, I felt so lucky to have met Kesara, who'd graciously shared her wonderful family members with me. Two hours of tennis with a nice man almost took my mind off the ridicule I'd felt after reading the sports pages this morning. The reporters had not been kind in their assessment of my abilities, berating me for not playing Wendell, for not shutting down the superstar on the other team, and for not having control of my own team. I'd expected some of it, but that didn't make it any easier to swallow.

I keyed in through the gate and made my way toward the front door. Within a few steps I'd nearly caught up to one of my neighbors. So far, I'd only met a couple of them. It looked like I was about to meet another. If I had my glimpses right, I was sure that the elderly woman in front of me occupied the townhouse next to mine.

Before I pulled up even with her, her foot caught on one of the flagstones in the courtyard. She tripped and would have dropped to the ground had my reflexes not kicked in. I grabbed her around the waist, pulling her against me.

"Oh, my stars!" she gasped, clutching my forearms. As soon as she had her feet back under her, I let her go.

"Are you all right?" I wasn't sure whose heart was beating faster at the near slip.

"Thanks to you, young lady." She turned to face me, tilting her head up to look me in the eye. "I would have broken something had you not come along."

"I'm glad we averted disaster." I looked back at the uneven ground, pressing my foot down on each of the flagstones. "There are a lot of loose and jagged edges out here. This isn't very safe."

"Not for someone my age. I'm usually so careful when I come through the front walk."

"You shouldn't have to be. We should get this fixed."

She laughed softly and I refocused on her. If I wanted to hazard a guess, I'd say she was in her eighties. Short white hair, round face, bright blue eyes with a welcoming smile. She came up to my sternum, but she wasn't intimidated by my height. "I've been trying to get the residents in this building to put in money to fix some of the common areas out here, but younger folks always have other things to spend their money on."

"Yes, but this is important. I'm having some work done on my place. I'll ask my contractors to give me a bid on resurfacing this courtyard." My eyes scanned the large courtyard. It wouldn't be cheap, but it would be worth it. When I looked up, she had another grateful smile on her face. "I'm sorry, I forgot to introduce myself. I'm Graysen Viola."

"Yes, I know. We share a wall."

"Oh, no, have the contractors been too loud? I asked them not to use the power tools until later in the morning."

"No, they've been perfectly fine. I just meant that I was aware the moment your unit was sold. The woman who used to live there was my closest friend. I miss her terribly." Sadness touched her expression for a moment, before she seemed to will it away.

"I'm sorry about your friend. I hope my being here doesn't make you miss her more."

She gave me a wistful smile. "Quite the contrary, young lady. I've been hoping for a breath of fresh air to give life to the place. Connie would want that. And by the steady stream of work and kind people you have going in and out of your place, I'd say we got what we wanted."

My head tilted. "You've met them?"

"The quiet one of the two young men helped me carry groceries from the bus stop one day. The chatty young man rearranged my porch bench for me. The girl with the fabric samples is lovely, always takes time to say hello, and the other young lady with the curly hair stopped to visit with me while she waited for the young men to finish up one day."

"I'm happy to hear that." I felt somewhat remiss that I hadn't made more of an effort to meet her. "I stopped by your place last weekend but didn't get an answer. I should have come by after work one day instead."

"Don't trouble yourself. I know how busy you've been, and I knew I'd meet you eventually. More times than not, I'm out here on my bench. I knew I'd catch you sometime soon." She smiled again, a little mischief creeping in. "I'm Mrs. Anita Emerson."

"It's a pleasure to meet you, Mrs. Emerson." I shook her hand.

"I'm glad to see you in good spirits. Those newspapers were pretty awful to you."

Surprised that she recognized they were talking about a neighbor she hadn't met, I had to laugh. "We did lose, so I'm happy to take the blame. Are you much of a sports fan?"

"I recognized your picture on the front page of the sports section. The next time they show your boys on the TV, I'll be sure to tune in."

"Well, thank you for that."

"Now, don't you worry about what those idiot reporters said. What you're doing is very important. I should know. I was the first female vice president for my bank. Breaking ground is never easy, but you seem to be holding up well." She nodded and gripped my arm. "Don't let them bring you down. Keep on, no matter what they throw at you, just keep on."

"Thank you. I appreciate the encouragement."

"I imagine you're running off again soon. I won't keep you, but anytime you feel like a visit, you just stop on by my place."

"I'll do that, thank you. And I will look into having this courtyard resurfaced."

"I don't doubt you for a second. Thank you for saving an old woman from a broken hip."

"I'm glad I was here. Bye for now." I watched as she walked carefully to her unit, feeling lighthearted from the conversation. There was something about that generation of women. Visiting was an activity they never took for granted, and I looked forward to our next opportunity.

Entering my place, I took stock of the still sorely bare room. Mirabella had made some purchases, but the major pieces would take a few more weeks before they were upholstered and delivered. For now, I had one club chair, two barstools, a bed on box springs, and two nightstands. And a newly finished shower, which I headed in to use. One hour stood between my current sweaty state and being picked up for my date.

After the shower, I ran the blow dryer over my hair, using the roll brush to smooth out my natural wave. I'd wear it down tonight because I wasn't coming straight from practice where I'd always have it in a ponytail or twisted into a bun. It was getting longer, almost to mid-back. I should make an appointment to trim a few inches, but my calendar didn't have an opening for weeks. Almost as a habit, I pushed on the tip of my nose back toward my face. A fraction of an inch off the tip and it might be considered perfect. Maybe a slight exaggeration, but still so much better than what I looked at every day. Not that I cared until something silly like a date with a gorgeous woman came into play.

Plunging earrings through my piercings, I made sure the dangling gold links and opals weren't tangled. I slipped on my silk blouse, and the daily battle of to tuck or not began. If I were wearing this under one of my suit jackets, I'd tuck it in, but with these pants that hugged my lower half, I wanted to avoid any bunching up. After trying both options, I decided on the tuck in. It looked dressier that way.

The gate chime rang as I was stepping into my sling backs. Bending to pull the straps around my heels, I pressed on the gate release and headed to open the front door. Darby was walking toward me in an elegant dress, looking stunning.

"Hi, Darby."

"Hello, gorgeous." She walked with purpose, not even bothering to take in her surroundings. When she reached me, she pressed on my shoulder to back me into my house. A determined look in her eye kept me from saying anything. Two steps inside, she stopped pushing and closed the distance between us. Her hands came up to cup my face, lips following soon after. I didn't have time to think before I was caught up in another cell-frying kiss. Wow, she was good at this. "I couldn't wait to have your mouth on mine. Hope you don't mind."

I let out a breath, blinking to regain my senses. "That was a nice hello."

"I'll say. You're looking gorgeous."

"As are you." I stepped back to gain control of the wooziness her kiss had brought on. "Did you have any trouble finding the place?"

"I wasn't sure this was the right address. It's so...ethnic. I figured you for something sleek and modern."

Ethnic? We were in California where Spanish architecture dominated. "Not really. My place in DC was a Tudor, but I saw this place and loved it. Once the renovations are done, I think it might be my favorite house."

She nodded her head, keeping whatever comments she had to herself. Perhaps it was the lack of furniture and fifties style kitchen that gave her pause, but something in her expression showed disapproval. "I know a good contractor if you need one. He specializes in remodels and has helped a lot of my friends on their flips."

"I have a great pair of contractors working on the place." But she knew that since we'd spoken about it at lunch together last week. Perhaps she'd forgotten the conversation. "Very reliable, and they do great work. They've really just started. In a few weeks it'll look completely different."

"Okay, but, if they don't work out, let me know. Are you ready to go out?"

Confusion knitted my brow. Guess she didn't want to see the rest of the place. I tried not to feel disappointed, but I could understand. With only one chair in the middle of the living room, it didn't exactly look inviting. "Sure."

"Great. I know just the place. You live in a nice area here. Great restaurants and shopping."

"Lead the way." I held the front door open for her.

She stopped in front of me. "I'm purposefully not bringing up your game last night. I'm usually in a lousy mood when we lose, so I didn't want to dwell on that if you're like me."

I wasn't, but I appreciated her concern. "It's fine, all part of the job."

Her smile made tingles spark in my stomach. "You're a sunny type, aren't you?"

"I like to think so."

She tilted forward and kissed me softly. "I can handle that. My fantasy woman has an upbeat outlook. Unexpected, but a nice surprise. Come on, sunny, let's start our night together."

I heard both a promising and ominous note in her tone. Not exactly the ideal start to a date night.

CHAPTER 16

Mrs. Emerson's bench provided a perfect view of the entire courtyard. We sat side by side watching Jose and Juan measure the area and test each of the flagstones. I'd already set my mind to fixing this courtyard, not only for Mrs. Emerson's sake, but because it would add about thirty grand to the resale value of any unit in the place.

"We can save a lot of these, but we'll have to clear out, grade the area, refill with gravel, then set the stones back in. At least a week," Jose said as he approached.

"We'll get you the bid tomorrow, but it's not nearly as much as we thought," Juan added.

"You're a miracle worker," Mrs. Emerson said, having watched me knock on all the doors and get everyone to agree to split the cost of the courtyard, citing potential lawsuits as reasoning. "How about some ice tea, boys?" she asked the J's. "You've been working hard out here."

"If you let me in on that action, Anita, I can make them keep working," Mirabella called out as she entered the courtyard. The smile I wore at her tease flared brightly when I spotted Kesara with her.

"You're all workaholics. Boys, help me bring out some chairs so we can enjoy a pitcher together. Sound good?" Mrs. Emerson got Juan and Jose to head into the house.

"Hi, Kesara, I didn't expect to see you tonight," I greeted. "And I swear, Bella, didn't I just give you a whole list of preferences the other day."

"Not good enough," she chastised, dropping into the first chair that Jose brought out. "I took a chance that you'd be here, and Kesara owes me dinner. I'm collecting on that afterward."

"I'm here. Lay it on me."

She fanned out another sample book on the bench between Mrs. Emerson and me. "I'm thinking wallpaper for the guest bedroom." I made some sort of noise that expressed my displeasure and Juan cracked up as he dropped into the chair he'd just carried out of the house. "I take it that's a no? Finally, a definite reaction to something."

"Drama," Kesara muttered under her breath, shooting me a conspiratorial glance.

"At least a five course meal, now, *prima*. Keep it up and you'll be on the hook for two." Mirabella cut her a look. "As I was saying, no wallpaper, so are we going monochromatic or some variety with wall color?"

"I like the idea of colorful," Mrs. Emerson put in after filling the last of our glasses.

I waited until she'd resettled beside me and taken a sip before saying, "I do, too. Have at it, Bella."

"You better pick a few or she'll make it look like a Mexican poncho," Juan warned me.

"Tacky." She reached over and smacked him. "Besides, Gray already said she likes the red and yellow hues, but get this," she elbowed Kesara, "can you believe with those beautiful eyes, that she doesn't like green?"

Kesara aimed her gaze at me, staring for a full ten seconds. "They are remarkable." Her tone was low, possibly meant only for her. With a slight shake of her head, she turned back to Mirabella. "Everyone has their own tastes, and there are a lot of shades in red and yellow than you can work with."

"Thank you." I wasn't sure if I was thanking her for steering Mirabella away from pressing me for more options or the compliment on my eyes. I'd never been complimented as much as I had since moving here. This place was definitely good for my ego.

"I peeked inside your place yesterday, Graysen," Mrs. Emerson told me, a little sheepishness slipping in. "I couldn't resist when Mirabella offered to show me her sketches."

"You're welcome anytime. She's going to make it look beautiful, isn't she? And what about these guys? Masters, don't you think?" I grasped Juan's shoulder.

"It will be grand when it's finished," she proclaimed, making everyone smile.

I shifted back to settle in for a nice visit. These people, whom I barely knew, made me feel like I'd found a home after all the years of traveling and temporary work situations. I liked every one of them, and could now feel the warmth that Kesara projected anytime we got together. She was a special lady, and I was lucky to be included in her group of friends.

* * *

The lobby of the dorm where most of my players lived needed an update from the eighties décor. It was like stepping back in time to my own dorm at North Carolina. A few students did a double take as they streamed toward the door, contemplating whether or not they should stop to say something to me, but knowing if they did they might be late for the game.

"Hey, Coach," Nate greeted as he and Eli walked toward me.

"Hi, guys." I looked over their cargo shorts and Piranha basketball t-shirts, wondering if I would be overdressed in my jeans and silver polo with a subtle university logo in green. Three others bounded up to us in jeans and LMU t-shirts, so I stopped feeling out of place.

Wendell, who lived in an upperclassmen dorm, joined us last. "I don't see why we have to go to this."

Ahh, a complaint from Wendell, how original. "We're supporting our sister team in their first home game," I repeated the reasoning I'd used at practice yesterday.

"We could have met over there."

"We're a team, we're walking in as a team, we're watching as a team. Let's go." I didn't wait to hear his sure retort, marching us out of the dorm and through the crisscross of walkways on south campus over to the arena. Seeing it full brought back memories of my own college days. I realized how lucky I'd been to secure enough seats for the whole team.

"It's a frickin' sell out," Ollie observed, looking up into the overflowing second tier.

"I believe they sell out every game," I told them. It wouldn't hurt to bash their egos a little. They'd have to be completely self-absorbed not to know that the women's basketball program was the most popular sports team at the school. They even beat out the football team in attendance. "This could be for us if we step up the play a little."

Wendell had taken the seat farthest from me, two rows back and at the opposite corner, so I couldn't hear what he said after his snort. I just hoped he stayed respectful during the game. As long as he didn't fall asleep, he'd might also learn something, too.

The head coach, Lindsay Meyers, spotted us almost as soon as we were settled. She smiled brightly and made her way over. I'd introduced myself when I was first hired and spent an afternoon talking basketball with her. Other than that, we hadn't had much contact. She was as busy as I was preparing for the season, but I looked forward to spending more time picking her brain over the season. "Thank you for coming, Graysen."

I took her hand in greeting. "We're happy to show our support."

"We appreciate it. Thanks, gentlemen, the team will be thrilled that you're here." They had the decency to acknowledge her words, not having a problem with this particular female coach.

"Good luck tonight." I gave her an encouraging nod as she turned back to the task.

For the next two hours the guys actually pulled their heads out and got caught up in the excitement. It was a good game until the second half, then our ladies pulled ahead and never looked back. I could tell that the crowd's reaction was a thing of envy with my team. I'd hoped it would resonate with them. Looks like I was getting my hope.

"Get some rest for tomorrow's game. I want the same kind of results that we saw tonight," I told them as we left the arena. They seemed pumped for the next game, even Wendell gave me a grudging wave as he left with the rest of the guys.

"You're not asking for much, are you?" Kesara's voice sounded from behind me.

I twirled to watch her approach. She was in jeans and a blouse, looking as casual and comfortable as she had in my courtyard the other night. I liked that she'd made an effort to go to the first games of all the sports teams. But I really liked that she hadn't brought several family members with her to this one like she had to mine. That had felt great. "It's all about the motivation. They don't like losing, but they really don't like being outdone by the women's team."

"Men," she scoffed.

"Yep," was all I could think to say. "I really like your family, Kesara." It was completely off topic, but something I'd wanted to tell her every time I saw her these days.

She beamed, not at all bothered by my offshoot. "They really like you, too. Enough that they want you to come to a Sunday picnic soon."

The invitation brought out my own smile. "That's nice."

"Soon? Or at least before everyone else in the family finds an excuse to descend on your place."

I laughed, liking the sound of that. "Hmm, I'm trying to think what else I need that I'm now sure you've got a cousin to help me with."

"Attorney, landscapers, beautician, manicurist, teachers, banker, cooks, waitresses," she ticked off on her fingers.

"How many cousins exactly?"

"Forty-two."

"Jeez, I don't even know forty-two people."

She laughed this time and the sound surrounded us, forming a comfortable place that only she and I seemed privy to. "We've pretty much got every occupation covered."

"I can imagine. Let me guess, you've got a car salesperson in there somewhere, which is why you and Santi are always giving me guff about not having one."

"We're giving you guff because you need one, especially once it starts getting colder." Her smiling face challenged me to disagree. Since I was starting to dislike getting on BART so late after dinner at Tavian's, I was going to give in. "But yes, we do."

"I knew it!"

She laughed some more. My, that was a nice sound. "Let me know if you want to look at something. He's a low key sales guy."

"I might take you up on that." As I was thinking of it, I asked, "Do you think I could get Mirabella to pick out some more suits for my games? I'm hopeless with shopping and she's so good with furniture and design, she'd probably be a whiz at clothes shopping."

She was biting her lip, trying to keep in a wide grin. "Bella could, but—"

"Oh, come on! Another cousin who's a personal shopper or clothing designer or something?"

"Nope...my sister."

"This is amazing." It really was. Her family was incredibly talented.

"She works at Nordstrom, so she gets a lot of good stuff in. We all use her. I noticed you were pretty high end the other night. Nordys gets some of that, but Neomi always knows where to get everything."

She'd noticed my suit. It was my best one. I had two others that were designers, too, but I decided I should wear only suits at the games this year because my adversaries would all be wearing suits. With the women's teams, I'd worn sweater sets, blazers, slacks, and the occasional suit. "If she has time to take me on as a client, that would be a big load off. I'm going to run out of things next week."

"I'll call her tonight when I get home."

"Thank you."

She waited a minute before teasing, "What? No offer of buying me lunch, dinner, or a new car for the labor intensive phone call I'm going to make?"

I laughed with her. "I'll think of something, my friend."

CHAPTER 17

By halftime of our second game, I wanted to wring my players' necks. Everything we'd been practicing these past few days, all the pregame instructions seemed to fly out of their little brains the second the ball was tossed for the jump. We were down by nine when we should be up by nine.

I looked them over as they slouched into their seats. "What happened to the press? Frank, the second they break through, you've got to drop back on your man or he'll continue to get that open dunk."

"The press isn't working."

"Your press isn't working. If you'd run it like we practiced, it would work." I took the time to redraw their positions on the board. "This team hates pressure. Hates it. The front court is doing a nice job of denying the inbound pass, but once they get it to the big man, it's like the rest of you forget you're supposed to be involved. You're not tired, so there's no excuse for you to be missing your assignments. Get it together and reapply after every made shot. Wendell, you're pushing too hard on offense. If a shot isn't there, you've got to swing it back out top."

"I'm doing all right." His smug look made me want to sit him.

"You're shooting twenty-one percent from the floor. That's not all right."

Two of the guys near me hid laughs behind their fists. "I've got more points than anyone else."

"Your role is to put the ball in the basket when you've got an open shot. Don't start thinking you can make room for your shot when you're double or triple teamed. Frank, I need more looks from you. Dash, if you have to, start throwing up threes. Make them spread the defense." I clapped my hands together. "We've got this game. Give me twenty minutes, as hard as you go in practice, and they'll be limping home."

Unfortunately, they didn't listen any better in the second half than they had in the first. And in no time, I was looking at my second loss as a head coach for this team. I'd never started a season 0 and 2. It was enough to depress even me.

By practice the next day, the team was again doing everything I asked. Running plays flawlessly, working together, and showing good defensive pressure. Some of the guys liked to showboat more than others, but that was to be expected. Wendell, though, acted like the rules didn't apply to him. He refused to give up the ball when it was passed. It didn't matter how many people I'd drop in on him. He thought he could shoot his way out of anything. When he missed and cleaned up his shot, he'd smirk in satisfaction. I had to get control of this.

"Come in, Wendell." I watched him approach my office after practice. He folded himself into one of my guest chairs, knees touching the back of my desk. "We seem to be having a problem communicating. You like ignoring my instructions and it's affecting the team."

"I have the best stats on the team. When I get the rock, it goes in the basket."

Really, really wanted to smack him now. I pulled my stat sheet in front of me. "Last year you averaged nineteen points, ten rebounds, and two blocks a game." He nodded, smirking more. "Oh, but look, zero steals, zero assists, five turnovers, and sixty-two percent from the line."

"Points, rebounds, and blocks, that's where I'm at. That's what the scouts look at."

"You know what else they look at?" I looked at him expectantly. "Field goal percentage and offensive versus defensive rebounds. Twenty-six percent and eight out of ten rebounds are offensive. You know what they'll think about that, don't you?"

"That I average a double-double?" he snarked.

"That you pad your stats."

Oh, he didn't like that. The steam coming out of his ears told me he really didn't like that. "I'm the best player on this team by far. Thirty percent is good enough when I average twenty a game."

I let him get away with rounding up. "Imagine how much more you'd average if you only took open shots?"

"We don't win unless I shoot. You need me to shoot."

"Wendell," I paused, making sure he focused. "You're a great player, but we need each other."

"Ha!" he snorted, slouching farther into his seat. "I don't need you."

"Yes, you do." I gave him time to let that sink in. "I need you to be as good as you think you are, and you need me for the NBA scouts."

He blew out a loud amused breath. "I can do that on my own."

"No, you can't."

"I did it all on my own last year." His chin jutted, challenging me to deny his claim.

"As amazing as it is to think you actually attend college, let me explain how things are. In a battle of wills, you'll always lose. Why? Because I have all the power."

He scrunched up his face before scoffing, "Screw you."

"You'll treat me like you've treated every other coach you've had," I said calmly, not believing that I was being so accommodating with this putz. If any of my female players had tried half the stuff he had, they'd be off the team by now. But I couldn't hold him to the same standards, not when he'd never been held to anything other than the expectation to play well. "If you don't follow the team rules, participate to the fullest in practice, follow my game instructions, and treat me with the same respect that I show you, you don't play. NBA scouts can't see you unless you play."

"You won't do that. I win games." He poked a finger into his chest as if I needed the visual aid.

"I'm not afraid to lose. You're not the only person on this team. You may think you're the best, but it doesn't mean you are. You are when I say you are. Until then, you can be the best at sitting the bench because you won't see any playing time." I challenged him to say something, but he sat there and sulked. "Do we understand each other?"

"Whatever." He got up from his seat.

"Once again, that's not a response." I stopped him. "If you want to play, you'll follow my game plan."

"Fine." He didn't bother to say goodbye.

Why did everything have to be so hard?

CHAPTER 18

The hand snaking under my shirt and streaking up to my breast felt so nice. Almost as good as the lips caressing mine. Kissing Darby had become a favorite activity of mine. Kissing Darby in her apartment was now my favorite location. After a couple of weeks, I'd succumbed to her wish to cook me dinner. She was pretty good at the cooking, but it was the movie time on the sofa that I really liked.

A gentle squeeze was followed by a fingertip swiping under my bra. That felt really good. Soon her hand had worked my bra cup down and she was teasing my nipple to rigidity. I moaned into her mouth. She pressed against me, swinging a leg over and pressing it between mine.

"Damn, Gray, you feel so good." Her lips moved down to nuzzle my throat, nipping and teasing along the column. I tilted my head back, unable to do anything but clutch at her back. When her mouth closed on my now exposed breast, I couldn't stop the groan. "Oh, yeah, you like that," she spoke against my breast.

I slipped my hands under her shirt and skimmed them up the sides. I liked feeling her in my lap, close to me, her hands and mouth making me forget where I was. Until that tongue flicked against my other nipple, I hadn't even realized she unbuttoned my blouse or popped the clasp on my bra. All I could feel was the intense heat her mouth stirred inside me.

"Jesus, Gray, I need you. All of you." She set her feet on the floor and pulled me up with her. In a haze, I followed, wanting more, wanting everything she promised. Needing that mouth back on me. "I've waited so long for this. For my fantasy." She kissed me again.

As if she'd popped a balloon in front of my face, I suddenly became aware of our surroundings. We were in her bedroom and she was stripping. My breath left me at the first flash of her exposed breasts. Red tipped, tilting upward, begging to be touched. Oh, God, this was it. I suddenly wished I'd not cared about the pool in college and just had as much sex as was offered. Or the hundreds of men or women who'd thrown themselves at me while I played pro ball. If I had, I wouldn't be starting to freak out right now. I would be able to appreciate every inch of flesh that she was revealing for me. I would be helping her shed her clothing instead of just staring dumbly at her. Thinking stupid things like how she must add color to her hair, something I should have realized when I first noticed she didn't have any freckles. Natural redheads had freckles. That so shouldn't be something I should be thinking when she reached for me, pushing off my blouse and bra. And when her body first touched mine, I should have relished the feel instead of panicking and wondering how I should respond when she touched me.

Okay, just breathe. We'd been dating for a while, and I liked her. This was the right time. I just had to get past the fact that I was a complete loser who'd only ever done this once before and never with a woman.

"You don't want to help?" A teasing smile played at her lips while her fingers continued to unbutton and unzip my slacks.

I definitely wouldn't be able to do this if she could tell I was practically a novice at this. She'd tried to get me to talk about previous relationships on other dates, but I'd managed to avoid that noose by mentioning that I'd never been serious with anyone.

Taking a deep breath, I stopped her hands and reached down to flick off my heels, then shimmied out of my slacks and underwear. Standing here naked with her naked, nope, not awkward at all, especially with her scanning every inch of me. I forced myself to calm down, but my heart felt like it would take flight.

"You're better than all my fantasies, Graysen." She stepped toward me and took me into her arms. The brush of her skin against mine helped stop most of the thoughts racing around my head. "So gorgeous, I can't wait to make love to you."

She pressed me back until I was sitting on her bed. Her face followed, pressing lips to mine before levering herself over my now prone form. She raised her head up and looked into my eyes. Her laser blue eyes seemed to look right inside me, a second away from finding out just how inexperienced I was.

I reached for the bedside lamp that lit the room, but her hand clamped down on mine. "Leave it on," she ordered.

I shook my head, but she wouldn't let up on her grip. I knew I couldn't do this with her being able to watch my reactions. She'd know, and I didn't want that. "Off." My voice sounded rough.

"I want to see you. I want you to see me."

"It's bright." The excuse sounded lame even to me.

"You're shy?" she teased. "No need to be."

I twisted the switch and the room went dark. "Please."

"You're lucky you're my fantasy, otherwise you wouldn't get your way on this," she sighed. "Next time, you can't hide."

She was already talking about the next time. If I could fumble my way though this effort, maybe next time wouldn't be so intimidating. Of course the fact that she thought of me as her fantasy added more pressure than I could bear. I'd be lucky if she didn't quit midway, sorely disappointed.

Her mouth started its slow torture again, for a moment, erasing all thoughts of doubt. I wanted this, she wanted this, just because I had no idea what I was doing didn't mean a thing. I knew what I liked. She was bound to like the same stuff. I let my hands slide down her back, gripping her hips as her leg nudged mine apart.

When her thigh pressed up against me, I jerked at the pleasure that shot through me. That definitely felt nice. My hands slid up to cover her breasts and she gave a responding jerk when I squeezed. Flicking my thumbs over those erect nipples, I had a hard time concentrating on the leg that now rubbed insistently against me. My hips rocked against her leg and she moaned encouragement.

With her face pressed into my neck, a hand snaked down to explore my sex. Fingers teased me, barely grazing my clit before plunging inside. "Damn, Gray, you're so tight, feels so good. Like that? Hmm?" Her hand started pumping into me and my hips reached for the friction I needed.

Her excited chatter continued, whispering erotic things she wanted to do and wanted me to do. She didn't seem to need any response, seemed completely involved in the pleasure she was giving and receiving. I slid one of my hands down to touch her. Wet heat spilled onto my hand. She grunted loudly, interrupting her chatter.

"God, yeah, Gray, make me come. Fuck me." She redoubled her efforts, thrusting into me, using her leg as better leverage.

I raised mine to fit between hers, which helped lift my pelvis into her pumping hand. Ah, better, right where I needed it. Dipping lower, I pushed into her with two fingers. Her slick tunnel gripped my surging digits, the feeling familiar even if the angle was foreign. Her exclamation told me that she liked it a lot. It only took two thrusts and she was coming, loudly. Her hand flexed against me as she went through her contractions and the added pressure helped tip me over the edge. The feeling was different from when I initiated a climax, not exactly better, but pleasant.

"You made me come so hard and felt so good coming in my arms, baby." She'd collapsed on top of me, breathing rapidly. Her heartbeat pounded against my chest, sweat making her slick and warm. Her lips trailed over my neck as she worked through her recovery. "Mmm, don't leave me yet," she whispered as I started sliding my fingers out of her.

Okay. I cupped her mound, staying inside her still fluttering channel. Wow, she took a while to recover. That had never been an issue for me. Quick flare up and almost instant dowsing once I hit my peak. Shudders were still rolling through her. I envied her ability to milk a climax like this. Maybe I'd have a heightened libido if this is what I went through every time.

"I want you again," she moaned, working her way up to kiss me. "You're body is so amazing. Flip me over and make love to me, babe. I want you on top this time."

Guess we weren't done. I rolled her over, pulling out of her, deciding that this time I'd take my time exploring her body. Just because I hadn't had a mind blowing time, didn't mean that I couldn't enjoy touching her.

My mouth and hands took the time to learn almost every inch of her. She felt good. She tasted good. I liked making her feel this good. When she climaxed again, I worried that she'd expect to make me orgasm again. I wasn't sure I could do that. As wonderful as it was to touch her, my own passion had pretty much died out after the first orgasm.

The sound of her deep breathing told me I wouldn't have to worry anymore. She'd actually fallen asleep almost as soon as she'd climaxed the second time. I thought only men did that, or at least that's what my friends had complained about in the past. It had been late, and she'd put in a lot of effort, so I shouldn't read anything into this. I shut my eyes, unaccustomed to her body weight pressing against mine, wishing I could use the restroom without waking her to clean up a bit, hoping most of all that I'd be able to sleep.

I'd had sex with a woman, successful sex, involved sex, sex that lasted more than thirty seconds. Did I feel different? Yes. Did I feel better? Not necessarily.

* * *

There had to be some notepaper around here somewhere. I went through another kitchen drawer. It was far later than I ever slept in, not that I'd slept, and Darby was still out cold in her bedroom. I'd been fighting my need to flee for over four hours. I just had to get some distance, allow me to think. I wasn't sure leaving a note was the right thing to do. It seemed kind of cold, something that might upset her, but I'd been awake for twenty-seven hours, my eyes were burning from not being able to sleep despite my fatigue. My mind wouldn't allow any peace until I could get some distance between us.

Not finding any paper, I headed back into the bedroom. Maybe I should just wake her. Or I could take that shower I'd ached for and maybe the sound would wake her. I didn't want to get back into yesterday's clothes after a shower, though. *God, just bite the bullet, woman.* I leaned over her sleeping form and shook her bare shoulder. The motion loosened the sheet down her chest. One of those gorgeous breasts popped free. I could almost feel the spiking nipple in my mouth, taste the perspiration of her skin. That part had been nice, great actually. All the rest, not as much.

"Mmm, morning, baby," she purred. Her hand reached up and pulled my neck down to meet her mouth. Yes, it was definitely morning. I'd rubbed some toothpaste on my teeth and tongue with a finger since I hadn't brought a toothbrush, and she'd just woken up. Yet another thing I probably shouldn't be thinking about that right now. "Why are you already dressed? Come back to bed."

"I've got to go." I edged out of her grasp.

"You've got to stay." She sat up, the sheet falling to her waist. Her hands grasped my arms and pulled me onto the bed.

"I really have to go. I promised my neighbor that I'd help with her party prep."

She frowned, sleep not completely clear yet. "Can't you help her later?"

"It's ten o'clock, Darby."

Her eyebrows rose, head turning to check the alarm clock. "Wow, you really wore me out." She smiled, lazy and sexy, reaching out to stroke my jaw. "I can't change your mind?"

"Not this morning."

"If you'll give me an hour, I could go with you to help. Two pairs of hands would get things done a lot faster, and we could be right back here before you know it."

Back here? Today? Oh, God. I so wasn't prepared for this. "That's nice of you to offer, but I think she's a little nervous to see all of her old friends. I wouldn't want to throw someone new into the mix. Thanks for being so considerate, though." I leaned forward and kissed her. It was an evil distraction, but I was using any card I could think of. My mind was about fifteen minutes from total meltdown, so I had to get away soon.

"Let me fix you breakfast, at least."

"No, thank you, I'm not a big breakfast eater." What would it take to get out of here? "Last night," I started, not really knowing what to say, but wasn't this what people said?

"Was spectacular, amazing, beyond all my fantasies." She crushed me against her and planted a smoldering kiss on me. Okay, forget the morning breath, this was a great kiss.

"You were wonderful," I said, meaning every word. She had been wonderful, even if the sex wasn't great. That wasn't her fault. It was mine. My first time after all these years was bound to be weird.

"I wish you could stay. We could spend our first Sunday together."

"Maybe another time?"

"Next Sunday and the next and..." she kissed me again, this one a brief parting. "What time should I expect you back later?"

"Oh, I hadn't thought, that is, I've got to get to work early and you've got a game tomorrow night."

She looked away briefly. "Okay, you're right, a game that I should be preparing for tonight. You're just so distracting. You'll come to the game, won't you?"

"I'll be there." I hadn't planned on it, but I didn't want to disappoint her any more than I already was today.

"See you tomorrow then." She squeezed my hand. "And, Gray, you really are better than my fantasies."

"Last night was special for me, too. See you tomorrow." I backed out of the room and resisted the urge to run to the door. When I hit the sidewalk, I'd forgotten that Darby had picked me up and I'd now have to trek to the station. Buying a car just ratcheted up the to-do list to number one.

By the time I made it home, I'd stopped freaking out. Okay, so I'd had sex with a woman I was seeing and it wasn't great. Many of my friends shared that the first time with a new person was often weird. It probably didn't matter that it was the first time I'd had sex with a woman. Since Darby hadn't been too disappointed, our second effort was bound to be better.

I just wished I'd felt a connection with her. Yes, she could make me a little lightheaded, but where was all that passion, burning, got to have it, would die without you, connection that everyone talked about? I should just stop thinking. That was always my problem, and the reason I'd avoided any romantic entanglements for so damn long. If I could shut down my mind, I would have jumped into bed with the first guy who approached me in college and every attractive sane fan while I was playing ball. God knew most of my teammates did. Instead I was always thinking about how I didn't feel anything for them, including desire, and they'd probably just wanted me because I played basketball.

The shower felt great. My muscles relaxed, and I finally washed off the smell that made me feel like I was branded on the way home. The scent of sex hours later didn't have any appeal, and I suspected the guy sitting next to me on the train could tell. Putting on fresh clothes, I felt like a whole new person. I wished I could fall into bed, but Mrs. Emerson was depending on me. She was someone who never pressured me, and helping her was exactly what my mind needed to work through my jumbled feelings.

CHAPTER 19

The only good thing about this road trip with the team was the posh airplane that the school chartered. The players had plenty of room to lounge in their oversized seats, trading iPods and DVDs, joking around and rehashing the two road games we'd just played. I was glad it was over, glad to be getting back, but we'd lost the games. I was being thrashed on a national news level now instead of just locally. I no longer wanted to watch the sports channels because the anchors were having a little too much fun with me right now. With four losses and a team that still resisted my every step, though, I was probably being a little oversensitive.

All I could think about was crawling into my bed and sleeping for at least six hours. I'd never felt this wiped out before. I was done with these childish babies, sick of the press questioning my abilities, and tired of trying to come up with encouragement for the guys on the team who were giving it their all when the others continued to fight my system.

Once we'd piled onto the bus back to campus, I'd given them all reminders about the next practice after the weekend. I could easily have them back tomorrow, but I really didn't want to see them, and it wasn't like they didn't know the plays or needed more shooting practice. They'd just have to start following my lead. If they did that, we'd pick up three fourths of the rest of the games.

As I was walking out of the North Berkeley station near my house, my cell phone rang. I looked down at the display, sighed, and opened the phone. "Hi, Darby."

"You were supposed to call me when you landed, sweetie. I was going to pick you up at campus. Ruin my surprise, why don't you?"

My feet stopped moving and I glanced around, expecting to see her. She'd called every day of my road trip. It was nice at first, but after the first loss, I didn't feel like talking about inane stuff anymore. "I didn't realize. It was a nice thought." I couldn't think of anything else to say. I wasn't too far from mental shutdown again. We had a date for tomorrow night, which would lead to our second attempt at sex. I didn't want to waste any more of what was left of my exhausted brain thinking about it.

"Turn around and I'll pick you up at the 12ᵗʰ Street station. I'm dying to see you, babe."

"I'm exhausted, Darby. I'm barely going to make it home as is."

"Please? It's not fair, you know. You blow my mind, make all my fantasies come true then get on a plane for more than a week. I'm barely hanging on over here."

I should be happy, right? This should make me happy. The woman I was seeing couldn't manage another minute without getting her hands on me. Ecstatic is what I should be. So why did I feel like a one-ton truck worth of pressure just landed on me? "We have a date tomorrow night, honey." I tested the endearment, but it didn't sound right to me. The iron gate in front of my building loomed. I felt like if I could make it through that, I'd be free.

"Graysen," she said in her husky I'm-going-to-kiss-you-then-rip-your-clothes-off voice. "I can't wait until tomorrow. Come over. I promise you won't be sorry. You'll get some sleep…eventually."

My feet stopped again. The gate was two steps away. All I had to do was key through it and nothing would keep me from getting to my place. But I'd blown her off the day after we'd first been together and run away on my road trip. That wasn't how an adult acted in a relationship. My brain issued the signal to turn around and start walking. "I'll be there as soon as I catch the next train."

Twenty minutes later, I rolled my suitcase down the front walk of her building. I still didn't feel any of the desire or anticipation that I should be feeling. Everyone I'd known had always bragged that once they'd had sex with a new lover, they couldn't wait to see them again. That wasn't what I was feeling. I wasn't feeling anything but exhausted and thinking that if I couldn't sleep tonight I'd be a basket case by tomorrow.

"Hi, baby!" Darby cried out, flinging her arms around me and dragging me inside. Her lips slanted against mine, letting me know everything she planned with that mouth of hers for the next few hours.

"Baby? Really? You're sticking with that one, huh?" My mouth spoke before my brain got involved.

She pulled back to stare at me. Hurt touched her eyes. "You don't like it?"

"I'm sorry. I told you I was tired. I get a little snipey when I'm tired."

Her face crinkled into a relieved smile. "That's okay. I'll make you forget all about being tired, baby."

"Let's choose another, really." This time I delivered the request softly, stroking her cheek.

"What? Too childish?"

"More like too *Dirty Dancing* for my tastes. Choose another, hon."

"Mmm, that's a nice one, but I'll come up with something good. For now, let's get these clothes off." She took control of that action, and I tried hard to shut down my thoughts and just let myself feel.

At least I'd slept, I thought when I woke the next morning. Not much, waking whenever she rolled or shifted, but probably three hours. Enough to slake my exhaustion and clear my mind. Last night had been much better, less awkward, but again, nice rather than explosive. She felt good, she tasted good, she could make me feel good enough, and she responded well to me. But was it mind blowing? Better than anything I could do for myself? No, to both questions, and that felt really wrong, like I wasn't being fair to her. Sometime around two in the morning, the thought hit me. If it wasn't exceptional, maybe I wasn't gay.

That thought followed me into the bathroom the next morning. I'd never reacted to anyone the same way I'd reacted to Darby. Would it be the same with a man, not the boy I'd known in high school? Could I do that with say...Santiago? Not even a second passed before the answer came to me. No. Definitely not, even as good looking as he was. So, gay, definitely, but apparently even a gorgeous woman who could make me woozy wasn't enough to ignite an insatiable libido. I'd just have to accept that about myself. Learn to live with it.

"You slipped out of bed without me again."

I jolted, turning to watch a naked Darby enter the bathroom. I'd left her sleeping and slipped into the bathroom for a shower.

"That's becoming a habit with you," she continued, flicking my towel loose and brushing up against me. "If you'd stayed, I would have shown you how fun mornings in bed with me can be." Her lips trailed across my shoulder blade before turning me to face her. "That's okay. The shower can be just as much fun."

The shower? She wanted to shower with me? No, thank you. I needed my shower. After all the years in athletics, my morning shower helped work out all the kinks and tight muscles. Now that I was forty, those aching muscles were a daily occurrence. After last night's activities, I was both sore and achy.

Too late, she pushed me in ahead of her. A few seconds of the glorious hot water sluiced over me until I stepped back to give her room. Now I was cold where the water had hit my skin. She pressed up against my front, steering us under the water stream. It hit her head mostly, turning the dark red darker. She stepped back and pulled my head under. I felt my long hair getting soaked and another instant of relief as the hot water pounded against my back. She squeezed some bath gel into her hands and started rubbing my shoulders and then onto my arms, intermittently pushing and pulling on me until she'd washed most of me. Her hands slid around my hips, one shooting between my legs. I jerked at the unexpected move.

"Ooh, you like that."

No, actually, I didn't. Not only did I want to shower alone, but I'd never been able to get myself off two days in a row, and certainly not twice in an eight hour period.

"I love how responsive you are."

I grabbed her wrist, stopping motions that were doing nothing for me. Her eyes flared at my fierce grip. Pulling her hand away, I knew I had two choices. I could tell her the truth, or I could give her what she wanted. With a tug, I whipped her around to face the shower wall. Her hands pressed against the tiles and she moaned something incomprehensible, feeling me push up against her back. This part I liked. Making her come, giving her pleasure, that made all this worthwhile.

Reaching for the shower gel, I soaped up her back from neck to ankle then I slid my hands around to wash her front. She growled when I spent time teasing her breasts, jutting her ass back against me. I took my time before I gave her what she wanted. Even more slick with the water from the shower, my fingers made easy work of tantalizing until she was begging. I switched hands and kicked her feet farther apart, snaking my other hand between her cheeks, sliding forward, under, until I'd found her core and slammed inside her with two fingers. She liked hard and fast, she'd told me with her body and voice.

"More, Gray, more," she panted after a few strokes.

I slipped a third finger inside on the next thrust, smiling at the unrestrained grunt that escaped her. My other hand alternated between teasing her clit and palming a breast. She was shaking, her sheath contracting against my invading fingers, and with one tweak of my fingers on her clit, she screeched in climax, gripping my fingers so hard they could barely continue the thrusts that would prolong her pulsations.

When the last of her ripples subsided, she collapsed against the shower wall, only my body pressing against hers held her upright. Her face was turned to the side, one eye blinking at me, trying to clear the haze of her ecstasy. "God, I love you, Gray."

The words rolled out of her so easily that I thought she'd said something else. Like all the other husky words that she said when we were making love. There was no monumental occasion to spur on these words. Nothing more significant than a statement made after she'd climaxed. It was possible she'd meant something else. She'd probably meant that she loved having sex, in the morning, in the shower.

Those thoughts were the only thing keeping me from stiffening against her or panicking because I didn't know how to respond. I'd always thought when someone finally said that to me, I'd trip over myself to voice the same sentiment. But unless I was willing to lie to her, I couldn't do that. Yes, technically, we'd known each other for a long time, but really, it had been a little more than a month. That wasn't enough time to feel so deeply for someone. Not for me anyway.

She managed to turn her boneless body around to face me. Her arms draped over my shoulders, a hand pressing to bring my face to hers. Her talented lips took hold of mine. "You are damn good at shower sex. Had that been an Olympic sport, you would have gotten the gold in that, too."

A nervous and relieved laugh left my lungs. "You're as biased as those gymnastics judges." I stepped back under the now lukewarm spray, reaching for the shampoo.

"Let me," she insisted.

I grabbed her hands before they reached my hair. "We're running out of hot water, hon." It didn't take long to lather my hair before I was passing her the shampoo and rinsing. I didn't bother to condition, something I knew I'd regret if I had to air dry, but I wanted out of that shower before she insisted on reciprocating.

"Wow, I've never seen anyone shower as fast as you." She stepped out after I'd already toweled off.

"Had a lot of practice from all those times the coach was so ticked after a loss that she'd give us five minutes to get on the bus."

Darby laughed and reached for her towel. While she was distracted, I slipped into her bedroom and headed toward my suitcase. At least this time, I'd have fresh clothing to put on. I kept the towel wrapped around my head and repacked the clothes Darby had slung this way and that on our way to the bedroom last night.

"Neat freak?" She was standing in the now open bathroom doorway. Her towel barely covered the important parts of her long body.

"Not really." Or at least I didn't think I was. I'd been wearing one of my better suits and now it was wrinkled after spending the night on her hallway floor.

"Are you as famished as I am? Feel like pancakes or omelets?" She strode to her closet, disappearing inside.

My stomach turned over. "I don't eat breakfast."

"Hmm?" Her voice was muffled for a moment. "Omelets?"

"No, thank you. I don't eat breakfast," I repeated.

"Just some cereal or a bagel, then? I've got a lot of stuff. I didn't know what you liked, so I got everything."

I squinted, wondering if we were speaking the same language. "Nothing, actually. I've never been able to stomach breakfast." It usually took a few hours before whatever I ate didn't immediately make my stomach queasy.

She resurfaced, clothed, looking sexy with wet hair. "You're an athlete. You must know how important breakfast is."

"I've heard, yes." I pulled the towel from my head and reached into the side pocket for the brush from my makeup bag. A few strokes through the thick strands tamed it enough to pull into a ponytail.

"C'mon, let me fix you something." She grabbed my hand, tugging us out of her bedroom. "So? What'll it be?"

"Just coffee. I'd be happy to sit with you while you eat, but I'm not hungry."

She let out a sigh, turning to open the refrigerator. "Have a seat. I'll bring you a plate in a minute."

I decided that an upset stomach was something I could handle if it made her happy. "Do you have the paper delivered?" Not that I wanted to read more about how under qualified I was for my job, but my skin was pretty thick, always had been.

"Should be out front."

I went to get it, leafing through to the sports pages. My photo was again on the front page, but at least it was only in the upper corner, teasing folks to an inside story. I agreed with the reporter's assessment that we should have won one of the two road games, and not all of the blame had been cast on me.

"You're braver than I am. I don't like reading my reviews. Not that we're covered very often, but it's been something to get used to." Darby came up beside me, placing a cup of coffee on the table.

"Oh, thank you. Do you need any help?" I offered, not wanting to be rude even if I didn't want what she was cooking.

"Almost done. You keep reading." She returned to the kitchen. "You're coming to my game later, right?"

Since we'd planned to see each other tonight, I had thought I'd go to her game and we could head out from there. But now, I was a little overloaded with Darby, and I still had yet to step into my own house after more than a week. I was dying to see what the J's had accomplished and if Mirabella had arranged any other furniture to be delivered.

"It's at three?" I asked, watching as her eyes narrowed momentarily, like she wasn't pleased I hadn't memorized her game schedule. "I can do that, but I really need to touch base with Tavian tonight."

"We're not getting together tonight?" She set a plate with an omelet and sliced cantaloupe in front of me. "But we had plans."

"We had plans tonight because I thought I'd get home too late to see you last night. Since I was able to see you, I should check in with Tave tonight. He'd never say it, but I know he's worried about my record. You understand, don't you?"

Darby flicked her eyes away. "He can't be upset. You're more high profile than any coach he's got on staff, now or in the past. You inherited a throwaway team. There's only so much you can do."

Throwaway? Sure, the best players from last year had all transferred to other schools to get away from the stigma of the violations the team had incurred. And yes, we'd lost nearly every promising incoming freshman to other programs after the head coach was fired, but they were still a good team. I was making them a good team, and I didn't appreciate that my, what was she?—girlfriend, significant other, lover, whatever she was—couldn't recognize that. Or at least be kind enough to fake enthusiasm.

"He won't be upset, but his college experience might give me some nugget of inspiration that I can use."

"And you can't get it on Monday morning at the office?"

"Honey," I started softly, "he's my best friend. I spend at least one night a week over at his place, and I haven't seen him for a while either."

"Okay," she sighed. "I can manage a night without you."

A night? Why was it every time she opened her mouth, I was questioning what she said? Jeez, I felt lousy. She was making me feel guilty when I had nothing to feel guilty about. Did couples spend every damn minute together? Was that what she was used to? If so, this definitely wouldn't work out. I'd spent too many years alone to suddenly find myself part of a Siamese pairing.

Avoid or confront? That was the question. "Thanks for understanding." I finally said. Avoidance, that would have to suffice for now.

CHAPTER 20

Initially, I'd been nervous about attending Kesara's family brunch. If I hadn't known five of the family members, I probably would have declined her invitation. But from the moment I rang the bell, Kesara took hold of my elbow and pretty much stayed in contact until I felt comfortable enough with the people I'd met that she could let me out of her sight.

As if I hadn't already guessed, they were a gregarious group. Affectionate, caring, considerate, and only ninety percent of them gaped at my size. Having gone through two plates of scrumptious Mexican delights, I settled onto a lawn chair to watch some of the smaller kids basically run after a soccer ball that very few of them actually kicked.

"Are you the one here with Kesara?" A man's voice sounded from my left.

I turned to see a wall of four solid men, ranging in height from five-seven to five-ten. They had short to sheer short black hair and each one had a different facial hair covering, but there was no mistaking they were related. "She invited me, yes. I'm Graysen."

"We're Kesara's brothers."

"Oh," I exclaimed, a smile forming as I moved to stand from my seat but didn't make it before one of them stepped close enough that I might have bumped into him if I'd stood.

"We don't care how much she likes you. If you hurt her like her last girlfriend, we'll hurt you. That bitch nearly broke her, and we won't let that happen again."

So many thoughts slammed into my head I had a hard time working on only one. They were threatening me, in an overprotective brother sort of way, but still a threat. Kesara had been badly burned by a previous relationship. And most importantly, Kesara was a lesbian. My insides fluttered, either from their menacing tone or the knowledge that this good friend was like me. Well, she was probably better at being a lesbian, probably had a lot more practice than me, and more than likely enjoyed sex better than I did, but I shouldn't be thinking about that. This was a family brunch and something else important was happening. Oh, yes, her brothers were threatening me.

"We're serious about this," the one with the sleek goatee insisted.

A laugh escaped before I could stop it. "How very cliché." My lack of fear made them step closer as one unit. "Really, you'll hurt me if I hurt her? What happens if she hurts me instead?"

"Get your own brother," mustache brother told me. He made it sound like I could go out to Brothers-R-Us and pick one up anytime.

I hid my smile at that thought with a quirk of my lips. "I have one, but he understands that my private life is private, hence the use of the adjective."

"That's your problem."

"No, it's yours, and I'll tell you why. I've known Kesara for a couple of months now. We've become good friends, but in all the time I've spent with her, she never once shared that she was a lesbian. She must have had a reason for that, and I'm guessing she's not going to be too happy that her brothers are airing out her private business while issuing threats to friends of hers." I took in their shocked looks. "But you guys know her better than I do. Maybe I'm wrong. Maybe she won't be as ticked as I think she will."

They all started with the menacing tone again, only this time in Spanish and aimed at each other. For meddling idiots, they were smart enough to figure out their sister was probably going to kill them for sharing all this with me.

"*Puedo entender todo lo que están diciendo ahora*," I let them know that that I could understand everything they were saying. They turned shocked eyes my way. "And let me give you a tip, the next time you threaten someone," I started, standing from the chair, watching as their heads tilted to follow my ascent. Two of them stepped back, and the other two had the decency to gulp loudly when I'd reached my full height. "You might want to make sure that your threats will be taken seriously. Seeing as I'm half a foot taller than most of you and I can bench at least one of you, I'm not too worried about the kind of 'hurt' you all can inflict."

"What's up, Gray, guys?" Mirabella walked up with a concerned look.

"The boys and I were just having a little chat. They were letting me in on some pretty private stuff about Kesara and throwing in a threat here and there, too. Good times."

Mirabella glanced at them and began to laugh, low, and taunting. "Oooh, Kesara's gonna kick your asses when she finds out you all are talking outta school."

"They did what?" Santiago asked as he approached.

"*Los hermanos* here decided they should try to intimidate Gray away from their sister," Mirabella filled him in.

"Jeez, morons, didn't you see how built this woman is? And man, I thought you would have figured out that you can't go around threatening people. Sara would kill you if she knew."

"Yeah, but she's not going to, is she, *primo*?" The tallest stepped into Santiago's personal space.

Sliding between them, I got the tall brother to back off. "He's not the one you should be worried about. How about we start over? I'm Graysen Viola. Are you Kesara's brothers?"

Still laughing, Mirabella introduced us around. "Ricardo, Arturo, Jorge, and Miguel, meet my friend and client, Graysen. Don't be idiots, make nice."

Their hands came out for me to shake, and I hid the strong desire to giggle at their supplication. "Nice to meet you all."

"Oh, good, you met my brothers." Kesara joined us.

"I sure did." I left them hanging for a while before I said, "Nice guys, you're lucky to have them. Not at all like my brother." I shot them all a meaningful glance. Jorge bit back a smile. Ah-ha, I'd won one of them over.

"Guys, did you hear that Graysen is practically keeping the entire family employed right now?"

Since hordes of other people swarmed around us, I smiled and made a point of looking around. "Not the whole family, and the work everyone has done is exceptional. I'd still be living in a temporary apartment with only two suits to wear at games and no house to renovate or decorate."

Another comment escaped in Spanish, this one not so flattering about me and how I probably treated the help. "*Cállate!*" Kesara and Mirabella scolded at once. Kesara turned to me, "I apologize for my brother. He thinks little of other people's feelings and seems to forget that it's possible for someone who isn't Mexican to understand Spanish."

I glanced seriously at Miguel. "I'm sorry that someone has treated you in such a fashion that you believe superiority is commonplace for people who contract the services of your extremely talented family. I'm not that way."

"Of course you're not." Kesara shot death glares at all of them. I was starting to believe that Mirabella was correct in who did the ass kickings in this family. "Stop being assholes to my friend. Go bother your wives."

As they wandered off, Mirabella exclaimed, "Damn, I'm glad I only have one of those."

"Same here," I agreed.

"Are your family get-togethers filled with such characters?"

I shook my head. "With only four of us, one who married into the family, it's pretty tame. Nothing like what you've got going here."

"Stick around. After they tap the second keg, things really get lively," Santiago joked. "We playing tennis again sometime?"

"Whenever you're free." I bumped his fist before he and Mirabella wandered off.

"Sorry about my brothers," Kesara needlessly apologized.

"Don't be. They were being brothers."

She cut a suspicious look my way. "How so?"

"Just protective. They love you a lot."

"Don't tell me that they told you…"

"They assumed we were…" Going out, getting it on, hot and heavy. The euphemisms assaulted me, shaking me to the core. Something about them was entirely too pleasant to dwell on. Then I felt guilty for even entertaining the idea. I was with Darby, and it wasn't fair to think about how Kesara's brothers' assumption felt really nice for a moment.

"Sorry about that. I told them we were friends, not dating."

"No big deal."

She tilted her head up to establish eye contact. "I'm not in a relationship, that's why I haven't mentioned it. I wasn't trying to keep anything from you."

"Kesara," I turned my full attention on her. "Your private life is yours. You can tell me as much or as little of it as you'd like. I don't believe I've told you anything either. So, don't feel bad."

Her arms came up to cross over her chest, sizing me up. "And if you were to tell me?"

I let out an amused breath. "You'd find out that we have certain things in common."

The smile that appeared got my insides running laps again. That was the first time I'd admitted being gay to anyone.

Having been a non practicing asexual for so long, I was glad to realize that the admission felt great.

CHAPTER 21

Darby's car slid to a stop in front of a large home in Marin County, an exclusive area just across the San Rafael Bridge. I was a little nervous to meet her friends, but we were in a relationship so I knew it was necessary at some point.

She grabbed my arm before I could exit. "I hope you have fun tonight, sweetie."

"I'm sure it'll be great." Better than being water boarded, at least.

"My friends and sisters are going to love you."

"I can't wait—hold on, your sisters?" Did I hear that right?

"Well, yeah, this is Kylie's place." Kylie was her oldest sister's name.

"You didn't tell me I'd be meeting your sisters. You can't just spring that on me a minute before we go inside." Or spring it on someone at all. There should be a discussion about the significance of such an event. No springing, springing shouldn't happen.

"What's the matter? They're really nice."

"I'm sure they are, but meeting your family is a big step. Something we should have talked about first."

"What's wrong? I love you, and I want them to meet you." She'd expressed that sentiment several times now since her first utterance. I no longer held onto the hope that she'd meant it in another way. A less emotionally tying way. It bothered me that I couldn't return the sentiment. I'd also been thinking that I must place a different significance on saying those words than other people since I wasn't about to say them any time soon to her.

"I just wish you'd given me the chance to be prepared," I sighed, resigned to attend tonight's party. What other choice did I have?

She leaned over and kissed me, making me forget my anger for a moment. When I felt a hand on my breast, I pulled back, irritation flaring back up. "What's wrong now?" Her tone expressed exasperation, like I was the one making her angry.

"We're sitting in a car in front of your sister's place."

"I've done far more in a car and in her house. Hell, in public even. I know you're shy, but a little fondling won't shock anyone."

"I don't feel comfortable being mauled in public. I don't care how innocent it may seem to you. This isn't what I'm used to and I'm asking you to respect my feelings on this."

She shook her head, rolling her eyes. "I've got to loosen you up a bit. Tonight's party will help. Let's go."

Before we reached the door, her hand slipped into mine, her expression challenging me to deny her this display. I gripped tighter. Holding hands, even kissing was fine, but when hands moved over breasts or butts, the intent was clear and broadcasting that in public wasn't something I was comfortable with.

"Holy smokes, she's taller than you, little freak," a woman with light brown hair, a less fashionable cut, expensive clothes, and an unmistakable resemblance to Darby said when she opened the door.

"I told you that, Ky." Darby leaned in to hug her older but shorter sister.

"Well, com'ere, you," Kylie instructed me, holding her arms up, expecting a hug. "It's good to finally meet you. Darby's been talking about you for years."

"Years?" I repeated, hugging her lightly before being ushered inside. I didn't get an answer because we were swarmed by the dozen or so people inside. Everyone else seemed equally grabby and it was ten minutes before I could stand upright. Not even the men were my height.

"Have some wine, grab a seat, and tell us all about you," Ashley, Darby's younger sister, instructed. "We're sick of listening to Darby talk about you. Let's hear how much of it's been true."

The group laughed as I fought my normal inclination to find an escape hatch. I didn't like being the center of attention when I wasn't working. Not that I liked it when I was working, but that came with the job, unfortunately. "I'm sure she's exaggerated greatly, but I wouldn't want to ruin the picture she's painted for you."

Darby smiled proudly, slipping an arm around me and turning to kiss my cheek. "She's perfect."

No one's perfect, I thought to myself. "See? Exaggeration, but I'm sure everything she told me about your kids was true. They're how old?" I already knew but get someone talking about her kids and there's no stopping the conversation.

Hours later, I found myself looking through the bookcases, ready to go home. Since this was Darby's deal, all I could do was amuse myself. Her sister had a nice collection, but judging from the pristine spines, I guessed she'd filled the bookcases without reading most of them.

"It's amazing to think after all these years that Darby was able to hook up with you."

I turned to find her friends, Paula and Ann, staring up at me. "It has been a long time since we first met."

"Did you carry a torch for her all these years, too? Is that how you hooked up?" Ann asked.

"Umm..." Torch? Years?

"She'd drag us to your games whenever you played in Phoenix where we all used to live. She'd be so heartbroken when she couldn't get past your team manager to get to you."

My face must have shown mild distress because Paula offered, "Oh, don't worry, she wasn't stalking you or anything." She laughed like the notion of stalking was funny. Seeing as I'd had trouble with one particular "fan" early on in my professional career, I didn't find anything amusing about the idea of stalking. "She just wanted to catch up with you. She'd told us all about hanging out with you at the Olympics and trying to keep in touch. Plus, we loved basketball, and you were something when you played."

"Thank you," I replied absently, wondering why Darby had never mentioned coming to see me play before. She'd given me the impression that other than the few televised games I'd been in, she'd never seen me play much after the Olympics.

"How'd it happen? Did she sweep you off your feet?"

"She has a tendency to do that," Ann inserted and got a smack from her partner. "Don't get me wrong, she's not a player or anything, but she's a prime catch. You're very lucky."

"She's lovely," I agreed. At this point it was best to just agree with them. None of what they were saying made any sense. It made me wonder if they were confusing me with someone else.

"Damn, right, she is."

"Hey, stop flirting with my woman," Darby called out from behind us. She wove slightly as she moved toward us. Her arms came around me, pulling my head down for a kiss. I tasted the wine on her tongue. If she'd snuck in another glass while I was over here looking through the books, then she was working on number seven. More than I'd ever seen her drink before.

"You're gorgeous," she whispered when she broke off. "Isn't she gorgeous? My Gray."

Her friends smiled and nodded, clearly happy for Darby. They also seemed amused by how tipsy she was. "Did you tell Gray about the time we stayed in the lobby of her hotel in LA hoping to catch her after her game?"

"Oh, shut up!" Darby giggled, gripping me tightly. "We were in the same hotel, baby, that's all."

"We sat around for over an hour waiting for your team bus to get there."

My eyebrows rose. Okay, maybe they hadn't been talking about someone else. She waited in the hotel lobby for me after a game? This discussion was becoming more uncomfortable by the minute. "We'd always catch the last flight home from LA after the game."

"Yeah, we figured that out when we didn't see you guys come back. But it was a good game, and Darby eventually got over it," Paula said.

"Yeah, with Margie," Ann added.

"Hey!" Darby exclaimed. "Nobody compares to my Gray."

Starting to get unnerved here. "Why don't we say our goodbyes and get going, Darby?"

"Oh, no, we just got here."

Three hours ago. "I've got a game tomorrow afternoon, honey." *Televised, against a ranked team,* I wanted to add.

"Isn't she darling?" Darby asked her friends. "And fine, and sexy, and—"

"She's a goddess, we get it," Paula cut her off, rolling her eyes at me.

"We should really head out," I said a little more firmly. Wrapping an arm around her waist and guiding her back toward her sisters and their husbands. "Thank you so much for inviting me. I had a wonderful time, and it was so nice meeting you all."

"She wants to go," Darby announced in a loud voice, confirming just how inebriated she was. "I want to stay, but my baby has a game to coach tomorrow. You know she's the men's coach, right?"

"You told us," one of her brother-in-laws replied.

"She's even more famous now," Darby continued.

"Okay, let's get you home." I steered her toward the closet where she'd left her coat and purse. "Thank you again." I was forced to give each a one-armed hug with my other arm helping to keep Darby from stumbling. Thankfully, she didn't put up a fight when I took her keys. No way I'd let her drive tonight. We said our goodbyes, and I loaded her into the car and drove her back to her place.

"Mmm, can't wait to get you in bed," she mumbled into my neck when I bent to help her out at her place. "You always feel so good."

"We're getting you into bed." I maneuvered her into her building and up to her condo. Her hands started roaming all over, intent very clear. I kept them at bay until we got to her bedroom. "Darby, come on, stop." I grasped her hands and shoved her gently onto the mattress. "Let's get you undressed."

"Sounds good, then you can crawl in here with me and fuck me."

"You're drunk. We're not doing this." I stripped her pants off after dropping her heels on the floor. When I reached for the buttons on her blouse, her hands gripped mine, those blue eyes boring into me.

"You want me as much as I want you."

"Honey, please, some other night when you're not out of it, okay? Now just sit tight and we'll have you ready for bed in a second." I proceeded to get her shirt off then unhooked her bra. She was beautiful, exquisite really, hard to believe these parts were forty-one years old. In fact, I sometimes wondered if there hadn't been a little surgical assistance. By the time I got her sleep shirt on, her fight had pretty much worn out. "Goodnight, Darby. I'll call you tomorrow."

"No, stay."

"I think you need a good night's rest. I've still got some game tapes to review at home. I'll call you tomorrow." I leaned down and kissed her, pulling back quickly before her hands could latch around my neck and not let me up.

Turning out her light, I made my way out of her building. Once again, I was at the mercy of the rapid transit system to get home. Maybe on Sunday I'd take Kesara up on her offer to introduce me to her car selling cousin. My face broke into a smile when I thought about that, and I kept myself from determining which made me smile more: meeting yet another talented cousin or seeing my good friend.

CHAPTER 22

When I turned back from the whiteboard, the team stared raptly at me. They were really starting to consider me as an authority on basketball, like they would any other coach they respected. A few wins will do that for you. But it was more than those easy wins in the last couple of weeks. They enjoyed practice, even when they had to run penalty laps, and they'd never had an easier time with school. As I'd suspected, the simple act of attending class made the papers and tests much easier to accomplish.

"They're ranked, which means what to us?" I prompted.

"They think they're better than us," Nate called out.

"They think they should win," Jeff offered.

"It means nothing," Dash shouted louder than the others.

I locked eyes with him and smiled before addressing the team. "That's right. It means nothing. We're in the same position we were for the first game. I know for a fact they're underestimating us. They don't know our offense or our defense, and we know theirs. That gives us the advantage. So, they're ranked. What happens if we beat them?"

The team hollered and high-fived. "We get ranked."

"That's right. Let's go get ranked." I watched as they jumped from their seats and noisily made their way onto the court.

"Coach?" Jason, the team manager, appeared at my side as soon as I stepped onto the court. "Ms. Evan would like to talk to you before the game."

My first reaction was to frown. Often I had people wanting to say hi during warm-ups before a game, but Darby should know better. After last night, I wouldn't think she'd be able to roll out of bed, much less attend a very loud basketball game. "Where is she?" I asked, and followed Jason's pointing finger to a row behind the scorer's table.

Darby was shifting from foot to foot as I made my way over to the bench, waving her down two steps. Her eyes were red and her skin a little pale. She had a hangover, a bad one, and the expression on her face looked like I was about to share it. "Why did you leave last night?" she hissed, at least having the decency to lower her voice.

Irritation flared. I so didn't need this right now. "I'm at work, Darby. If you want to have a personal discussion, you'll have to wait until I'm done."

"Wait." She reached out and kept me from turning back to the court. "You're right, but I was so hurt when I woke up and you weren't there. You didn't even leave a note."

"You knew I wasn't going to stay before we left for the party. I had to prepare for this game. Now, if you don't mind, I need to get back."

"God, you're not even upset by this." She grasped my shoulder, her eyes pleading. "We're having our first fight and you're all business."

"We're at work. If we weren't, I can assure you, I'd be suitably upset by your accusing manner."

"Coach?" Wendell called over to me from the court.

"Ten seconds, Wendell," I told him and turned back to Darby. "If you want to continue what you're calling our first fight, give me a call after work."

"You don't think it is?" She looked so hopeful and unsure of herself.

I relented because I had to get back. "I think you're making a bigger deal out of this than it is. Call me later, okay?"

Her smile was weak, but it was a smile. *Cripes, relationships! Was this really worth it?*

"What's up, Wendell?" I asked after moving around the bench and over to him.

"I don't get why you're having me post up on the right side. I'm always on the left unless we're running motion. We can beat this team, but I'm better on the left."

I smiled slowly. "I know that. So do the two NBA scouts who are here tonight." His eyes lit up and glanced over my shoulder to scan the crowd. "In fact, all NBA scouts know that about you. They also know that you resist going left, which to them, means you can't go left. It's one of the reasons they passed you over last year. We're going to show them you can go left, that you're just as good on the right side as you are on the left."

"How do you know there are scouts here?" He eyed me suspiciously.

"Because I invited them. They worked for the owners of my old team."

"You invited them?" His eyes popped wide.

"I noticed that you tend to follow my game plan and generally give me less hell when there are scouts in the crowd." I grinned when he couldn't hold back his own. "See? I believe I told you that we do better working as a team. I can help you get what you want if you give me your best effort in every game."

He nodded but it was grudging. I'd win over this kid if it was the last thing I did. "You'll get it, Coach." He sprinted back to the three-on-two sets the team was running.

From tipoff until the last two minutes of the game, it was close. So close that the other coach was sweating. He'd been yelling at his players all game, and now, he'd turned his fury on the officials. If we could break up one more play, he'd get a technical.

"Dash," I called out when the other team got lucky on a charging call. He trotted over from watching the player line up at the free throw. "Run two-down on this next set, and when you get plugged up in the middle, Jeff will be open on the three."

"A three ball?"

"We're taking control of this game. We're not sneaking away with a win. We're going to beat them. Get the three; then drop back to a box-and-one on the defensive set. Take away their outside shooter and make the rest of them deal with our zone."

He raised his brow at the idea of using a rare zone defense. "Will do." He raced back to the top of the key and flashed upside down rabbit ears with his fingers to everyone on the team.

With the made free throws, we were down by two. Dash received the inbound and sprinted up the court ahead of Jeff. He passed up to Nate who returned the ball as soon as he passed the half court line. Frank and Wendell jockeyed for positioning on the blocks as Jeff seemed to float down to the outside spot unnoticed. When Dash started to penetrate the key, Jeff's man stepped up on help side defense and Dash dished the ball out to an open Jeff. With perfect form, Jeff drained the three from the baseline.

The crowd went crazy as we took our first lead of the second half. The arena was full and had been ever since it became clear they had a novelty on the sidelines. I didn't blame them for their curiosity, especially since we put on a good show most games.

"Highlight!" I yelled my code word for our box-and-one defense. Frank and Wendell had to make eye contact with me to get confirmation that they heard me correctly. "Highlight!" I repeated and watched as they took up at the four corners of the key while Dash followed the shooting guard as closely as if he were his shadow.

As is usually the case with a zone defense, the offense started making passes, a lot of passes and on the fifth attempt, Frank got his big paw up to swat it away, right to Dash. Dash got on his horse and took it down court, me yelling at Wendell and Nate to give him a target on the wings. A beautiful no-look pass at the rim and Wendell slammed one in. The other coach called his last timeout.

"Very nice," I said as the team gathered around. "Get another stop with a two-one-two. They can't handle a zone and I want them scoreless for the last two minutes of the game." I stuck my hand in and was surprised when Wendell was the first to cover mine for the team chant. He'd played well, better than usual, but most importantly, better than he expected.

The rest of the game went as I'd hoped. We stopped them twice more and scored on each of the following drives, winning by seven. The distracted handshake the other coach gave me at the end of the game told me he had no idea how that game had slipped away. I had to keep from grinning like an idiot as I shook the hands of the other coaches and some of the players.

After a rousing locker room wrap-up, I headed back out to the viewing room. Tavian, Jacinda, the girls, and Kesara all waited for me in the hallway.

"Yay! Aunt Gray, you did it," the girls jumped up and down, tag-team hugging me.

"Good game, Coach." Tavian beamed. "Box-and-one, old school, my sista."

"Whatever it takes," I told him, getting a hug from Jacinda. "What are you all doing here?"

"Family sports day," Alicia told me, reaching around my waist with her sister taking up the other side. "We usually go play something, but we wanted to come see your game instead."

"Well, thank you. It's nice to have you here. And you, too, Kesara. Thanks for giving up your Saturday."

She smiled, glancing at the clinging girls then up to me. "It was our pleasure. I tried to get my sister to come, but she just wanted a picture of you in your suit."

"Her sister is my personal shopper," I told Tavian's family. And a damn good one. Shopping had never been so easy before Neomi starting picking things out for me.

"That's a job? I'm going to do that when I grow up," Dameka said.

"You'd be great at it, pookie," Tavian encouraged. "Come on, the game tapes will wait. We've got an ice cream celebration to attend."

"Ice cream! Ice cream!" The girls released me to dance their ice cream dance.

"Before you race off, the cousins would love to congratulate you," Kesara told me, gesturing back toward the stands where several of her family members sat.

"Join us, Kesara," Jacinda offered. "I'd love to meet your cousins. Gray has spoken so highly of all the work they're doing. I can't wait until the housewarming party."

"What housewarming party?" I asked.

"The one you're going to throw so we can see the finished product and bring you lots of gifts."

We laughed at her order. I knew better than to argue with her, not that I wanted to. I'd thought about cooking dinner to thank everyone for all their hard work, so a party wouldn't be a bad idea.

"I'm afraid that we're all off to a baby christening tonight, but come say hello before we have to leave," Kesara said as she led us over to where her cousins and their spouses were sitting. It felt so great having this kind of support. Tavian hadn't been lying when he told me I'd feel at home in no time if I took this job.

After ice cream with Tavian's family, I made my way home. I was thoroughly wiped out from the emotional win. Over the next two weeks, we should pick up three more games and have a winning record. Today had been a breakthrough with the team. They hadn't fought me on one decision and really started to act like the team I'd been trying to shape them into.

As I was keying into my gate, I heard a car door open and close. I turned to find Darby stepping out of her car. "Hey, this is a surprise."

"I couldn't wait for you to call. I've been here for a while. Did you go into overtime or something?"

"No, Tavian's family took me out after the game."

"Oh," she said quietly, following me through the gate and toward my place. "I shouldn't have —"

"Way to go, Gray!" my neighbor, Rick, shouted from his open doorway.

"Great game," Mike, his roommate, shoved through from behind.

"Thanks, guys." I waved to them, thankful that they'd only wanted to shout encouragement rather than rehash all of the game with me. They did that all too often.

"Wow, it's looking like a home now," Darby commented when she stepped inside my place. I'd taken to waiting out on the curb whenever she picked me up for our dates because it was clear she hadn't been impressed with the place before. Plus the construction zone had moved into the kitchen so it hadn't started looking pretty until midweek.

"Almost done. The rest of the furniture should be in place shortly." I offered her something to drink then guided her to the couch. "You were saying?" I encouraged her to finish whatever she'd been saying when Rick had interrupted us.

"I just feel like we're not connecting lately. When I woke up this morning and you weren't there, I felt rejected. I know I shouldn't have brought this up before your game, but I wasn't thinking straight."

I gave a slight nod, letting her calm down before trying to reason with her. "How much did you drink last night? Do you remember?"

"A few glasses of wine."

"Closer to a couple of bottles, honey. You weren't yourself at the end of the party and completely out of it by the time I got you home."

"You could have stayed with me," she pleaded.

"You were very insistent that we make love, and you weren't in any shape for that."

Her eyes widened. "Oh, God, did I make a fool of myself?"

"No, but you weren't yourself."

"I must have passed out at some point. You still could have stayed."

No, I couldn't have. "I told you before we went to the party that I couldn't stay over."

"Why do I feel like I'm the only one vested in this relationship?" She wiped angrily at the tears that welled in her eyes.

"You're not, Darby. I'm sorry if I've made you feel that way. You caught me off guard today by showing up at work trying to pick a fight. We can't be together if you're going to do that. I would never interrupt your work, especially not right before a big game to discuss a misunderstanding or anything about our relationship. It's not how I'm wired. I hope you can understand that."

She stared at me for a long time, breath pumping in and out of her chest. It bothered me that I didn't feel horrible for making her so upset, but this was all in her head, and I didn't sign up for being a therapist in this relationship. "I can, and I'm sorry. I just feel so raw right now. My head is killing me. I've got my friends calling to rave about you, and all I can think about is that I woke up alone."

"Maybe I shouldn't make plans with you on nights that I can't stay over. And, honey, not to be cruel, but I won't stay over if I think you're too tipsy to remember it."

Her chin tucked into her chest before she raised her head to reestablish eye contact. "I don't usually drink that much. I must have been more nervous about them meeting you than I thought. I'm sorry."

"Are you okay with us going out but not spending the night together, or should we only make plans when staying together is possible?"

"I won't lie. I want you in my bed every time we get together, every night actually, but I understand that this first season is important for you. I can contain myself until after the season ends."

Assuming we're still together. The thought zipped through my head, bouncing around like a pinball in play. I glanced away, hoping my eyes didn't betray my guilt. "Thank you for understanding."

"We're here now. You don't have a game tomorrow." She leaned into me, wrapping her arms around my shoulders to press up against me. "We could try out your new bed."

I kissed her, savoring the feel of her mouth pressed against mine. "You just said that your head was killing you." I cradled her gently. "I bet your stomach isn't feeling much better. Why don't you head home, soak in a tub for a while, pamper yourself. You could use a quiet day, couldn't you?"

She smiled, kissing my cheek. "You know me so well. This has been a terrible day, but now I feel so much better. As long as we're okay, I think I will take off."

"We're good," I assured her, not knowing if I was telling the truth but not wanting to dwell on it either. I stood and reached down to help her up, taking her in my arms for a comforting hug, before walking her out to her car. Leaning in through the open car door, I kissed her lightly. "Thanks for coming by, Darby."

"I'm glad we cleared the air." She kissed me again. "Bye, my love."

Watching her drive away, I thought I should feel bad about how upset she'd been and the fact that she was convinced that she loved me when I wasn't sure I felt anything more than fondness for her. But with a call out from a neighbor across the street, I decided I wouldn't let anything bring down my mood from our win today. Basketball season meant thinking about basketball not relationships. Darby would just have to understand.

CHAPTER 23

The doorbell rang as I was dropping the last appetizer onto a serving dish. I still had the entrées to finish, but I figured Jacinda and the girls were here early to help me prep for the housewarming party.

The door opened to reveal a smiling Kesara. I blinked, not expecting her for another hour. "Please don't tell me you can't make it to the party later."

She laughed at my note of panic. "I figured you might need some help putting together some of the food."

"You didn't have to do that. I've got everything under control." I lied like a good host.

"I just bet." Her eyes scanned the new kitchen, nearly every cabinet open, plates stacked, pretty much chaos. "I can't believe you're doing this, and I can't believe you didn't just make them all bring a dish. We do it that way every Sunday. It wouldn't be any trouble for them."

"Then it wouldn't be a thank you party for all their hard work, would it?"

"Here we go with the thank you's again."

"Here we go with you not getting the whole purpose of a thank you again," I shot back, a chill racing over me at the smile she flashed.

"I hope you know what you're getting into, mixing my family with your friends."

"Your family are my friends, at least the ones that worked on the place, and other than Tavian and Jacinda, I don't know the neighbors well enough to call them my friends."

She regarded me, serious at first, then a peaceful look came over her. "Let's see what we've got in here." She stepped around me toward the kitchen. "My word, this is a gorgeous kitchen. Did they tell you that their brother Julio is the cabinetmaker?"

"Yes. Can't wait to meet him."

"May I look around? I was here to pick up Mirabella two weeks ago, but not everything was finished."

"Make yourself at home." For the first time those words sounded genuine to me. She and her family had become part of my life over the past couple of months. I was used to leaving just as Juan and Jose arrived, coming home as Mirabella was finishing up, seeing Santiago or Kesara waiting for one or the other to go out for the evening. Even Neomi had taken to dropping off wardrobe pieces from time to time, waiting for me to try them on before she'd return them if they didn't work. I'd miss having them be a regular part of my everyday existence. I wasn't sure how to deal with that.

From the other rooms, I'd hear her call out compliments as I continued to put together the marinade for the chicken and steaks. When she resurfaced from the guest room, she said, "It's wonderful, Graysen. Looks like it must have when it was built."

"Except for my shower and this kitchen."

"I definitely have shower envy. If I wasn't in an apartment, I'd have the boys do the same to my bathroom."

"With a realtor for a cousin, you're in an apartment?"

Her brown eyes darkened for a moment, looking away. "It was a temporary fix that turned into a home. I don't like moving, so I'm not eager to jump into something else even if I'd rather have a place to own."

"It's much easier to move when you sell everything heavy," I joked.

"Good tip." She moved up beside me, taking the spoon out of my hand and loading it up to pour over the steaks. "You're going to spoil these people with all this great food. Don't you know that a BBQ is supposed to be cheap hotdogs and burgers?"

"I've got those, too." I pointed the knife over my shoulder at the stacks of buns.

"How many people are you expecting?"

"Everyone that worked on the house, their families, Santi and any guest he wanted to bring, Neomi and her husband and kids, Tavian, Jacinda, and the girls, my neighbors and their guests, and I believe I told you to bring a guest."

She faced me, smiling again. "No one to bring. I figured I'd need to help you referee my family. Especially if all that beer I saw on your back porch is for them."

"They'll be lucky to get one beer if Rick and Mike bring any of their former frat brothers over as guests."

We both laughed and settled in to finish up the prep before people starting arriving. Not long passed before Tavian and family arrived, then people started trickling in. I offered tours where everyone seemed duly impressed and Juan, Jose, and Mirabella wore proud smiles and puffed up chests as everyone raved about their work. What astounded me was how pleased they were that I was hosting this party to thank them. Apparently showing gratitude for your contractors and designers wasn't really done.

Sometime later when we'd all been mostly fed, the girls, my neighbors' kids, and Juan and Neomi's kids started a game of kickball in the courtyard. I went to supervise and keep them from kicking the ball through a window. A waving figure caught my attention from the other side of the gate. I leaned over enough to look through the archway and saw Darby trying to get my attention.

When one of the kids raced over and let her in, I called out, "Hey, I thought you had your sister's thing today?"

She smiled broadly as she approached. "I cut out early. I felt bad that I couldn't make it to your first party here." She stepped into my arms and planted a hello kiss on me that turned far more intense just before I stepped away.

"Darby! There are kids here." Who thankfully were too involved in the game to watch her eat my face.

"Like they care. I missed you. I wanted to say hello."

I resisted the urge to sigh. Lately she'd been getting bolder in public, almost like she was trying to get people to notice us wherever we went. I wasn't ashamed of our relationship, but I wasn't into exhibitionism even if I weren't as visible as I was becoming. "I'm glad you're here. You can meet everyone who worked on my house."

"I thought you said this was a housewarming party?"

"It's more of a thank you for all the hard work party."

Her brow knitted, but I coaxed her toward the house. We met Mrs. Emerson and her grandson first, two of my other neighbors, and eventually all the people responsible for making the place look so good. For once, Darby wasn't overly talkative and didn't seem to command the attention she normally garnered. Within moments, she was gravitating toward Tavian and Jacinda. Perhaps she was a lot more shy than I'd ever given her credit for.

Familiar voices had me turning to find Kesara coming in from the back door. She and Santiago were headed toward me, fight in their eyes, probably about to ask me to resolve another of their mock conflicts with the reason they couldn't seem to find whenever they were together.

Kesara glanced over at the living room to smile at Tavian and stopped, all trace of amusement leaving her face. Within seconds it seemed like every emotion in the spectrum had crossed her face before she shut them off and what I'd come to know as her professional face fell into place.

"Everything all right?" I asked.

"Great party, Gray," Santiago said, not noticing any change in his cousin.

I smiled but turned a concerned gaze to Kesara. Before I could repeat my question, the kids swarmed inside, distracting all of us for a moment. "Kids!" Tavian's booming voice got every one of them to snap to attention whether they were his or not.

"It's okay, guys, just try not to hurt yourselves on any sharp corners," I warned them, getting them to slow down to a trot through the house.

"You're so great with kids, babe," Darby said, slipping an arm around my waist. "Hi, I'm Darby, Gray's girlfriend," she told Santiago.

His eyes widened momentarily before taking her hand. "I'm Santiago and this is my cousin Kesara."

"Good to see you," she nodded to Kesara, but her tone didn't sound genuine. "Excuse me a moment, sweetie." She turned and headed back to Tavian. All I could do was stare at her quizzical behavior.

"She seems nice," Santiago offered. "I didn't realize you were involved with anyone."

I let a laugh escape. "You mean you didn't realize I was gay?"

He laughed with a tilt of his head. "She work at the university, too?" He looked at both Kesara and me.

She stayed silent, so I answered, "Yes, the volleyball coach."

"Convenient," he mimicked an old SNL character and got us laughing again. When his nephews appeared and dragged on his hands, he excused himself, leaving me with Kesara.

"Would you like another ice tea?" I offered, noticing that she looked a little out of it.

"Actually, I think I'm going to head out." She started toward the door.

"Wait, what?" I hustled after her out into the courtyard.

"I think I ate a little too much. I've got a stomachache."

"Would you like to lie down? My bedroom has thick walls. Close the door and you'll have all the peace and quiet you need."

"No, I think I'll just head home. Thank you for a lovely party."

"Wait, Kesara." I reached out to grasp her arm. "Are you okay to drive? If you're queasy, maybe I should take you home?"

"God, you're sweet," she said softly, her head shaking. "You've got a house full of guests, and you're offering—"

"Baby? What are you doing out here?" Darby appeared in the doorway before walking toward us. She slipped both arms around me, leaning against my frame. "Are you leaving, Sara?" She used the American pronunciation of her name.

"Her name is Kesara," I corrected, fighting back the surge of anger I felt toward her.

"Oh, sorry. Are you leaving so soon?"

Kesara flicked a glance at her. "Yes." Her brown eyes landed back on me. "Thank you for the party. I had a wonderful time."

"Should I get Santiago to drive you home?" I called out to her retreating form.

"I'm fine, thanks. See you at work." She pushed through the gate and disappeared down the sidewalk toward her car.

"I didn't realize you were friends with her," Darby said in a suspicious tone.

"Yes. In fact she's the reason I found this place, have it remodeled, and decorated. Most of those people in there are her family."

"That explains it." She nuzzled my neck, tightening her grip.

"Explains what?" I pulled away. Something about her was really ticking me off today.

"Never mind. Come on, let's get back inside. Tavian was just about to tell us about your first meeting, but he wanted you to hear it."

I shook my head and scoffed, upset that I couldn't pinpoint what was making me so angry with her and irritated that Tavian was going to try to embarrass me in front of a house full of people. I should be used to it though. He loved coming up with highly exaggerated stories about our college days.

I gave one last look in the direction of Kesara's exit, wondering what had caused her sudden mood swing, but with Darby's tug on my arm, I didn't have time to dwell on it.

CHAPTER 24

Back from our third road trip, I made my way up to Tavian's suite of offices. We now had a winning record, and if I had anything to do with it, we'd maintain one for the rest of the season. I wondered if that was what Tavian wanted to talk to me about.

Kesara sat at her desk, phone to her ear, dealing with what sounded like a complaint. I felt a pang of regret when I saw her. I hadn't seen her since my housewarming party, having missed her at our usual weekly lunch for the last two weeks. I'd missed her smiling face but could see that I wasn't going to get to speak to her before I had to meet with Tavian.

She caught sight of me and smiled politely, tipping her head at the door to indicate that I should head inside. I stuck my head through the open door and found Tavian clicking through something on his computer. "Checking the sports line?"

"Hey there, get in here. Congrats on the games. You're turning this team into quite a force."

"Thanks. They don't seem to be fighting me as much."

"I knew you could do it." His way of saying, "I told you so."

"We're not into smooth sailing yet. We've got a lot of tough games, and Ollie and Frank are still having trouble with school.

If they don't make it through their finals, we're without them for January."

"You'll get them through it. The mere fact that you know they're having trouble before they have it tells me you've got a handle on it."

I narrowed my eyes at him. "What's going on?"

"What?"

"Don't what me, junior. What do you want?"

His hands clasped against his heart. "I'm hurt, Gray. I don't always want something from you. Can't I just be nice?"

"No."

"You punish me, woman. Okay, there is something, but it's nothing big."

"Mm-hmm." I slouched into one of his chairs.

"No really, it's just that my office has received about fifty requests for interviews over the past couple of weeks." He looked up at me expectantly, but I didn't bite. "Yeah, well, obviously, it would be great if you'd agree to some of those."

I took my time blinking at him in silence, trying to make him sweat. "No, thank you."

"You've got to do some of these." He held up several pages.

"No, I don't. We talked about this when I accepted the position."

"Yeah, but who knew we'd have this many?"

"I did," I held up a finger then added another. "And so did your wife, which is why we agreed to no interviews when I accepted this job."

He scrunched his brow. "How could this hurt?"

I scoffed, wondering if he'd been paying any attention to how the media was handling the team. "The required press conferences are becoming a circus. Only half the questions are about the games now. I have to sit through those because it's part of the job, but I'm not doing an interview unless it's a commentary on the game we just played."

"You're killing me here." He looked exasperated, but I'd calmly explained to him why I wouldn't do interviews when I signed the contract. He was so happy I agreed to take the job he would have let me get away with anything at the time. I knew this day would come, which was why I'd put it in writing. "This program needs all the support it can get. One interview? *Sports Illustrated*, maybe? Just one, for me?"

"I'm not doing anything that would highlight me. I made that decision when I became a coach. It's all about the team now. An interview like the one you're talking about will have very little to do with the team."

"You could dictate the subjects you'll cover. I mean, I know you're private and everything. Hell, how long have I known you, and I finally meet someone you're dating? But, it doesn't have to be about stuff like that."

It would be about all that stuff and more. "I don't care if the only personal question they ask me is when I started playing basketball. If they aren't asking me about a game, it's personal, and I don't want to discuss it. You should know this about me."

"I can't persuade you?" His hands flipped up in pleading.

"No." I didn't even try to joke about this.

"I should have insisted on it for your contract."

"Then I wouldn't have signed."

His head shook before he sighed, resigned. "God, you're tough."

"Always have been," I retorted, wiggling my eyebrows. He was used to losing most of our disagreements. "Anything else?"

"I'm going to string these guys along."

"You do what you have to." I rose to leave.

"Would blackmail get you to agree?"

I laughed. "You've got nothing on me, Tave. You were the wild one in college."

"Get outta here." He flicked his hands, having accepted that he'd never win.

With a wave, I made my way back outside, thrilled to see Kesara was off the phone. I stopped in front of her desk, making her look up from her computer screen. "Hey there. How've you been?"

"Fine, you?"

"Good, thanks. I didn't see you at our regular lunch meet last week." I left out how disappointed I'd been.

"I've had a crazy schedule lately."

"Coaches wanting stuff?" I joked.

"Always." She graced me with a smile but didn't say anything else. This was so unlike how our friendship had progressed. I didn't know how to handle it.

"Did Santiago call you about the comedy club for this weekend?" He'd called to invite me yesterday and said he'd call her, but I wanted to make sure she'd come.

"He did, but I'm busy."

I knew the comedian was in town for the whole weekend, so I offered, "How about some other night?"

"Maybe."

Okay. I stared at her for a moment, her attention divided between the screen and me. "I'm sure this will sound egomaniacal, but did I do something to upset you? I mean, I knew once the house was done and Neomi had me dressed properly that I wouldn't get to see you as often, but when I can't even catch you on campus..." I faltered, not wanting to voice my suspicion.

Her eyes bounced back and forth between mine, as if searching for something to say. "Sorry, I've just been in a little funk."

That didn't sound good. "Something recent? You seemed fine until your stomach got queasy at my party."

Her glance flicked away then to the phone when it rang. "It's nothing to do with you."

My hands came up on their own. The ringing phone pressured me into backing off. "Okay, well, I'll leave you to get back to work. But, please call or stop by whenever."

She nodded with another polite smile as I retreated. I'd find some excuse to call or stop by every other day until I wore down her mood and we got back to being good friends.

CHAPTER 25

Sometimes a look was all it took to let me know I'd just screwed up. Darby was giving me that look from across the table at her favorite restaurant. I'd become accustomed to various expressions she'd show me, but this look always surfaced when I said or did something that displeased her.

The sigh didn't help either. "You're upset." I said for her.

"I can't believe you won't change your schedule."

"We've discussed this before."

"I'm getting tired of the fact that we still only get together once a week unless I give you a month's notice."

Actually only a week, but I wouldn't make that clarification now that she was just getting warmed up. Another thing I'd learned, never stop Darby when she was on a roll or the roll would never end.

"I mean, are we in each other's lives or not?" she persisted.

"Your season may have ended, but mine is still going on for another few months. Almost all of my games are at night, and we agreed that coming over after a game doesn't work. So, what are you asking from me?"

"You still see Tavian one night a week. You're going out with Santiago at least once a week, and your neighbor always has something she wants you to do for her. Add that to all the games you've got and I barely get to see you."

It was probably just my imagination, but it seemed like the restaurant got quieter all of a sudden. I glanced about making sure that everyone else was as consumed in their chatter as Darby seemed to be in ours. Then I started wondering if everyone else's girlfriend always waited for public venues to have what should be a private discussion.

Returning my attention to her, I tried to remain calm. "I won't give up everyone else in my life for my girlfriend. I'm not one of those women. You wouldn't either, so what's really going on?"

"You don't have to see your friends and your neighbors as much as you do, and you could invite me to Tavian's every once in a while."

I resisted the urge to tip my head back and let out a huge sigh. "Tavian's our boss. If I weren't his friend, he wouldn't invite me over. And I will continue to see my friends and neighbors as much as I want to, just like you're free to see your friends, sisters, neighbors, colleagues, and anyone else you want to go out with."

"You never invite me to go out with your friends." Her blue eyes turned into accusing laser beams.

"I invited you to my housewarming party, but you didn't seem to have any fun. In fact, you barely said a word to anyone but Tavian. I figured you wouldn't want to go anywhere with me and Santiago or any of his cousins."

"Well I don't know if I would," she agreed, and I felt a short burst of relief that she saw things my way. It didn't last long, though. "But you never ask me to go."

"Okay, I'll own my part of this." Mentally, I counted to five so that I wouldn't sound as sarcastic as I felt. "Would you like to go to the symphony with Santiago, Mirabella, and me?"

A man who wasn't the waiter approached our table, interrupting Darby's sure decline of my invitation. This was becoming more frequent as the number of televised games increased. "Hey, you're Graysen, right?" Like we were best friends or something. "You know how you can win more games?"

I looked at Darby and said softly, "Pardon me." Then I turned my attention to him. "Is this a riddle?"

He didn't catch my sarcasm. "See if you put Wendell and Eli in at the same time, you'll win more games."

I didn't bother to point out that they played the same position. That would only prolong this interruption. "I'll keep that in mind. Thanks."

"Yeah, you'll definitely win more. They were a good team last year. This year they suck, but not if you play both of them at the same time." When my blank stare didn't seem to drive him off, he asked, "Can I get an autograph?"

I refrained from laughing, both for his request when clearly I sucked as a coach, and for the fact that he didn't have anything to write on or with. "Not while I'm having dinner, sir. Come to the next game and I'll sign your program."

His brow furrowed, not sure how to react when I'd declined his request. "Just sign your menu or something."

"The menu belongs to the restaurant, and I don't sign autographs when I'm not working. Please respect that."

He glanced at Darby as if looking for her help. She'd gone from the oddly excited expression she usually got whenever someone recognized me to stewing in frustration. Realizing she would help, he asked, "A picture at least?"

"At the next game. Come up to the bench, I'll remember you. Have a good evening, sir." I made a show of turning back to my coffee and taking a sip while staring at Darby. He finally took the hint and left, grumbling all the way back to his table. "I'm sorry. You were going to tell me whether or not you wanted to join us on Wednesday at the symphony?"

Her blue eyes narrowed before shooting a look over my shoulder at the retreating man. "What a dick."

That's unnecessary, I thought to myself. Annoying, I'd give her, but her mood made her harsh. "Sometimes people don't understand how rude they're being by interrupting."

"Telling you how to do your job, jerk-off," she muttered, still scowling at him.

"Darby?" I got her attention back. "The symphony?"

A sigh blew across the table. "I don't want to go to the symphony. I want you to come to my sister's Christmas party since you won't come home with me over the break."

"Darby." I clenched my teeth to keep the frustration from overtaking my tone. I almost wished the guy would come back. That would be so much easier to deal with than an unreasonable girlfriend. "I have games over the break. I don't have a vacation like you do."

"And you won't ask your mom to come a day earlier so that I can meet her, either."

Ahh, so that was part of it. Like I'd have my girlfriend meet my mother before I knew if we were serious or not. "She works, too, you know."

The waiter came over and I let him know that we were through and would like the check. Darby ignored him, something I'd noticed about her the first time we went on a date. I always thought you could tell a lot about someone by the way they treated service industry folk. What I saw from Darby, I didn't much like.

"I feel like I'm taking a backseat in your life."

"And I feel like you're putting pressure on me to act a certain way. We're dating. We're not required to spend every single moment together."

"But that's the point. I want to spend every moment together." She was starting to whine, always an attractive feature of hers.

"Well, I can't offer that to you. I'll never be able to offer that to you."

"You could make more of an effort to see me every week. You could cut out the dinners with Hailey and Kesara and every other woman you see alone without me."

Ah-ha, yet another piece of the puzzle. As it turned out, Hailey, one of my former teammates, was also Nate's sister, which explained how he'd seen me play so often. I hadn't recognized him to be the cute kid I'd met back then, but it was a nice surprise to find out. When I'd first mentioned running into her, Darby seemed thrilled for me. Then I mentioned meeting Hailey's partner, and Darby adopted a scowl whenever I brought her up now. "You're not jealous, are you?"

"Do I need to be?" she asked without pause.

"It's so heartwarming how much you trust me."

"We're talking about jealousy, not trust."

"Jealousy and trust are intertwined." I tried not to sound condescending, but the continual slights about my friends were starting to get to me. "If you trusted me, you 'd know there was nothing to be jealous about."

"So you're not spending time with other women because I don't give you everything you need?" Her insecurity was rearing its ugly head.

"I spend time with friends because they're my friends. I don't make their gender a requirement for whether or not they'll be friends."

"It should be if they're lesbians," she shot back.

I placed some money into the check folder and got up from the table. Without waiting for Darby, I started toward the door. She rushed to catch up with me, surprised that I'd left without saying anything.

"It doesn't because I'm not an animal," I reasoned when I reached to open the car door for her. "I can actually control any impulses that might occur. Plus, I'm in a relationship with you, and if I've never made it clear, I don't cheat."

"That's the sweetest thing you've said all night, but I don't trust them." Her eyes followed my progress around the car, waiting for me to get in before she joined me.

"Neither Hailey nor Kesara are interested in me, and even if they were, they aren't the type to go after someone else's girlfriend."

"How do you know?"

"Because that's an underhanded thing to do," I retorted without giving it any thought. "Neither of them are like that, and Hailey's been partnered for nine years."

"Kesara's not."

Taking my eyes off the road briefly, I looked at her. She was focused on the passing scenery, but her hands were clenched. "How do you know? Are you two friends?"

"No, but I know she's not with anyone."

"They're my friends, and I won't give them up because you're feeling insecure."

She didn't like that characterization and proceeded to tell me so for the rest of the drive to her house. These conversations were getting more and more exhausting to endure. If it wasn't something I was neglecting about our relationship, it was something else. Recently, it seemed like I couldn't measure up to all of her expectations.

"You still haven't said whether you'll change your plans on Wednesday for my sister's party?" This question came as I pulled up to her curb.

Biting back a growl, I answered, "I have told you, and I won't. Mirabella got these tickets for us months ago. I'm not going to cancel for another of your sister's parties."

"They finished working on your house. Why are you still friends with them? You don't have to continue being polite after they've finished working for you."

"We are friends, Darby. Friends. Yes, both she and Santiago did some work for me, but they became my friends then and I'm keeping them as friends now. Just like I'm going to keep seeing Hailey and her partner, and Kesara, and my neighbors, and anyone else I want. This will be the last time we discuss this. I'm serious. If you can't keep your insecurity in check, then I can't help you."

"That's not a nice thing to say," she huffed as she exited the car. "That's like saying you don't care about me."

"No, it isn't." I followed her out of the car. "It's saying that your insecurity about this is unattractive and not something I'm looking for in a relationship."

She whirled to face me, fire in her eyes. "So, either I be a good girl and let you go out on pseudo dates with these other women or you break up with me?"

"They aren't pseudo dates." I waved my hands to erase the notion from the air around us. "Nothing about them is romantic at all. Don't say you're one of those people who think you can't be friends with another lesbian?"

"I'm just saying that I know how easy it is to find yourself in a situation where you can stray."

I reached out to stop her. "Are you telling me you've cheated on a girlfriend before?"

"No!" she practically shouted. "But I have had a girlfriend who left someone for me when I was just her friend."

I guess I could see where she might have some worry, but I'd never given her anything to worry about. It took me forty years to finally get into a relationship. I sure as hell wasn't going to drop her for someone else who showed attention. "Did you encourage her to leave?"

"Not really, but she did, so I don't take relationships for granted. You're putting yourself in that kind of situation often enough for me to be nervous."

"There's nothing to be nervous about."

She sighed again, the look resurfacing. "Well? Aren't you coming inside?"

"I don't think so. You're ticked, you're not listening to me, and you're aching to keep fighting. I'd rather not spend my night like that." Watching a marathon of *Real Housewives* of some overindulgent city sounded like a less torturous evening.

"So, not only are you unwilling to change your plans on Wednesday, but you're giving up on our only date when you know I'm getting on a plane soon for a two-week vacation?"

"We're seeing each other the night before you leave, or did you forget that?"

"Fine, I get to see you once, then nothing for two weeks?"

"We're not going over this again. We've both got work tomorrow, and I'm tired. Maybe we can have lunch together this week when we're in a better mood." What had she expected? That if she pouted enough I'd give in and do whatever the hell she wanted?

She shook her head, that displeasure showing again. "You can't just walk away when we haven't resolved anything."

"We have resolved things, just not to your liking. I'm leaving before I say something to upset you further. You can either deal with the disappointment you feel and have lunch with me later in the week or you can live with the disappointment and stay pissed at me."

"Sometimes, you're impossible," she huffed.

"I know." It was easier just to agree with her. "I'm sorry about that, but it's the way I am, and you either accept me or you don't."

She gave a weak smile before clutching at me, hugging urgently. "I'm sorry. I'm just a mess. I always get this way before I go home for the holidays. I really hoped that I could introduce the woman I love to my parents." She waited for me to say something, but I didn't know what to say. "At least we'll get to see you on TV for two games. Give me a signal to let me know you're thinking about me."

"I'll be thinking about you." I pulled back slightly and tilted her chin up for a kiss. "How about lunch on Thursday, so you can tell me all about your sister's party?"

"If I can't get you to go with me, then I guess lunch will have to do." She kissed me again, a little desperation this time. "Goodnight."

CHAPTER 26

The box was small, made of blue velvet, exactly the size of a ring box. When I'd finished unwrapping Darby's Christmas gift, I stalled, staring at the box. She'd already opened my gift, the newest iPhone that she'd been saying she couldn't live without. There was no way I'd be able to swing her attention away from me completing this reveal. My eyes nervously flicked to hers. They stared anxiously at me, urging me on. But this couldn't be what I thought it was. That would be crazy.

Beyond crazy, actually. When I opened the lid, I saw a diamond solitaire on a gold band. It would be beautiful if I liked diamonds, which I didn't. It would be beautiful if I was in a place to commit to her, which I wasn't. It would be beautiful if it were coming from someone who'd stolen my heart, which it wasn't.

Darby slipped to a knee in front of the sofa and reached for the ring box. Oh my God!

Before she could say a word, I snapped the lid shut and waved a hand. "Darby, this isn't…please, don't."

She looked at me, uncertainty in her eyes. One blink, then the confidence returned. "Graysen, I love you."

"Darby—"

"I want to spend the rest of my life with you."

"Darby—"

"Marry me?"

Again, would have been beautiful if I'd ever thought about this moment, but I hadn't. The whole not attracted to anyone thing sort of kept me from dreaming about marriage. That hadn't changed while I was dating Darby, either. I'd been hoping that after a while I'd feel more deeply for her, but it hadn't happened so far. "This is...unexpected."

"But good, though, right?"

I tried to let her down as gently as possible. "I'm not ready for this. I don't mean to hurt you, but we've only been dating for three months." Less than, actually.

"I've been in love with you for almost twenty years."

My head was shaking on its own. "You can't know that."

"It was love at first sight for me, Gray. I thought it was the same for you." Hurt swam through her eyes.

"I was certainly attracted to you, but I told you that I take a little longer to get to where you seem to be. It's been less than three months. I can't tell in such a short time if I want to spend my life with someone."

"Dammit! We're good together. We have fun together. We love each other. What more do you need?"

"Okay, you're upset," I said the words I seemed to be saying at least once every time we got together.

"Stop it! You're so damn rational." She stood and started pacing in front of me. "Can't you, for once, just react? Show me some of that passion I've seen in you."

I stood to be eye level with her. I reached to take her hand, but she ripped it away from me. Okay, she was pissed. She had a right to her feelings, but she was the one who'd brought this on.

"Fine, you want a reaction?" I started, knowing that what I had to say would make her even more angry, but she wanted passion. "What are you thinking asking me to commit to you after only three months? What are you thinking asking me to commit when we seem to get into an argument about spending time together or my friends or my schedule almost every time we have a date? What are you thinking asking me to commit when we've never discussed things like where we'd live, whether or not we want kids, what would happen if one of us lost our jobs, and all the other important things that couples who've been together for a few years know about each other? And really, what are you thinking asking me to commit to you on the night before you go away for two weeks? What kind of timing is that?"

She looked surprised by my candor. I couldn't blame her since I'd been repressing these types of thoughts from the beginning of our relationship. "I thought I could convince you to join me over the holiday."

"You thought...?" I stared at her, dumfounded. "What about my job? What about the games I have to coach?"

"Well, you could come back for the games. The televised ones, at least."

Just the televised ones? Who thinks like that? "What about the other one? What about practice?"

"You have assistant coaches."

Surprise leapt from my lungs in an audible breath. "You think I should turn my team over to my assistant coaches so that I can spend a two-week vacation with you at your parents' house? What are you thinking? You know that our jobs are not something you can just decide to take a vacation from. You know that only a death in the family or severe illness would excuse our absence from the sidelines."

She tucked her chin against her chest and mumbled, "I thought Tavian wouldn't mind. I thought he'd be so happy for his best friend that he'd let you take a little time off."

"I see." And I did, but it was a startling thought. "You expect me to take advantage of my friendship with our boss to neglect my job, disappoint my team, and join you on a trip that I told you a month ago I couldn't go on?"

The mouth that had often made me dizzy with kisses dropped open. "You don't have to make it sound so malicious. I would have understood if you still couldn't go, but I wanted to ask you. I wanted to give you a ring for Christmas. I thought it was romantic."

"Honestly, Darby," I began, so shocked by her proposal that I was letting all my thoughts go unedited. I couldn't tell which of us was more surprised. "Did you think all the things we've been bickering about over the last month would magically disappear if I agreed to marry you?"

"Since we'd be living together, yes, I did. I'd get to see you every night, not just once a week, and you'd have to cut down on the outings with your friends."

"Marriage doesn't mean that we'd live on an isolated island. We'd still have evenings out with friends. We'd still spend some time apart." Unless she locked me in a basement. I was beginning to wonder if that action would be so farfetched for her now.

"We could go out with friends. My friends are always inviting us places."

"I get it. It's okay to hang out with friends as long as they're yours?"

"Well, I don't really know yours. Plus you've really only known them for a few months, so they're all new friends." She made it sound like they were throwaway minutes on a cell plan. "You like mine. We'll have plenty of time to get to know them better."

I shook my head, finally feeling like I'd had enough. I'd been hanging on since our first night together, hoping that I'd feel more for her, hoping that I'd start to crave being with her, hoping that I'd feel like I couldn't wait until we jumped into bed at the end of a date, but that hadn't happened. I'd continued to feel only fondness for her and surface enjoyment from the sex we shared. "Darby, I'm sorry. We're obviously in different places. I can't accept your proposal. I care about you, and I've enjoyed being with you, but this isn't working anymore."

Blue eyes blinked in rapid bursts. "What are you saying?"

"I'm saying that I think it's time we recognized that we're better as friends." Was that a standard I'm-dumping-you line? I so didn't want to be that kind of jerk, but it was the truth. I did and still do like her, a lot, but as a girlfriend, she was exhausting and self-absorbed.

"Friends?" Her voice was shaky.

I let out a long breath and spoke the absolute truth. "You want more from me than I can give you." Which I'd known from the beginning, and had I not been pressured into a something so deep so soon, I would have stopped this before she got terribly hurt.

"And you think throwing away three months of love to be friends is the answer?"

"I think that when a proposal isn't accepted, there's no going back. You're ready to get married. I'm not, and I don't see that changing anytime soon."

Tears started in her eyes. I wished I could feel something other than dread by the sight of them. She'd cried over little things in the past three months. I was getting used to her strong and often short-sighted reactions to things. Tears didn't upset me as much anymore.

"I can't believe you're doing this. I was so sure you'd be as excited about this as I was. I feel like I don't even know you at all."

"I'm sorry, Darby, really." The impulse to hold her was strong, but that would only complicate matters. "I haven't meant to hold back, but I guess I have been. I thought I'd start feeling a little more like someone in a committed relationship would feel. But right now, I feel like we're still just getting to know each other, still trying to work through the kinks of where we are as a couple. The fact that you don't feel that way tells me that we're not in sync as a couple. You have to see that now?"

"I don't know what I see. I'm still reeling from not being able to slip this ring on your finger." She turned away, slamming the lid of the ring box closed. "I think you should go."

"I'm sorry for hurting you. You mean a lot to me. I hope we can work through this and become great friends." Lame, but all I had to offer.

"Just go. I can't handle any more tonight."

"Okay, I'll go." I grabbed my jacket from the back of the couch. "I hope you have a good holiday." Her only response was a slight nod with those weepy eyes.

Well, one thing I hadn't missed by never being with anyone was how awful it felt to break up with them.

CHAPTER 27

My mother and I made our way across campus to my office. She'd arrived late last night but had time to inspect my new place before she tried out the guestroom. Today, she'd insisted on coming to work with me, something she hadn't done since my first job as an assistant coach. It had been embarrassing then, but now that I was the head coach, I was excited to show her around my work.

"Beautiful campus. I was expecting California modern."

"Not like your Yale, Mom, but it'll do."

"Yale didn't have much of a basketball team when I went, so I'm glad you've found a good fit."

"It's only temporary." I'd been thinking that for the past month. I thought I might be able to make it a few seasons, but now I thought I'd start looking again soon.

"Oh no, you're not unhappy here, too, are you?" She wrapped an arm around my waist. Nothing ever felt as comforting as my mom's hugs. She was always ready with one, no matter how minor a problem I might be having. "I thought with Tavian running the department that you'd avoid some of those problems you had at the last college."

"He's been great, but this wasn't what I had in mind when I started coaching. Maybe I'm out of sorts, but you'll see what I mean at practice later." I led her to my office, passing a few occupants on the floor. Only the winter sports were left in the building. The rest had taken the two-week winter break.

"De-luxe." Mom raved, looking around my spacious surroundings. "Did Mirabella decorate this, too?" She'd raved about my place, wanting to hire Mirabella for her own house.

"No, this was all here. The former coach was pretty spoiled so I've been trying to tone it down since I got here."

"How is it that you're the modest one of my kids? Ken doesn't have a lick of athletic talent and that boy is the biggest ham I've ever seen." We both smiled at my brother's usual attention getting antics.

"You make sure you say that when he gets here in a couple days." Ken and his wife would be joining us on Christmas Eve. I felt very lucky to have my family join me for the holiday when I couldn't leave work. Ever since I'd gotten my first head coaching gig, they'd made an effort to visit me either on Thanksgiving or Christmas and I always appreciated it.

The intercom buzzed and Tavian's voice boomed loud enough for us both to hear. My mom smiled as he ordered us up to his office. His spies on the floor must have called to tell him we'd arrived. He loved my mom almost as much as I did. They'd met during my first year of college and hit it off instantly. Of course, the fact that he was the eighth of eight children — hence the name — meant he was always craving any type of maternal attention.

Up two flights of stairs, we'd barely even stepped onto his floor before he stormed out of the office and swooped my mom up into his arms. "Mom V, took you long enough to come visit. I didn't think I'd have to lure your daughter here to see your smiling face again."

"Con her daughter, don't you mean?" I muttered.

"Quiet," Mom said. "Don't interrupt the man when he's telling me he missed me."

"Ha!" Tavian exclaimed, shooting an elbow into my side. "Told you she wouldn't think I'd done anything wrong."

"Don't start with me, young man, you're not off the hook. My angel told me how you withheld pertinent information when it was too late for her to do anything but take your job." He looked dutifully shamed. "Aw, Ally, I was in a bad place and I needed my Gray to get me out of it."

"And she has, hasn't she? You two have always been so good for each other." She smiled up at him, squeezing him into another hug. "Now, when am I going to see Jacinda and the girls?"

"Dinner tonight."

"Perfect. So maybe you better show me—oh, excuse me," her eyes flicked over to Kesara's desk, "I was so caught up I didn't—"

I cut her off, waving Kesara closer. "This is my friend and Tavian's executive assistant, Kesara Luz. Kesara, this is my mother, Ally Viola." Over the last couple of weeks, Kesara had shaken her so called funk, and we'd gone back to weekly lunches and get-togethers with her cousins on weekends. I was glad that whatever had been bothering her seemed to have disappeared.

"What a pretty name," Mom was telling her. "It's nice to meet you."

"Thank you, and it's nice to meet you, too."

"Mirabella is Kesara's cousin and her other cousins helped make my place beautiful, but I wouldn't even have it if it weren't for her good eye while we were out house hunting."

"How fortunate. I love her place. The renovations and décor are astounding."

"I'll make sure my cousins know you said so." The phone rang and Kesara rushed back to pick up the receiver.

"Did she tell you about all the changes in her life, Ally?" Tavian wiggled his eyebrows as he dragged us into his office. "Have you met Darby yet?"

"Tave!" I admonished, upset that he'd brought this up while we were in a work setting. We'd managed to keep up a professional relationship for the most part while we were at work, but this was a massive gaffe.

"What? You know your mom and I have been worried about you for years." He and Mom exchanged a glance that made me think they'd been having secret phone calls about my love life for years.

"You never needed to be." I gave him a stern stare. Turning back to my mom, I told her, "And it didn't work out with Darby."

"What?" Tavian took over, his shock matching my mom's. I'd planned to tell her tonight when we could talk more about it. I wasn't going to tell Tavian until I had both him and Jacinda in a room alone. "You broke up with Darby?!"

"Jeez, Tave, shout it a little louder. I'm not sure everyone on her floor heard you." This wasn't the way I wanted him to learn about the breakup of two people on his staff. I knew he'd be surprised that it ended so soon, but as my friend, he probably knew it would end at some point. "It was a mutual decision and for the best. We're better as friends, and that's all I'm going to say on this subject."

He looked at my mom. "Did you make her this private, Ally?"

"I had very little to do with this one. She practically raised herself. Her brother, on the other hand, we barely managed to survive that upbringing." She rubbed my back, smiling fondly at me.

"I can't believe you didn't say anything, Gray. Is this going to—"

His certain chastisement was interrupted by Kesara appearing at the open door. "Graysen, Coach Meyers just called to say that one of your players is wandering around your floor, probably waiting for you."

Coach Meyers, Coach Clem, the football coach, and all our assistants were the only people left on our floor for the holiday. I certainly didn't want one of my players disturbing their office days.

"Thanks, Kesara. Mom, I'd better go deal with this."

"Handle it," Tavian ordered. "I need me some quality Mom V time. We'll be fine here until you're done."

I smiled then took leave. From the moment I introduced them, they'd acted like family and it warmed my heart to see. I'd have to pry them apart by the time I got back. I just hoped that my nonexistent love life wouldn't be all they discussed.

"Hey, Coach," Jeff called out once I reached my floor. His eyes darted around me. "I was looking for Damon."

"He won't be in until practice later this afternoon."

"Oh." He looked a little lost, glancing back at their offices then over the cubicle area.

"Come inside." I motioned to my office.

"That's okay. I can wait."

"You hiked over from your dorm at nine a.m. You obviously can't wait. I didn't even think you guys got up until the crack of noon." He gave me a weak smile, glancing back at the lobby area. "Let's sit down." I walked into my office and didn't look back until I'd had a seat at my desk. With one last glance back toward the exit, he came inside, shutting the door behind him. Uh-oh, this was serious. "What's on your mind?"

"It's, you know, guy stuff. I can wait until Damon gets here."

Guy stuff? All I could do was guess. "Do you need to see a doctor?"

"No!" he rushed to say. There was a pale tint to his dark skin tone today, and his normally tight curls were frizzy for lack of product this morning. "No, it's just something that only guys have to deal with."

Christ, I hope he wasn't talking about erectile dysfunction, but I was the mentor in this exchange. I should act like it. "You'd be surprised how understanding both genders are when it comes to problems. Why don't you try me? What we say in here doesn't go anywhere else unless you want it to."

He flicked his glance away, heaving a huge sigh. "My girlfriend's pregnant."

I'd heard a lot of problems over the years of coaching, so I didn't even bother with raised eyebrows. I also didn't bother to point out that this problem was, in fact, universal to both genders. "Congratulations."

He scoffed. "I don't know if it's mine."

I gave one nod, letting that statement hang between us. Now that problem *was* unique to men. "Has she given you a reason to suspect it isn't?

"She says it's mine, but how do I know? She could be sleeping with everyone."

I held up my hand to get him to stop. "Were you under the impression that you were in an exclusive relationship?"

"Well, yeah, I don't share my women."

"Then the baby is yours."

"She could have been sleeping around."

"That's a strong accusation, Jeff. You must have some reason for it." I eyed him carefully. "Are you sleeping with other women?"

His head turned to the side, breaking eye contact. So, that was it. He was sleeping around, so of course, he assumed his girlfriend was as well.

"I'm not going to judge you, but I will say that, if you were in what was supposed to be an exclusive relationship and your girlfriend ends up pregnant, then you have to believe the baby is yours. Suggesting otherwise is kind of sleazy."

Another huge sigh, but he turned back to look at me. "Damn, Coach, I know, but I don't want to deal with this."

"It's overwhelming, yes," I agreed.

"She needs to get an abortion."

I let five seconds pass. "You understand that you have no say in the initial decision about the pregnancy, right?"

"What?" He leaned forward, giving me his full attention.

"I'm saying that it's the woman's choice whether or not to carry the baby to term. Your job is to support whatever decision she makes without telling her what to do. Please tell me you understand that. I like to think that I've had more than just a basketball influence on your life."

He shook his head and sighed again. "I know. I just wish we didn't have to deal with it."

"How would you feel if she decided to put the baby up for adoption?"

"I don't know, better than me raising it, I guess, but I don't know if I'd want a kid of mine running around without knowing me, you know?"

"And raising the child with your girlfriend?"

"I'm not ready for that." He waved defensively.

"Okay, but please tell me you know that, at a minimum, you'll have to be financially responsible for the child, right?"

His look told me that he felt like that was really unfair, but he didn't want to be lectured on the consequences of sex. "Yeah. You're probably going to tell me to marry her, right?"

"That's not for me to say. What some people call 'doing the right thing' isn't right if there isn't a solid foundation for getting married. You can decide on a co-parenting plan that doesn't involve you being married or living together. Or you can decide that your only influence in this child's life will be monetary. Either way, you cannot manipulate her into making the decision you want. This is all part of becoming a man. You accept the consequences for all choices you make."

He actually smiled, laughing softly. "You're kinda big on that, aren't you?"

"My job is to turn you all into high functioning adults. If you become decent basketball players in the process, all the better."

"Okay, I get it. I freaked and have been since she told me last night."

"You're entitled to your feelings, but hopefully you get that the 'girl stuff' part of this equation is a little more involved than the 'guy stuff' part. She's probably freaking out even more than you are, even if she seemed happy about it."

"You think?" He looked up at me in earnest.

"I know. A woman can be ecstatically happy about the prospect of having a baby one minute then be panicked about what it will do to her body and career path, what kind of mother she'll be, what will her friends and family think, and all that with the added component of hormones she's never had to deal with before." I got him to smile again. "Your job as the boyfriend is to let her know that you're there for her, no matter what she decides. Let her make the initial decision, then whatever it happens to be, you need to be honest about how involved you'll be."

"I can do that."

"I know you can. You're a good man, and you will be a great father when you decide you want a family."

"Thanks, Coach." He stood and managed not to let out another sigh. "This really helped."

"I'm glad, and I'm here anytime you need to talk."

"Cool." He turned to head out but stopped before he reached the door. "Appreciate the help." Then he was through the door.

I let out my own huge sigh. One good thing about coaching a men's team was that news of this nature didn't mean they'd miss an entire college season.

CHAPTER 28

New Year's Eve. Usually it was a quiet evening for me, but Tavian was having a party and Jacinda wouldn't accept no for an answer. I'd roped Santiago into going with me since Kesara had brought Mirabella. We'd been chatting and making fun of several of Jacinda's colleagues until Tavian would get yelled at by his wife for not being sociable. He'd slink away to deal with their combined guests but would find his way back within thirty minutes.

I'd been nursing my glass of wine for more than an hour, knowing champagne was coming up at midnight. I wasn't a big drinker to begin with, but on New Year's it was never a good idea to get sloshed when I had to rely on public transit to get home.

"Still having fun?" Kesara leaned in to whisper as the infamous Leo finally finished yapping about yet another sales issue and wandered off to find more victims.

A chill skittered down my spine as I turned and found her face inches from mine, eyes hooded with her alcohol induced relaxation. She looked so sexy in her little black dress, and I felt guilty for thinking this of my friend. "Jaci actually tried to set me up with that guy at a dinner a few months ago."

Her hand clamped around my upper arm, eyes widening. "You're kidding?"

"Nope. To her credit, he was the first of many she planned, and when I told her that I wasn't interested in men, she had several women lined up for the next dinner. I swear, she could run her own matchmaking service. Don't tell her if you're looking because she'll have a parking lot full of women ready to date you within a week."

"Good tip." Her hand brushed down the length of my arm as she took another swig of her wine. "This is a nice party. I'm glad you're here and thanks for bringing Santi."

"Of course, it wouldn't be a party without Santiago. Plus it gave you the opportunity to bring Mirabella."

"Ulterior motive. I want her away from that loser boyfriend of hers. Maybe we should get Jacinda to help us."

"Don't tempt her."

"She did so well with you and Leo, though." Her tease made me laugh as she bumped her shoulder against me. "Yet somehow you ended up with Darby Evan." The way she said her name startled me. Almost venomous. "I'm sorry," she backed off. "That was uncalled for. I'm sure she's very nice."

"You two know each other somehow, don't you?" I'd surmised this after the way Darby treated her at my party and Kesara's reaction.

"Not really. More like we know people in common."

I waited for more but nothing came. "That you're not going to tell me about?"

"I don't like to talk about it." She took her hand back. I missed the warmth immediately.

"All right, but if you ever want to unload, I'm happy to listen."

"You are too sweet for your on good, my friend." She nudged me. "Are you getting over your broken heart?" My eyes popped wide as she rushed to say, "Tavian wasn't exactly quiet when your mom was visiting last week."

I had wondered if she'd heard. Now, I knew. "No broken heart to get over."

"Really? Darby usually leaves people in devastation." Alcohol had to be contributing to Kesara's uninhibited commentary.

"Neither of us is devastated. It just didn't work out."

"Wow, well, I'm glad you're not terribly upset." Kesara glanced at me then looked away. "She managed to break my heart and I never even went out with her."

My brow furrowed. "What?"

Her hand clamped over her mouth as if just realizing what she'd said. "Nothing."

"Kesara," I started but was interrupted by Santiago and Mirabella approaching.

"You guys missed that idiot Leo getting into a beer chugging contest with absolutely no one," he told us. "I'm hoping he's single. He'd be perfect for Bella."

"*Cállete, primo,*" she ordered. "You ladies doing okay? Need more wine?"

"I'm good," I responded and Kesara nodded the same.

"Come with us. I bet he's going to do something really stupid as soon as the clock strikes midnight."

I laughed, shaking my head. "I'm going to head out into the backyard for some fresh air. You guys go ahead." They tried to coax me once more but gave up once raucous laughter sounded from the living room. I locked my hand around Kesara's arm, tilting my head toward the backyard, hoping she'd join me. I wanted to finish our conversation. "Tell me how she broke your heart," I urged once we'd cleared the patio door.

"It's not worth the effort."

"That didn't just slip out. Please tell me."

Her head bent, a sigh slipping from her lips. "I'm sure Santiago told you I was in a committed relationship for ten years." She waited for my nod. "I thought I had the perfect relationship until I found out she'd been cheating on me for most of the last year."

Whoa. "I'm sorry to hear that."

"Live and learn, I suppose."

"How does that relate to…Jeez, it wasn't with Darby, was it?" She nodded solemnly and I felt the dread landing heavily in my stomach. I didn't know what to say. Darby had said that she'd been friends with someone in a relationship and the woman traded her spouse for Darby. "Did she know your ex was married?" I asked the question I wasn't sure I wanted the answer to.

"They met at a department meeting that Elena and I were attending together. So, yeah, she knew we were partnered." She waved a hand through the air. "But it's not her fault. My partner strayed, probably due to how much I was working that first year I became Tavian's EA. I'm as much to blame as my ex. Darby isn't at fault, but I guess I still resent her. It doesn't affect our working relationship, but when I saw her at your place, I let my irritation run free. Sorry about that."

I usually didn't like to judge people's behavior when it came to love, but that was a low thing for Darby to do. I had a hard time believing it, yet I knew Kesara wouldn't lie about this. "You know, we've been arguing about a number of things over the past month, but your name came up more than once. She didn't trust me having you as a friend."

"She probably thought I'd try to pay her back."

"You'd never do something like that."

She shook her head and let out an amused breath. "No, and it doesn't matter how gorgeous you are."

Startled by the easy compliment, I joked, "You're a little tipsy, aren't you?"

Her eyes landed on mine, blinking slowly, but the amusement faded. From inside, I heard the ten second countdown start. I couldn't look away from her eyes. They twinkled in the low patio lighting. Her big curls fell around her face and brushed her shoulders in a way that looked professionally done. With a nose as refined as her prominent cheekbones, she was the one who deserved the gorgeous label.

At the count of one, Kesara's lips pulled into a soft smile. "Happy New Year, Graysen."

"And for you as well," I returned the best wishes, watching her eyes drop to my mouth. The heat of her gaze warmed me throughout.

Inside, people were shouting New Year's wishes, giving and receiving hugs and kisses. I stopped thinking about anything other than how her plump lips beckoned. With a tip of my head, my lips brushed against hers. A friendly buss that jolted me rigid. Breath pushed out at the shocking sensation. I couldn't stop the second lean in, eager to have our mouths meet again.

"Happy New Year!" Jacinda's voice boomed out from the patio door as she rushed forward and wrapped me into her arms, planting a loud kiss on the corner of my mouth. She turned and pecked Kesara on the cheek as Tavian, Santiago, and Mirabella made their way over to us as well. After several hugs and kisses went round, I finally felt a little more like myself instead of the kiss-crazed woman I'd been moments before. It had been a friendly New Year's kiss. I shouldn't read anything more into it. Plus, I was slightly inebriated, so that probably added to the fabulousness. Not to mention it had lasted less than three seconds, so it wasn't really even a kiss, more like a peck.

I caught Kesara's gaze. She was smiling at our friends crowding around us. No sign that the kiss had affected her at all. Yeah, tipsy. We probably wouldn't even remember it tomorrow.

* * *

When the phone rang at three a.m., I'd only been asleep for two hours. The first conscious thought I had was of soft, pliant lips grazing mine. The second ring forced me to focus. I snatched up the receiver before realizing it was my cell phone. Fumbling around, I grabbed it and flipped it open. "Hello?"

"Coach?"

Thanks to the glass of water and aspirin I'd taken before hitting the sack, my head didn't pound as much as I'd thought it might from that extra glass of champagne I'd consumed. Hearing one of my players on the other end of a phone call at this hour, though, ramped up the pressure on my brain. "Who is this?"

"Oh, thank God, you answered. You gotta help us out."

It sounded like Jeff, but I wasn't sure. He also sounded drunk. "Jeff? Where are you?"

"Jail! We're in jail. You gotta come get us out."

I popped up in bed, more alert now that I'd heard the magic word. "Calm down, and tell me exactly where you are?"

"Embarcadero, in the city. Can you come?"

"I'm on my way." I slid out of bed and walked into the bathroom. Downing another glass of water and two aspirin, I pulled my hair into a messy but manageable bun, then donned khakis and a cashmere sweater. Stepping into my loafers, I headed out to the garage for my first trip ever to pick up a moronic player from jail. I'd been asked to retrieve players from an airport, train station, a bar after drinking too much, a mall after shopping too much, but never jail. Men!

It wasn't difficult finding street parking at 3:30 a.m. A few doors down from the police station, I parallel parked the car I finally let Kesara goad me into buying. Gathering my wits, I stalked toward the front door and pushed through. It was relatively quiet for a night I would think would be their busiest.

There was a lone officer standing behind the main counter. "May I help you?"

"Yes, I'm here about Jeff Andrews."

He punched some keys on his computer, held up a finger, and picked up the phone. Murmuring into the headset, he glanced back at me then did a double-take with his eyes. Nothing else moved, just his eyes, and I knew he'd just recognized me. I only hoped that wouldn't hurt Jeff. "Have a seat. The Captain will be right out."

This couldn't be good. I sat, trying to keep my hands from fidgeting. A burly older man in uniform pushed through the security door. "I thought I recognized one of those idiots. You're their coach, right? Ms. Viola?"

I resisted the urge to sigh. "There's more than one of them?"

He laughed and it looked like it surprised him, releasing some tension. "Three and their girlfriends. Come on back."

I followed him to his office. "Jeff didn't say much on the phone."

"I bet not. Those kids were barely standing when we picked them up."

Maybe this wasn't so bad. "Are there charges?"

"No, I figured if they could find someone decent enough to come get them in the middle of the night, they can't be all bad. Drunk college kids are a common occurrence around here. If you'll take them off our hands, I'll bring them up now."

His smile prompted mine, but I held a hand up. "Any chance I can see them in lockup? I'd like to make them sweat a little longer."

"I like the way you think, Coach. Sure, come on." He led me through the squad room and down the stairs. Voices got louder as we approached the cells. "They're in the last cell. I tried to keep them separated from the real criminals."

"Thank you, Captain. I appreciate your patience and understanding."

"Just let the Sergeant here know when you want them out." He shook my hand and turned back to the stairs.

"Jeff," I said when I stepped up to the last cell and saw his bulky form in the corner.

"Coach!" he yelled too loudly, reaching out to clutch the bars between us.

"Damn, dude, you called Coach? We're so busted." Wendell slammed up against him, bringing them both into the bars.

"Calm down and tell me why you're here?"

"Oh, man, it's so bogus, dude," Jeff slurred.

"First, I'm neither a man nor a dude. You're drunk, and it looks like Frank and Wendell are, too. Anyone else you have in there with you?"

"Our women, but listen, listen, we're, like, drinking in a bar, minding our own business, and these assholes start telling us we can't play worth shit, that we'll never make the NBA, that you suck as a coach. What were we supposed to do?"

"Walk away?" I posed calmly.

"Oh, hell no!" Frank bellowed having moved up behind Jeff.

"I won't ask you again to calm down." I shot him a glare. "Do you have any idea how much trouble you're in?"

"We didn't start it, and we didn't do any damage. Don't tell me those dickheads are pressing charges?" Wendell asked.

"Watch your language, guys. Better yet, all of you, just shut up. Here's what's going to happen. In order for you to walk free from this, you'll agree to five hours of community service every week until the end of the school year. Agreed?"

"Yeah, whatever you want," Jeff agreed.

"Good, then let's get you out of here." I turned back to the smiling Sergeant and indicated that he open the cell.

When the door slid open, Jeff actually bounded out and drew me into his arms. "Told ya she was cool. Thanks, Coach. We owe you."

I pulled out of Jeff's loose embrace. "Remember that when we're running five miles tomorrow morning and cleaning up the courtyard around the athletic department."

"What?" Wendell demanded.

"You didn't think I'd let a rule violation go without punishment, did you?" I started walking not worried about whether or not they'd follow.

"We're already doing community service," he whined.

Upstairs I pushed through the exit and into the cool night air. They crowded out into the street behind me. "That's in exchange for not being arrested. What did I tell you about drinking while you're in training?"

Frank gathered his girlfriend close. "Come on, Coach, it was New Year's Eve."

"What did I tell you?" I asked again.

"That we aren't allowed to drink." His head bent in an attempt at shame.

"Actually, I told you not to get caught." I knew asking them not to drink was never going to happen. Thankfully, all three of them were able to drink legally or this would be a whole different problem. "You all got caught. Any other complaints or can we get you home?"

Wendell's girlfriend shot an elbow into his ribs when he opened his mouth. "Thank you for rescuing us," she offered.

"You're welcome. Now, get in." I unlocked the Land Rover's doors and they arranged themselves into the backseat with Frank riding shotgun. I glanced into the rearview mirror at the sullen looking Wendell and the now happy Jeff. His arms were around his girlfriend, whispering into her ear. Looks like he'd managed to work through the pregnancy issue with her. I resisted the urge to shake my head at them and started the car.

I'd sleep for a few hours on the couch in my office before waking them for a five-mile run that should make them sorry they'd gotten caught. After an hour or two of picking up trash, I'd have plenty of time to make it over to Tavian's for the Rose Bowl later in the day.

CHAPTER 29

The building had been gloriously quiet for two weeks. Only the winter sports coaches and our assistants had to work during the break. Now that it was over, everyone was back, talking about how wonderful their breaks were and how much fun they'd had. Some had taken the time to say they'd watched us win our games, but I was craving the quiet.

Until Kesara walked into my office. Then suddenly, I was happy to have someone else on the floor. "Morning, Gray, heard your New Year's Day was full of fun."

I took a breath and shook my head to clear the sensation of her soft kiss. I'd managed to go nearly all of two days without thinking of it. "Which of the morons complained to Tavian?"

She laughed, the accompanying smile crinkling the skin around her eyes. "None. Kat told me she saw you dragging them out of the athletic dorm and forcing them into a run around the lake. She said they looked like death warmed over."

"Oh, yeah." I joined her laughter, knowing the soccer coach of all people would appreciate running as a form of punishment. "Halfway around the lake, they're all puking their guts up, vowing never to drink again. Overall a pretty good day."

"I like that you're a little evil." She wiggled her eyebrows at me.

"Nothing little about it, my dear."

She kept smiling, but the look in her eyes told me she wanted to say something else. My heart started pounding, thinking that she might bring up the kiss. It couldn't have just affected me. No way. Not the kind of kiss that I'd felt everywhere. It didn't matter how long it lasted.

"There you are!" Darby's voice sang out from the doorway.

My eyes leapt from Kesara's intense brown to Darby's giddy blue. I didn't have time to greet her before she'd reached me and pulled me out of my chair for a hug.

"God, I missed you. Did you have a nice break? How come you didn't return any of my calls?"

I pulled back from the clingy hug and stared at her, confused. Why was she acting like this? I could feel Kesara's frown before I saw it. Yeah, well, I felt the same way. "Hello, Darby. Did you notice that I'm not alone?"

"Oh, yeah, hi, Kesara. Listen, Gray and I have some things to discuss in private. Do you mind?"

"I mind," I interjected, completely perplexed by Darby's unnatural warmth.

"No," Kesara said at the same time. "I'll talk to you later, Gray. Welcome back, Darby."

"Yeah," Darby brushed off the greeting. "You didn't answer me. Why didn't you return any of my calls? I texted and called at least once a day. I missed you so much."

More like five or six times a day. My fingers got tired of deleting all the inane texts and voicemails. "I wasn't interested in having another argument. I thought the break would be good for both of us."

"I know we went through a rough patch, but I realized how much I loved you, and I don't want to give that up. I can live with the fact that you're not ready to get married yet, but we don't have to break up."

I tried to keep my face from showing the confusion and frustration coursing through me. I had to break up with her again? The first time sucked. I didn't want to go through that again. "I thought I was clear. You're a wonderful person, but I feel like we're better as friends."

"We're better as lovers." She reached for me again.

"No, Darby." I made sure she'd heard me. Something told me she hadn't heard that word very often in her life. "I'm not what you're looking for. I started realizing that a while ago, but the two weeks apart helped to clear my head. I really like you, but that's it."

Her brow furrowed. "You don't love me? You can just turn it off like that?"

"I don't want to hurt you, but we're not meant to be together."

"How can you say that? I waited almost twenty years to be with you. It was love at first sight for me. Don't throw away what we have because I pushed too soon."

Her voice had started to rise, and now that the cubicles were filled, I decided I'd better shut the door to keep this conversation private. I gestured for her to sit with me on the sofa. She was breathing hard, strain in her eyes, probably close to tears.

"I can't help the way I feel any more than I can help the way you feel." I tried to calm her down. "You talk about love at first sight, wanting to be with me for all those years, and I'm just amazed. We hardly spent any time together then and didn't keep in touch. I don't know how you can be so sure of how you feel." She looked like she was going to interject, but I cut her off. "But that doesn't really matter. I'm just not in the same place as you. We can't be together if we don't want the same things."

Her head bent to lean onto my shoulder. "But I can want anything that you want, Gray, please."

I wished she could hear herself and understand just how much she was compromising with that statement. I wished that I could feel something more for her. I wished that I'd had time from the start to get to know her before she'd pressured me into a romantic relationship. Perhaps then, I wouldn't be stuck having to break up with her twice. Hurt her twice.

"I want us to be friends. I want you to be happy. I want you to find someone who can love you the way you should be loved. And I want you to realize that you deserve that, not force yourself to bend to someone's will just because they want something significantly different from you."

She clung to my arm, nuzzling my neck, trying not to let me see her tears again. I knew she'd figure out that what I was saying was true. That she'd been settling for our relationship all along because I'd never wanted everything that she wanted. It might take a month or two, but she'd realize that I wasn't good for her as a girlfriend. I just hope she would realize that I would be good for her as a friend, even if it took a lot longer for that.

CHAPTER 30

By mid-January, the team had started picking up speed. Hardly any guff from even Wendell anymore. Winning had helped ease his doubts, as did the steady flow of NBA scouts I kept bringing in.

"My legs are gonna fall off," Jeff complained on his last wind sprint, passing close to me but grinning the entire time. I really liked him now, and with a few other office visits, I'd started to get to know him better as well. He would be a good dad, and he seemed to be buying into the idea of it.

"Might make it hard for you to play tomorrow night if you don't have legs, Jeff," I retorted, blowing my whistle as soon as the last of them crossed the line. "Need me to sit you?"

"No way, Coach!" he shouted.

"Okay, then. If running's too much, I can make you swim at Monday's practice."

"No!" they all shouted, having fallen for that alternative form of conditioning way back in November. Swimming laps for an hour nearly killed them, no matter how great of shape they were in.

"Fine, then we're going to work on something that I've been waiting all season to perfect with this team." I flashed a big grin. "The three-minute game."

"Hell, yeah, 'bout time!" Dash cheered, abandoning his earlier winded state.

"We've been ahead too much these past few games not to get this down. I want it like clockwork by the time tournament season rolls around. Bill, take Team Silver down to the other end of the court and work the plays you suggested last week. Damon and I will be with Team Green on our plays and we'll switch in a half hour."

The players split into their respective teams and positioned themselves at their usual places. It was time to institute an unstoppable strategy for maintaining a lead and solidify the idea that we were a winning team. Sometimes, attitude was all it took to win. I hoped with this extra piece, these guys would start thinking they were unbeatable.

* * *

It had been a good day. A really good day, and it felt great to get out of the gym and not worry about basketball. All I cared about today was making sure the kids were having a good time. Tavian and Jacinda had gone out of town for the weekend and roped me into staying with the kids. I'd been a little intimidated by the thought of two long days with them when Kesara suggested that she get Neomi's kids and go with us to Alcatraz for the day. I knew Alicia and Dameka would love it with or without the extra kids along, but I was so grateful that she suggested it.

The kids had a great time crawling all over the cellblock, being locked into solitary confinement, hiking out into the exercise yard and getting the special tour of the medical wing. I was fairly certain they would have volunteered to stay overnight if they could. Kesara and I shared smiles and laughter all day, happy that the kids were happy, but really just relaxing in each others' presence. I'd liked spending time with her alone, but it was fun to see her in the favorite aunt role, too.

"Can Nora and Sefina spend the night, Aunt Gray?" Alicia asked after finding me with Kesara alone in the kitchen.

I had to commend her for not asking in front of Kesara's nieces in case I said no, but I wasn't sure I could handle two more kids for the night. "We'll have to call their mom, sweetie. They may have plans." I looked the question at Kesara who smiled and nodded.

"Can we? They want to stay over, please, please?"

"One more?" I teased.

"PLEASE!" she shouted, giggling the whole time.

"We'll call her and see, okay? For now decide what you guys want on your pizzas."

We watched her sprint out of the kitchen and hit the stairs at a dead run, taking them two at a time. Yeah, she was going to be an incredible athlete, just like her dad. I planned to see what she had in her on the basketball court out back tomorrow. I looked over and caught Kesara staring at me with a faint smile on her face. She'd been doing this all day, and I bit down on the natural reaction to question what had her smiling.

"Are you sure you want to deal with all four of them all night and tomorrow morning?" she asked, that teasing smile playing at those enticing lips.

"Maybe I won't let you leave, either," I shot back before I blanched at the innuendo of the statement. I shouldn't be saying anything like that. We were colleagues, and I've recently discovered just how complicated relationships at work can be.

"You and what army?" She stepped up close. Without the heels she usually wore at work, her head tilted at a severe angle, taunting me to make fun of her stature.

I stepped back, waving my hands, acceding her victory. Unlike with her brothers, I wasn't entirely sure I could take this little spitfire. "Do you think Neomi would mind if I kept her kids the night?"

"She'd probably jump a plane to Reno for a night of wild fun."

"C'mon, Neomi? Really?"

"Really." Kesara's serious face had me doubting we were talking about the same person. Neomi was always so professional with me, lightening up just a bit once she'd gotten to know me, but responsibility and family were tops on her list of priorities.

"Interesting." I pulled the phone from its stand and handed it to Kesara.

"Are you sure you're up for all four of them? By yourself?"

"It's not like they're all in diapers. I'll be rid of them after breakfast out tomorrow morning." I rolled my hand in the air in the direction of the phone to get her to make the call. As she was punching in the numbers, I added, "Plus, you'll be here until they fall asleep after dinner and a movie, so other than rousing them in the morning, I won't have to do anything alone."

Her expression told me she had some great retort to launch, but Neomi came on the line. They spent the next five minutes chatting about sleeping and drop off arrangements. I turned back to search through the menus in the junk drawer for a nearby pizza place, trying not to stare at Kesara. That had been a conscious decision all day.

When I fished the right menu out and turned back to see when I could get on the phone, a flash of heat flooded my senses as an image played out in my mind. Bare skin, lots and lots of it, Kesara's beautiful face taut with unexploded ecstasy, her mouth grazing my neck, her body writhing under mine, her hands clutching at me as —

STOP IT! I screamed at the image flickering through my mind's eye. I reached out to grip the counter, regaining some balance as I came to grips with the first erotic fantasy I'd ever experienced about someone I knew. Hell, the first conscious one I could ever remember having. And it was about this friend, this colleague, this nice woman who was so off-limits. How frickin' unfair. Maybe if we didn't work together or maybe if I didn't suck at relationships or maybe if I knew what the hell was expected of me in a relationship, but none of those things were true, so I had to shut this down right now. It didn't matter that I could still feel the brush of her lips from that brief New Year's kiss but barely remembered the sensation of any one of Darby's kisses. What kind of girlfriend would that make me? A lousy one, and Kesara deserved so much better.

"Gray?" Her expectant look made me think I'd missed something.

"Huh?" Was all I could manage coherently.

"Neomi says it's fine for the kids to stay. She'd be happy to pick them up in the morning."

"Oh, okay, but we'll probably hit a pancake house in the morning so I can swing them by. They're over in Emeryville, right?" I knew my tone sounded nervous, but I was still working through my completely irrational behavior.

"I told her you'd probably insist on dropping them off."

"I'm that predictable, huh?" I turned a friendly smile her way now that I'd managed to contain the alien bout of lust that had poured over me.

"Hardly." Her eyes lingered for a moment on mine before sweeping gently over me and turning away completely. "Kids?" she yelled up the staircase. "Sleepover!"

"Yay!" all four girls screeched and danced, hopping down the staircase to put in their pizza order and riffle through the available DVDs.

"Yay," I mumbled to myself, hoping I knew what I was getting myself into tonight. Although it couldn't be much harder than trying to deal with these inappropriate feelings for Kesara. Maybe a little distraction wouldn't be a bad thing.

CHAPTER 31

For the third time the same woman passed by my office door. I was on the phone, checking on two recruiting prospects, talking to their coach. As soon as I set the phone down, the woman's fist rapped on my open door. I motioned her inside.

"Hello, Ms. Viola, I'm Nadine from Human Resources."

I stood and walked around my desk, my hand out to shake hers. "Nice to meet you. Please call me Graysen."

"Thanks." Her head swiveled to take in the sofa and chairs off to the side.

"Can I help you with something or just wandering through the offices talking to the coaches?"

Brown eyes flipped up to meet mine. They were lighter than Kesara's with a yellowish tint rather than the red I was used to staring into. Discomfort seemed to be the prevailing emotion in them. "I'm hoping you can if you have some time."

"Certainly." I gestured to the sofa seating area.

"This is an unofficial visit, mind you," she began, her eyes darting to the still open door.

I started to feel a little uncomfortable myself, getting up to close the door so that we were the only ones privy to this discussion. "Okay."

"It's about Darby Evan." She waited for me to respond, but I didn't have anything to say. "She's been telling me things that I wanted to follow up on. She hasn't made a formal complaint or anything. We've just been talking as friends, but as her friend, I don't like the way you're treating her. As someone whose business it is to keep the work environment comfortable for everyone, I don't like it at all."

I understood the words she was using, but they made no sense at all. All I could do was sit and stare at her, blinking while I tried to piece together what the hell she was telling me. "Are you saying that Darby feels I'm making her uncomfortable at work?"

"I know you two were in a relationship and now, apparently, that relationship has changed. Darby isn't happy where it's going and feels the effect at work."

"Huh," I said softly, anger and sorrow filling me. "Let's call in Tavian and take care of this formally."

Her hand reached out as if to clutch at me, but she pulled it back. "That's not necessary. Like I said, this is an unofficial visit and won't be anything unless Darby makes a formal complaint, which I'm not certain she ever will."

"Well, I'd like this resolved, and I'd like it resolved with my supervisor."

"I'm not sure it's wise to air this out in front of your boss, Graysen."

"Oh, I think it is." I reached for the extension on the coffee table and punched in Kesara's line. "Hey, Kesara, does Tavian have a quick minute to join me in my office?"

Nadine looked perplexed as I listened to Kesara get Tavian moving at my rare request. I knew it would only be a minute before Tavian arrived and I could tell it confused her. Most people would not want their bosses to listen to an HR lecture on sexual harassment. She stood the second he hit the doorway.

"Hi, Nadine, I didn't expect to see you here." He came forward to shake her hand and dropped into the chair next to me. "What's up, Gray?"

"Nadine was just telling me that Darby is having a problem with the way I'm treating her at work, complaining about, what's the term, Nadine? Hostile environment?"

Tavian's snort practically eclipsed her saying, "Yes." Her brow furrowed at his reaction.

Because I knew this would resolve things, hopefully once and for all, I punched in Darby's extension and put her on speaker. "Hi, Darby."

"Hey, sweetie, it's so good to hear your voice."

Nadine's brow furrowed even more at the eager tone that came from the speakerphone.

"Any chance I can pull you away for a second?" I asked.

"Right now? Sure, where?"

"My office if you don't mind."

"Anything for you, sweetheart."

I tried not to look too smugly at the highly confused look that now adorned Nadine's face. Darby hadn't sounded like she felt I was harassing her at work. I knew I was going to blindside her, but whining to an HR rep, she needed a little lesson.

One step inside my office, Darby's smile slid off her beautiful face. She came to a stop, her gaze pinging back and forth from Tavian to Nadine. "What's going on?" she asked.

"I was wondering the same thing," I told her.

"So am I," Nadine inserted. "Darby? Would you like to elaborate on your seemingly amicable relationship with Graysen?"

"Uhh," Darby said, looking at me to help her out but realizing I wouldn't.

"I can't believe you did this. I almost wrote Graysen up," Nadine stood to address her.

"I didn't want that," Darby assured emphatically. "I just miss her."

"That is so inappropriate, my God!" Nadine scolded.

I didn't bother to say anything. Tavian and I shared an awkward glance. I felt a little relieved that Darby was getting dressed down in front of her boss and an HR rep, maybe she'd stop trying to "bump" into me in the halls. But I also felt a little guilty because I did want to keep her friendship when she finally spiraled out of this somewhat pathetic idea that we might get back together. I didn't want that and she didn't want that. She just didn't know it yet.

"You're right. I know. I'm sorry, really. I wasn't thinking. You misunderstood what I was saying, and I should have corrected that, but I..." Darby drifted off, looking over at me.

"I think it might be wise to steer clear of each other for a while," Tavian suggested.

Darby looked like she wanted to protest, but her good sense seemed to return to her. She nodded her head before turning to me. "Sorry, Gray. I didn't mean for it to go this far."

"Please don't let it happen again," I hoped my grave tone told her how seriously I was taking this.

Nadine grabbed her elbow and propelled them both out of the office with an apologetic look at me. I waited until they'd closed the door and had enough time to make it down to the elevators.

"I know." I turned back to Tavian. "No relationships at work, I get it."

Tavian snorted again. "I practically shoved you two together, but I didn't know she was a psycho."

"Tave! She's not psycho. She's just..."

"Heartbroken?"

I ducked my head, letting out a huge sigh. "I hate this, you know. You should have warned me that relationships can get so messy."

"You didn't already know?"

Oops, my big mouth. "I've never had one that serious before," I admitted the half-truth. Tavian didn't need to know that Darby was my only relationship. He'd always given me the benefit of the doubt, assuming I'd been in several semi-serious relationships that weren't involved enough to warrant introductions to my closest friends. I'd never bothered to change his impression for fear he'd realize how big a loser in that department I really was.

"Well, I hope she stops trying to pull this crazy stuff."

"You and me both," I admitted.

CHAPTER 32

Staples Center, an arena I'd played in several times before, somehow had a different feel to it with the NCAA Final Four banners on the floor. I could feel the excitement starting to build already. This place would be hopping with mostly California fans eager to route for the only remaining west coast team left in the tourney. As a Cinderella seed at 14, we'd also get the crowd's usual tendency to root for the underdog.

It had been a long road to even make it into the tournament, but with our last winning streak against very good teams, the selection committee gave us a fairly good seeding. The team felt we should have gone higher, but now that we'd made it to the Final Four, they didn't seem to care. They'd performed well, incorporating all the new plays seamlessly, and their conditioning was the basis for these tournament wins. Tomorrow, we'd be playing the best ranked team in the league. They won't have underestimated us like our last four opponents. It was going to be exciting, and I hoped the guys would be able to handle all the pressure.

I gathered up the basketballs to rack them. Damon and Bill had retreated to the locker rooms to change out of their sweats. I was going to wait until I got back to the hotel. I still had a couple hours before I'd be meeting up with Kesara and Santiago for dinner. They were driving down to watch the games, but mostly to give me some moral support. Tavian and the family wouldn't be in town until tomorrow morning.

Before I racked the last ball, I took aim from the NBA three range and let it fly. Muscle memory and good form produced a perfect swish, and I had to stop myself from eagerly rushing in for another shot at the rim. That, too, was muscle memory.

"Nice shot," Dash called out from the tunnel leading to the locker rooms.

"Luck," I brushed off his compliment.

"Ha!" he barked, hustling over to grab the bouncing ball. "Were you a three-point specialist?"

"It's not considered a specialty for the bigs to hit threes in women's ball." I watched his eyes sweep over me and knew what he was thinking. He stood at six-one as a point guard. "And yes, six-three is considered a big."

"I've watched enough women's games to know that the fours and fives aren't usually money from three." He paused, shooting me a grin. "By the way, Tavian showed me a game tape."

"Oh, yeah? He managed to rope you into watching one of his games, huh? From college or the NBA?"

"Nope. One of yours. Your first Olympics."

I gulped, not sure how I felt about that.

"Thirty-two points, thirteen rebounds, six blocks, a gold medal, and you only played twenty-five minutes. Damn, Coach!"

"We had a good game, that's for sure." I grabbed the ball from him and racked it. "Get the rest of the team, will you? We've got to get out of here before our competition shows."

"Sure thing." That playful expression lingered a bit but he could tell that I wasn't in a playful mood.

I waited for the team to gather themselves so we could get the bus back to the hotel. In that time, I hoped that Tavian hadn't shown that game to anyone else. I wasn't sure how the rest of the team would take it. I'd never liked accepting compliments, but they came a lot when I played. Now that I wasn't a player, I shouldn't have to be subjected to it anymore.

By dessert that night, I would have gladly listened to any compliments anyone wanted to give me just to get out of sitting through the rest of dinner. I would have watched every single game I'd ever played with anyone on my team. Hell, I would have reenacted every single game to avoid more of this dinner.

"Oh my God, tell me you didn't have to endure that for six long hours in a car?" I turned from the sinks when I saw Kesara walk into the restroom where I was hiding out.

She started laughing, a wonderful sound, especially after the two hours of dining torture we'd just been through. Santiago really needed help picking his girlfriends because that airhead at the table with us was a nightmare. "It was even worse." Kesara reached out to clutch my arm and get a hold of her merriment. "For at least three hours she had her bare feet dangling out the window, giggling and waving at truck drivers as we passed them. Then when we tried to stop off for a quick snack because she said she was hungry, we had to drive twenty miles off the freeway to find a supermarket because she wouldn't eat at any of the fast food places right off the highway."

"What is Santi thinking?"

Her eyes bored into mine, a knowing gaze made me lose the smile. "Come on, look at her."

"What?" I shook my head, not understanding what she meant.

"She's gorgeous, Gray." She must have spotted the confused look on my face. "Not your type, I guess."

"But she's yours?" I was silently crossing my fingers that the buxom blonde out at our table drooling all over Santiago wasn't Kesara's type. She and I couldn't be farther from same type. If that was what attracted Kesara, I didn't stand a chance. Not that I did anyway because we worked together and we were friends and Kesara didn't like me like that and I shouldn't like her like that.

She let a mirthful breath leave her mouth before her eyes swept over me. "No." Her voice was low, seductive, or it would be if we weren't hiding out in a restroom trying to avoid spending more time with the ditz back at our table.

"I thought I knew Santiago pretty well, but clearly I had no idea what he went for in a woman."

She shook her head. "When Santi decides he wants to settle down, he'll go for someone with substance. This woman is just another pleasurable distraction. He usually hangs on to them for three or four months them goes on a six month dating hiatus."

"I'm not sure I can handle that for three or four months."

"I don't think he'll make it three or four more hours. If she wasn't dependant on a ride home with us, I have a feeling he'd be crashing in my room tonight."

"You could fly home with the team," I offered. "You're part of the athletic department."

Her hand moved up to touch my cheek. "You're very sweet, but I better keep him from dumping her body along the way."

My face tingled where she touched me. I tried not to lean into her touch. Friends didn't do that. "We better get back out there or she might start having sex with him at the table."

That got another wonderful laugh out of her. I'd been noticing lately that every time she laughed my whole body felt lighter. "That wouldn't surprise me at all." She slid her hand down to clasp mine, tugging to get us moving. It felt so good in mine, smaller but strong and soft and warm. I tried not to grip it too tightly, not wanting to seem like I was clinging to her.

Once we'd rounded the wall cutting off the bathrooms, she reluctantly dropped my hand, or at least I hoped it was reluctantly. Seeing as the restaurant was likely crawling with fans and press, it probably wasn't a good idea to flaunt public displays of affection, especially with a f-r-i-e-n-d! God, I really had to stop this.

"Oh, good, we can ask them," the blonde said, slurring her words after what looked like her fourth appletini. "How long have you guys been going out?"

Kesara shot a look at me as we both sank back into our chairs. "We're not," she informed Bambi without a single longing look, or remorseful tone, or even a wishful sigh, much to my disappointment.

"C'mon, you're both lezzies, right?" Barbie swished her blond tresses back and forth between a guilty looking Santiago and an angry Kesara. "You better be, or at least you," she pointed her long bony finger at me, "better be. I'm not okay with my man having a woman as his 'friend' if she's straight."

"Jesus," Kesara muttered, shooting a glare at Santiago.

"Babe, that's not fair." Santiago tightened his grip around her shoulders as if trying to rein her in.

"I'm just staking my claim, that's all."

That even made Santiago swallow roughly. His pained look made me turn away before I started laughing. Unfortunately, Kesara turned toward me and we couldn't help it. The laughter just came out. I hurriedly grabbed my wallet, dumping enough money onto the table to cover the dinner and waved apologetically at Santiago and Buffy. Kesara rose with me and we left before our stifled laughter erupted into the loud knee-slapping kind.

CHAPTER 33

Entering a gym after the season just ended was probably the most depressing thing I went through every year. Especially after a heartbreaking loss. As if savoring it, I walked slowly across the hardwood floor toward the locker rooms. Some of the guys should be in there. I wanted to remind them of the exit interviews, or that was the excuse I was using.

I was decked out in sweats, but under, I had on practice gear. The same gear I wore for years with my WNBA team. Gear that had brought me luck during all those years and would hopefully be put to use today.

Knocking on the locker room door, I called out, "Coach coming in." I waited for a responding call before entering. Five of the guys were packing up their lockers. "Hey, guys."

"What's up, Coach." It was a greeting, not a question.

"Just wanted to post the exit interview times in case any of you forget."

"Hour and a half hour for mine," Dash inserted with his characteristic grin.

"Sounds good." I put the reminder sheet up on the white board and wandered back to where my arena office would have been had I been a man or wanted to disregard my players' locker room privacy. "Should have asked Tavian to have a partition built or something," I muttered to myself. It was a shame I couldn't have used this space all season.

"Something wrong?" Wendell turned from the locker closest to this office.

"Come in here a second."

He frowned, looking at his watch. I wasn't due to talk to him until after Dash. With a shrug, he followed me into the office. "Yeah?"

"Have a seat." I gestured to a guest chair. "It hasn't been an easy year, has it?"

He actually laughed. I smiled at the rare sound. He had a nice laugh. "Sure hasn't, but we did good in the tourney. Almost had 'em." A one-point loss. One point and the team would have advanced to the championship game, a place they'd never been before.

"On to greener pastures for you, though." I made sure to catch his eye. "You've earned it, Wendell. Once you started applying yourself, you really excelled. It was actually a pleasure coaching you some games."

"But not all games, right?" he teased, which told me all I needed to know.

"Enough," I confirmed. "You're going to do well in the NBA. Do me proud, play well, and stay the decent man you've become over these last couple months. A little humble pie never hurts anyone."

He smiled sheepishly. "I'll try."

I nodded. "Do you remember what I told you during our second team meeting?"

"Aw, Coach, really? We've had a million of 'em this season. Am I gonna have to run if I don't remember?"

We laughed together and it felt nice. "Not today, but let me remind you. I said if I ever thought you were mature enough to handle the consequences, we'd play one-on-one if you wanted." His eyes widened, body shifting forward in the seat. "You're mature enough."

"Game on! Hell, yeah!" He sprang out of his seat without another word, rushing over to his locker and whipping off his t-shirt.

I followed almost as quickly. "You might want to let me leave before you pull a striptease."

The guys laughed, but Wendell was determined to get out on the court. "You better get changing, too. You're about to take a massive beating."

"What's going on?" Dash asked, pausing in his task.

"I'll leave Wendell to explain." Pulling on the door, I rushed through before he was completely naked. Gah! I didn't need to see that to throw me off my game.

When I entered the gym, I slipped off my sweats to my basketball shorts and practice jersey before my opponent joined me. Grabbing the ball from my earlier warm up session, I took some practice shots. I hadn't expected Wendell to jump at the opportunity so quickly, nor did I think he'd say anything in front of his teammates. He must still think I wasn't even a challenge, but the fact that he'd taunted me the same way he taunted his teammates told me he'd reassessed his opinion on female ballplayers, or at least of me.

"Really, Coach?" Dash burst through the gym doors. "Dub's not full of crap?"

"Well, I can't speak to that," I kidded.

"No way." He reached into his pocket and pulled out his phone. "I'm telling everyone."

"That might not be a good idea." I didn't want to turn this into a spectacle.

"Oh, they're going to want to see this. You're going to kick his ass, right?"

"You think I can?" I was genuinely interested to know because I was no longer sure.

"You would have right after that Olympic game I saw. If you've stayed in that kind of form, hell, yeah, I think you can." He was busy texting as he said this, glancing up for a wink at the end.

"Prepare to be spanked, Coach," Wendell taunted when he, Jeff, Ollie, and Eli walked into the gym. "Oh, wait, should I have Jeff run get a nurse in case you fall and break a hip?"

"Ha-ha," I barely suppressed my laugh. "I may have some years on you—"

"Twenty or forty," he tossed out with a snicker.

"But," I interjected firmly, "I'm still the only one of us that's seen me play. Not too late to back down, junior."

"Like you said, you're older, haven't been playing for eight years, and..." he paused, his dark eyes twinkling. "You're four inches shorter than me, which gives me a half step advantage."

Now that made me smile broadly. He had remembered and not once did his one-time sexist attitude rear its ugly head. "That's right, but I don't plan on losing, young man. Let's go." I tossed him the ball and gestured to the free throw line. We'd shoot for outs.

On only his second time at the line, he missed his free throw. I hit mine. We turned and smiled to each other, and then I headed out to the top of the key. With a quick ball check, he backed off me by three steps, expecting me to drive at him. I waited for him to crowd me, but he stayed in his defensive crouch. I took one dribble then set up for a three-pointer. All net. The now seven guys in the stands applauded my shot.

Wendell's eyes flipped back to me from watching the ball. "I see how you're gonna play it." He collected the rebound and grinned. "You're getting smoked now."

He took a few dribbles toward me as I stayed low waiting for his move. He tried a step around me, and I stripped the ball from him on the crossover, hustling to catch up to it. He was still reeling from the ball no longer in his hand so I was able to take a free shot. 2-0.

"Wicked, Coach!" Nate called out as he led the rest of the team into the gym. Six of the women's players were mixed with them. This was drawing a crowd. I hoped I didn't live to regret it.

"Ball," Wendell barked, waiting at the top of the key. Levity was gone now that I'd gotten off two easy shots.

When he checked it this time, he was sure to keep his guard hand up to prevent another cherry pick. But like all big men not used to dribbling more than a couple steps before a dunk, he wasn't as sharp as I was fast. With a quick flick of my hand, the ball was flying back behind him and I chased it down. This time, he wasn't as shocked and charged me. Faking left, with a dribble behind my back I slid past him and went in for an easy layup.

"Oh, yeah!" One of the female players yelled out, slapping the hands of her teammates.

The crowd had expanded again, several more of the women's team, three football players, and at least eight softball and soccer players. I should have locked the gym doors. This was something I needed to do for Wendell to show him that women were his equal whether I won or not. I hoped he could handle me taking three points off him.

"Luck," Wendell muttered as he held out his hands for my pass.

He didn't try to dribble this time, just let a quick shot fly. When it banged off the rim, he bodied up on me, grabbing the rebound from my swatting hand. If I lost, it would be because of this rebounding difference. With his extra four inches, he could grab the ball when I would have to swat it out and chase it down. As soon as he landed, we both went back up, my hand brushing his wrist as he got off a good shot.

"That's what I'm talkin' 'bout!" Two of his teammates yelled.

"No inside game, like I said," Wendell smirked.

"We'll see about that, son." I headed back to the top of the key just as Tavian came running through the door, Kesara following close behind. I smiled at both, happy to see that I'd have at least two genuine fans of my own.

Wendell set up a step away from me. He wasn't going to let me get off any more free shots. Too bad for him that my three-point shot wasn't as good as my drive and pop. 4-1, and Wendell was starting to get antsy.

"You see my girl shoot?" one of the female players called out, slapping the hand of one of her teammates.

"That's Coach Viola to you, Stacey," Coach Meyers called out from the doorway, beating the young woman into submission. She waved me over as the football, soccer, wrestling and all our assistants came in behind her. The circus had officially started. "Beat this little punk, Graysen," she whispered in a firm tone before stepping up the aisle and dropping into the seat next to Kesara.

No pressure there. I hustled back over and took up a defensive stance, swiping at the ball any time it came near me. Wendell had gotten careful though and launched another to bounce off the rim, out jumping me to the rebound and stuffing it home.

Not a word passed between us as we went back to the top of the key. Six more outs later, my lead had diminished to one. He was using his body exactly how I'd trained him to use it. Powering up, muscling out, checking, and finishing. He would become a fine NBA player if he didn't let his mouth get ahead of himself again.

"Nice move," I complimented on his hand switch layup.

"Coach Damon's been working on it with me."

I liked that he gave Damon credit. At the start of the season, he would have been all talk. I decided it was time to break out my trademark move. Driving to the hole, I let him body me up, pressing against me to keep me from squaring up at the basket. Instead of stepping around and into him to muscle up like he always did, I spun away and launched a fade away jumper. 7-5.

"Damn!" Wendell boomed, staring at me as the crowd applauded whether they were rooting for me or not. "You're gonna teach me that move."

I laughed because he'd stopped being so miffed every time I hit one. "Be glad to."

With the ball in his hand, he made a direct move and dunked over me within thirty seconds. That was a killer shot if a player had it, almost indefensible, but especially for someone shorter.

"Now would be a good time for a dunk, huh, Coach?" he started with the trash talk again. Since it was said with levity, I didn't mind. It was the kind of player he was.

"Don't need it. I'm still up one." I drove at him, spinning and lifting a shot one step to his left, his bad side. 8-6. "Make that two."

"A little trash talk from the coach. You hear that, fellas?" He looked at his teammates, who were split evenly down the middle. Half were on the side with the female athletes, nearly all the coaches, Tavian, and Kesara. The other half were with the football players and a couple of wrestlers who'd wandered over from their practice. "I'm dunking this one, too. Thought I'd give you a heads up."

He managed to get that dunk and the next two shots, one without an answering basket from me. That put us even and at game point. "I've been holding back." Everyone heard that smug announcement, prompting razzing taunts from the crowd. It wouldn't break my concentration, though, not when it all came down to one basket.

"Game point," I said, making sure to get his nod and checked the ball at the top of the key. I knew that I didn't have to make this shot, that it would be okay to lose, that Wendell and all the men in the crowd now understood that gender did not automatically dictate athletic prowess. But I wanted this win. It'd been eight years since I'd played for anything other than a fun pickup game.

His big paw came out and swiped at my hand three times as I charged and retreated, looking for a hole or a way around his big body. I thought about taking a jump shot, but I knew if I missed, he'd likely get the rebound, clear it then jam it home. I had to win this one in the key, a place I'd practically lived during my college and professional career.

Backing down on him, I felt him push against me, trying not to give up an inch. I took him left again. He still hated going left, but I was using every advantage I could. I took a ready dribble, faked a turn right, came back left but he adjusted, thinking I was going for my fade away. Instead, I ducked under his raised arm and took a big step to his side, leaping up and finger rolling the ball into the basket.

The crowd went crazy, applause, laughter, and good natured taunting. I collected the shot and headed back toward a stunned Wendell. He looked like he wanted to say something, but I cut him off, keeping my voice low so that he was the only one to hear. "How's that Y chromosome feeling now, big guy?"

He couldn't do anything but shake his head and chuckle. "Good game, Coach. Let's go again. I guarantee I won't give up those first three easy points."

"No, you wouldn't, but one game is enough for this elderly lady." I said loudly, letting him save face a bit. Because I was feeling good, I winked at him and took off, driving to the basket. Three steps from the backboard, I launched into the air, scooping the ball into my left hand, and executed a reverse dunk off the right rim. It wasn't as sensational as some of his, but it was still a dunk. This time when I turned around, Wendell's wasn't the only face in the crowd that had a shocked look. Only Tavian and my former teammates knew I could dunk. I didn't have to raise my voice to be heard this time. "Just because women don't dunk in every game, doesn't mean we can't."

"Holy shit!" he gasped, still looking up at the basket. "Do that again."

"Practice isn't officially over. I could make you run for that kind of language."

His hands shot up as his teammates surrounded us, calling out congrats and telling us how much they liked watching us play. It felt good, almost like I was with my own team, and I allowed myself thirty seconds to soak it up.

Tavian pulled me out of their clutches. "We are so never playing again," he stated. "You little cheater, you've been playing every day, still, haven't you?"

"Guilty." I smiled up at him.

Kesara wore a proud smile, clearly happy that I'd had fun and taken out the once smug kid on my team. "Nice," she said simply, squeezing my arm. The zap of pleasure that accompanied the squeeze was even better than the adrenalin rush from winning the game.

"Way to put him away, Graysen. Haven't had that much fun watching a basketball game since we won the whole show a few years back." Lindsay Meyers looked back over at the stands and called out to collect her team. She was running exit interviews today, too.

Time to get back to work, but I would wear this smile for the rest of the day.

CHAPTER 34

Or so I thought. Five minutes into the meeting with my favorite player, I lost that smile. I was looking at the one guy on the team who had made my whole season worthwhile, who had kept things lighthearted, eagerly accepting any new change, and he was leaving early. Very early. Dammit.

"This is a surprise, Dash." A shock, more like it. He was a sophomore. I should get to have him for two more years.

"I know, but I've got to try." He glanced away, swallowing roughly. "My gran is sick. I can't waste another season in college."

My head began shaking, for his situation, for next year's team, for my success as a men's college coach. Pretty much all of it rested in his hands. And he was leaving. Once again, dammit. "I'm sure we could get special permission from the NCAA for your situation that would allow you to earn some money."

"Yeah, right. The same kind of money I'll make in the NBA?"

No, of course not. No one made the kind of money the NBA paid except male golfers or top box office stars. "I hate to tell anyone they can't do something, but you know how difficult that league is." I watched as his eyes widened. He wasn't expecting this from me, but I was his teacher as much as his coach, and he had to hear this. "Don't get me wrong, you'll be drafted, but you're a sophomore. Sophomores rarely make the team. Give me another year, and I'll increase your chances by eighty percent. Give me two, and you'll go in the top five picks."

"I'm making the team. I learned a lot from you this year. There's no way I'm not making that team."

Actually, there were a lot of ways and a lot of similar stories to prove it. "You've talked this over with your gran?" I knew his grandmother held a lot of weight with him. She liked him being at school, had told me herself on her last visit.

"She's not happy, but we don't have a choice. She needs a nursing home, and Mom can't pay for it."

Dammit. He'd made up his mind. My point guard, the best player on my team now that Wendell was graduating, was declaring eligibility for the NBA draft, two years early. So was Frank, one year early, and Jeff was headed to the European league to start earning an income for his unexpected family. Four of my starting five were leaving and the sole remaining starter wasn't a star. He was a position player, good enough to fill out the lineup but not something to build a team on.

As if I hadn't already wanted to stop being the coach of this team, this pretty much solidified it. I stood to wish him luck. He hugged me, wished me the same, and with a wave, a sophomore with tremendous potential walked out of my office and off my team. Yet another difference between men's and women's college ball. God, this sucked.

I picked up the phone and called Tavian's office to get him to meet me outside. It wasn't entirely professional, but since he'd lured me here under less than professional circumstances, I felt I could bend the rules this once. He needed to know what I was thinking.

"I still can't get that game out of my head. You handed him his ass today. Way to go, my sista!"

I smiled, reaching up to slap his extended palm then got us moving away from the exit. "Dash is declaring."

"What?" Tavian turned to face me, walking backwards along the lakeside path. "As a sophomore? He's good, but not that good."

"That's what I told him, but he's in a bind financially to help his family. He'll make the D-league, but he won't be guaranteed a spot."

"That blows," he declared, almost as frustrated as I was by this situation.

"Yep."

He glanced over at my defeated tone then came to a stop. "Oh, don't do this to me. You took a hopeless team to the Final Four. The stigma from last year is gone. People are lining up to buy next year's season tickets. I've got interview requests from every sports mag out there. You can't be thinking of — "

"Leaving?" I cut him off. "You know this was short-term for me. I did what I promised to do, took away the stain on your program. Now you can shop around for a prestigious coach. Someone who won't be so upset when he or she loses a player because he's idiotic enough to think he can make the NBA as a frickin' baby." I was practically shouting by the time I finished.

"Wow, haven't seen you this upset since our old AD decided to remodel the men's locker rooms only."

I didn't rise to his bait. He loved bringing that up to jolt me off whatever track I was on. "This isn't for me. I told you that when I took the job. It's so different from what I'm used to. I struggled all season. It wasn't exactly enjoyable, and I like liking my job, you know?"

"I do because I like liking mine too. Of course you're a big reason why I'm liking it so much this year." He squeezed my shoulder in sympathy, but his eyes showed the worry that comes from having to start another coaching search. "Are you sure about this?"

"Pretty sure, but don't worry because I've set everything up for the next person to step right in."

"Of anyone who's ever said that I believe you. I'm sad to think that you'll be gone. I liked having you a floor away."

"When Coach Meyers retires, give me a call. I'll be right back here in a flash." That was a promise I could easily make.

* * *

About ten minutes before I was supposed to dash out to meet up with Kesara for dinner, the doorbell rang. I was surprised to see her on the doorstep. She matched my smile but glanced away quickly.

"Wasn't I meeting you there?" I motioned her inside.

Her eyes pinged back to mine. After a slight nod of her head, she came across the threshold. Something was worrying her. She turned to face me, opened her mouth, then shut it again and headed into the living room to plunk down on the sofa.

"Are you okay? Can't make dinner?" When she didn't respond, I continued, "That's okay, another night. Anything I can help you with tonight?"

She took a breath and locked eyes with me as I sat in the chair next to the couch. "We work together."

I squinted in confusion, not sure where she was going with this. "Yes."

"That's the problem with us."

The problem? "We have a problem?"

"Yes. We work together."

"What am I missing?"

She blew out the breath. "I'm—we're..." She waved her hand between us. "We could have something really great here."

Her words made my heart start pounding. Heat swirled through my stomach, and my mouth went dry. She probably wasn't talking about what I thought, but I couldn't help my hope from surfacing. "Yes." It was the only thing I could think to say that didn't sound moronic and desperate.

She smiled, letting a soft breath escape. For a moment, it looked like relief rinsed through her, but then another emotion flared. One that amped up my heat index just before she exhaled and said, "Screw work."

She popped off the sofa and came toward me. Before I knew exactly what was happening her face was an inch from mine. My hands reacted by gripping her head and bringing her mouth to me. God, those lips. So soft in that brief New Year's kiss had turned insistent and caressing. They grazed and tantalized every inch of mine. She was a master kisser. Really. If there was a cult of kissers, she'd be their leader.

When her mouth released its Svengali like hold on me, I melted back into the chair barely able to sustain a thought. My heart pounded and my limbs felt heavy. "Wow," I breathed and heard her chuckle. Great, I'd said that out loud. How suave.

"My thoughts exactly."

I broke into a smile. She had such a way about her. I never felt like I had to live up to her expectations. "You should have told me you were such a good kisser," I teased.

She laughed that wonderful laugh. "That would have changed things, would it?"

I laughed with her. "I might have attacked you in the hallway at work."

"Yes, 'cause that's not inappropriate."

We sobered a moment. "I like you, Kesara." I had to say it. More than liked actually, but I definitely couldn't share that yet.

"I like you, too, Graysen. What we have, it's worth the difficulties of our work environment."

"Actually," I hesitated telling her, but since Tavian already knew, I didn't want to hide anything for her. "That may not be an issue for much longer."

"What?" She sat back against the armrest of the couch.

"I'm waiting to hear back from Berkeley."

"You...what?"

"I interviewed for a head coaching position with Berkeley. I'm waiting to hear back."

Her mouth sagged open before a smile crept across her beautiful face. "You won't be working at LMU anymore? You'll be just up the street at Cal?"

"That's what I'm hoping."

"Hmm," she let out a sound that said she was contemplating what I'd told her. Then her knee slid onto the chair next to my thigh, a hand pressed onto my shoulder as she set her other knee in place to straddle me. "Well, then, problem gone."

Her face lowered to press another kiss onto my lips. My hands moved up to grip her hips and hold her in place. She felt so good straddling me, her mouth exploring mine. Before I realized it, my tongue pushed out and licked along her bottom lip, seeking permission. Her mouth opened, allowing me entrance. My tongue slipped inside, teasing at first, then stroking hers. Hands gripped my back and neck pressing us closer together as her pelvis dragged along my lap, connecting with my hips. With a soft cry, she pulled back, breathing hard and staring wide-eyed at me.

Suddenly, her body was gone and she was standing before me. "I'm not sleeping with you on the first date." I was so shocked by the loss of her I hadn't registered what she'd said. If it weren't for the grin and soft chuckle, I might think I'd done something wrong. "C'mon, you're taking me to dinner. A proper date." Her hand reached down to pull me up with her. Stunned that I somehow managed not to screw up my chance with this amazing woman, I could only follow her lead out the door on our "first" date.

CHAPTER 35

"**S**o, it's true?" Darby leaned against my doorjamb. It was the second time I'd seen her since that meeting with the HR director. She'd bumped into me in the lobby a few days after we'd come back from the Final Four. Surprisingly, she'd congratulated me on taking the team as far as we'd gone, wished me luck in the recruiting, and headed on her way. It finally seemed like she was moving past our mistake of a relationship.

Without needing to ask what she meant, I glanced down at my last box of personal items. "It was a spectacular offer."

"Of course it was," she agreed, moving inside a step. "They're lucky to have you, Gray."

I smiled. "Thanks, but I'm the lucky one. It's what I was made to do."

"A top ten squad at a top twenty university. Amazing."

We locked eyes for a moment. The heat I'd once felt was gone and so was the hazy feeling I often experienced in her presence. It felt nice not to regret having broken it off with her. It looked like she was finally okay with it, too. "That's what I was thinking."

She nodded, finality in her eyes. "I wish you luck. I know you won't need it. I'll keep my eye on your schedule and try to make a game."

"I'll look forward to it. Thanks, Darby. Good luck to you as well."

Her hand rose up and gave a quick wave before she ducked back out into the hallway. For the first time since breaking up with her, I didn't feel the guilt I normally experienced whenever I caught a glimpse of her in the lobby or overheard someone talking about her. I was really glad she'd stopped by on my last day.

"Everything okay?"

The voice this time brought a flush to my face and my heart started thumping. Kesara stepped into my office, a private smile on her face, eagerness in her beautiful eyes. "Hey," I greeted softly.

"Hi there." Her head tilted, studying me. "Anything you have to worry about?" Her eyes glanced back and down the hallway that Darby had followed.

"She was wishing me well."

Kesara's face sagged in relief. Tavian had told her about the meeting with the HR director, and I'd noticed her checking the hallways whenever we walked through the department as if needing to shield me from anything else Darby might try. "I'm glad, for both of you."

"Me, too," I told her honestly. The urge to hug her had me grabbing my last box of possessions. We adhered to very strict rules while at work. No touching, no lingering glances, no hugging, and definitely no kissing. It would be so nice not to be colleagues anymore, and starting Monday, that would come true. Tonight we had a celebratory dinner planned. It would be our fifth date. Unlike with Darby, I'd found it difficult to keep from ripping her clothes off every time we had a date, but it was nice to take it slow.

"Are you ready?" she asked, her eyes twinkling with promise. "We're no longer coworkers when we walk out that door, you know."

My lips pulled into a wide smile. "Our problem won't be a problem anymore, will it?"

"No, ma'am, it will not." Kesara fell into step with me as we headed down the staircase and into the night air. "I'm looking forward to our date."

We walked to my car and loaded my last box inside. "So am I." I reached for her door and opened it, watching her get into the passenger seat.

When I took my seat, she leaned over and kissed me lightly. "Shall we be good and go out to dinner or just skip it?"

My stomach felt like it burst into flames, very pleasurable flames, very not nervous or anxious flames. I'd been having more frequent fantasies about Kesara, all types of fantasies, and the heat had never amped up to this level. With a simple question, I was practically panting in my seat. "Order in?" I asked, hoping she'd go for the compromise.

"Oh yes," she said softly, reaching across to grab my hand as I steered us onto the street that would eventually get us to my place.

I didn't have time to get nervous, and even if we'd been stuck in traffic for an hour, I don't think I would have gotten there. Everything about Kesara was comfortable and right. No pressure, no guilt, no worry that I'd upset her with anything I said. Only heat, anticipation, and excitement.

Without words, we came in through my back door. I didn't bother with the boxes. I could get them later. Turning back from locking the door, I found Kesara right in front of me. Her arms came up and pulled me into her. Brown eyes spoke volumes in the time it took before I couldn't stand it any longer and leaned down to kiss her.

God the things she could do with her mouth and tongue. I'd had to break off kisses on our dates before or I'd never be able to stop until she was stripped bare before me. This time I didn't have to stop. This time, I'd get all of her.

We stepped our way into my bedroom, staying mostly attached. Her hands roamed my sides and skimmed across my butt, squeezing to tantalize; then they were gone, back to my waist. Every movement of her hands shot sparks of heat from her touch to the rest of my body. I felt like I couldn't catch my breath but wasn't about to stop. I'd waited for this moment my whole life. Waited to find someone who could make me feel so much and overwhelmed me with desire that I'd missed out on.

"It's crazy how much I want you," Kesara whispered, sliding her lips down my throat, nipping and licking a spot that I'd never known was so sensitive until her mouth first grazed it. She'd been doing things like this to me for weeks while we dated. I had a feeling tonight I'd find out a lot more about my body under her skillful hands and mouth.

I reached for her top button and slowly revealed the golden tan skin beneath. White lace popped against her skin tone and the three little red bows on her bra made my fingers ache to trace them. My palm slid from her throat down the center of her chest, the heat of her skin contrasting with the shiver I felt under my hand. My fingers started to undo her slacks as I felt her hands begin to strip off my clothes. Soon I discovered her matching panties with another taunting bow and took a moment to take it all in. She was beautiful, perfectly proportioned, magnificent skin without one blemish, toned legs, fit arms, firm tummy. Magnificent.

"You are so beautiful," she spoke, drawing my eyes up to hers.

I somehow stood before her in my underwear, not having realized that I'd assisted her in getting nearly naked. I also realized that I was eager to shed the final barrier, lay everything out for her to see. I cared so much for her already, this final step might plunge me into the depths of love. "You are stunning, my darling, more beautiful than I fantasized."

Her brown eyes lit up before a smile played across her lips. "You've been fantasizing about me? Hmm, wonder if they were as good as mine?"

I laughed, feeling happiness overwhelm me. She was perfect for me, decisive and compassionate, caring and firm, demanding and accommodating all in one. I enjoyed every moment I spent with her, craved more time together, and hung on her every word. I couldn't imagine growing tired of anything she did or said. This woman was the one for me. I was certain of that fact, and nothing about the thought scared or pressured me.

She reached around me to unclasp my bra, her eyes dropping to watch my breasts spring free. She licked her lips and swallowed roughly. A moment passed before she moved to slip her fingers under my panties and slide them down my legs. "Beautiful," she breathed.

Standing naked in front of her, I felt liberated, not awkward, and the feeling spurred my movements to shed her bra. Her breasts were gorgeous, small and round, with already rigid brown-tipped nipples. I dipped my head and took one into my mouth, sucking gently, then licking to the sound of her moan. My hands slid down her hips and slipped her underwear off. I brought my head up to look at her. A dark trimmed triangle of soft curls covered her core. I clenched my eyes shut at the perfection of her.

A hand pressed against me, urging me onto my bed. I didn't resist, almost leaping back so that I could feel her skin against the length of mine. She followed, waiting until I'd settled before she lowered herself onto me. I gasped at the sensation, overwhelmed by warmth and softness. Her mouth slanted over mine, ramping up the fire already blazing inside. My hands journeyed over her sides and back, positioning her hips between mine. She let out groan as we fit together.

She kissed my sternum, moving to a breast, closing over my nipple with her teeth at first. My back arched into her, feeding her more as my hand slipped between us, cupping her fully. I didn't know which of us was more excited. She drenched my hand as I gently rubbed a wide circle over her.

"God, that feels so good," she moaned, kissing her way across my chest to lash her tongue against my other nipple. "Please, Grace, please."

Oh, that sounded nice. She'd called me Grace once before, and I loved the sound of it. Mix that with the torment in her voice as she asked me to make love to her, and I was a goner. I whipped her over onto her back. Time to get serious.

I kissed my way down her body, spending lots of time on her nipples before settling between her legs. She was swollen and hard, no longer hidden between her folds. Lightly, I licked one stroke across her protruding clit. Her hips bucked under my hands. One more lick brought her taste onto my tongue. She began a slow undulation of her pelvis, seeking relief. I smiled then lowered my mouth to latch onto her. My groan was probably louder than hers as I sucked her into my mouth, stroking her clit with my tongue.

Her soft cries told me she wouldn't last, but this first time, I wanted to look into her eyes as she fell. I released her clit and climbed up over her, fitting one thigh between hers to keep the contact. Her eyes popped open at the loss of my mouth, watching me rise above her. I kissed her softly, then more insistently while my fingers delved between her lips to circle her swollen nub. Her kiss lost focus as she rose toward climax. I watched her gorgeous brown eyes roll back when she shattered beneath me. I'd never seen anything more beautiful than that.

"Oh, Graysen, you're amazing," she panted through her recovery.

"You're the amazing one, Sara."

A lazy smile spread her mouth wide as fire sparked in her eyes. "You're mine now."

With that declaration I found myself rolled onto my back, a fiercely determined lover hovering above me. Her smile promised sinful things before it disappeared from sight. I expected her to torture me with butterfly kisses on my breasts or inner thighs, but she must have known how far gone I was. She didn't bother trying to rev me up. She went in for the kill. Lips closed over my clit, tongue stroking in time with my clattering heartbeat.

"Kesara, I need to…" I didn't get to finish before she pulled off me and slipped her legs between mine. I looked down to watch her triangle press onto mine and saw her head lift from watching the same.

"Come with me, Grace," she whispered then started to thrust her hips, grinding hard against my need.

I felt the tingles turn into a swirling charge before I exploded against her. I gave a hoarse shout, but I have no clue what I said. Pulsations wracked my body over and over as she thrust and ground against me. My name passed her lips as she came again, seizing up over me before ripples made her body tremble and finally sag down on top of me.

It was a long time before I caught my breath, before I stopped feeling the indescribable pleasure of the climax she'd drawn out of me. I spent the time squeezing her to me, running my fingertips across her back and feeling her shiver in delight. I marveled at how spectacular that was. Finally, I understood what I'd been missing. I never wanted to go without again.

She lifted her head off my shoulder to look into my eyes. "That was incredible." She dropped a languid kiss to my lips. "I'm so far gone for you, you know?"

I let a soft laugh escape. "I'm right there with you, Kesara." Yes, completely with her on that sentiment.

CHAPTER 36

The guy with the tape recorder had been annoying me for the past hour. We'd already done a photo shoot and preliminary questions for his article. Despite my aversion to publicity, I felt that this issue needed to be put to rest. I'd chosen a preeminent sports magazine and would be sitting in for a short satellite interview with one of my former colleagues on ESPN later.

After all the background questions were asked and answered, none of which I thought would actually make it into the article, he hunkered down and began the expected topic. "Why?"

Really? That was how his years of experience taught him to ask the zinger questions? But, who was I kidding? I knew exactly what he was asking. "This is what I enjoy doing. When I pictured myself as a coach, it was at a prestigious institution like this one, with a team that has the same kind of passion that I do about basketball."

He leaned toward me. "Are you saying your last team didn't?"

"No, I'm giving you my reason for leaving my job as coach of a men's team to be the coach of a women's team. Your question implied that it's a step down."

"Technically, it is. You went from being the only one of your kind to being one of a few hundred."

I refrained from scoffing in his face. "The issue is not whether I was the only one, but whether or not it was the job that I had envisioned. Teaching and coaching kids for one year was not what I signed on for. It may work for my former colleagues, but for me, a coach is someone who brings a player along, helps develop more than just a fade away jumper, breaks down every single bad habit, and forces that player to get better and mature on court and off. One year is not enough time to do that. I'm invested with these kids. I want to see them succeed in whatever they choose to do. I'm not interested in getting my hands on them for a few months just to watch them wander off into the sunset and hope they do well."

He seemed to contemplate that response for a while. "Do you regret taking the job with LMU?"

"Absolutely not. I was brought in for a reason: to banish the stigma from the program and build up a squad that had been pummeled by violations. Those players didn't deserve that. They needed a fresh start, and I think I gave them that."

"But don't you think that quitting will send a message to other women who may want to coach in the men's league?"

I pushed a breath through my lips. I should have insisted on only television interviews because a magazine interview puts you at the mercy of the writer. If he didn't like me, anything I said could be framed negatively. "No, I don't think it will. Leaving LMU for a women's team does not signal failure on my part. If I'd come into a team that had four returning starters and two superstars, the success we had might have been a fluke. But I took over a team that had been plundered of nearly all its best players and recruits. I had to make them believe they were a team that could win while you and every one of your colleagues were saying they'd be lucky to get two games all season. We did a lot better than that, a lot better than anyone expected."

I watched his mouth quirk, knowing I'd nailed his estimate on our team's win rate. He nodded once to encourage me to continue. "The team I'm going to be working with now is ranked at a top university. Do you know how much more difficult it is to recruit players for a leading academic university? Leaving my former team to take over this one is not a step down or moving backward."

"Okay, I can see your point," he agreed grudgingly. "But I still think that by staying on at LMU you could have proven without a doubt that women belong in the position as head coach of a men's team."

I gave a short laugh. "I have proven it. There were four coaches standing at the end of the tournament last year. Three of the four had been there many times before. Three of the four had superstars on their team. Three of the four have the best players in the high school ranks clamoring to be part of their team. They barely have to do anything when it comes to recruiting. I took a team from infamy and obscurity to the Final Four. I gave them the tools and support they needed to become winners. In one year, I coached a team that set a win record, a conference tournament record, a NCAA tournament record, had four of five starters leave to play professionally, have every single one of my players with a GPA of 2.6 or better, and have recruited better prospects than ever in the history of the university. I did that. A woman coaching a team of fine young men. Women can do this, and I hope that many women will want to in the future. I could have stayed on indefinitely coaching that team, but it wasn't what I wanted."

I could tell he was trying to formulate another argument, but I cut him off. "Female basketball players play for the love of the game. We both know that because the money isn't there. Sure, they can now make a nice living playing basketball year round, but they do not have the luxury of playing a season or two and being set for life. They have to love the game more than they love the prospect of becoming rich. That's the kind of passion I signed on for. That's the kind of passion I want to lead. My guys were a wonderful bunch, and I wish them all the best with their new coach. I know I made an impact on their lives as much as they have on mine, but it's time for me to continue with my passion."

Having helped Tavian hire the highly experienced coach we'd managed to edge out in the Elite Eight game, I no longer doubted my decision to leave. I felt good that my guys would be left in very capable hands. His coaching philosophy was similar to mine, so it shouldn't disrupt their development too much, and he was a great guy. I could tell he'd become a friend.

The reporter had a few follow up questions, all of which told me that he'd started to see my point of view. He knew I was excited for my new job and that I'd found a comfortable home. By the end of this upcoming season, I'd prove to everyone that this was where I could do my best work. Let someone else manage the year or two or three that male college basketball players put in. Let them worry over those kids, try to make them better men, coach them to wins, but feel the heartbreak of watching them leave too soon, knowing full well that they would likely fail. That wasn't for me. I wanted a full-time coaching gig, not just part-time coordination until my players found something better to do.

After finishing with the magazine reporter, I sat for the satellite television interview. The questions were similar, but my former colleague knew me much better. When I explained why I'd moved on, he didn't second guess me. I felt good when I was done. Exhausted but good to have it behind me.

An hour later, I walked into the viewing room behind my new boss. The faces that stared back at me looked both familiar and foreign. I'd watched game tape of every single one of these players, but I'd never met them. Now, I was their coach.

"Good afternoon, team," I greeted them after the introduction from the athletic director.

"Hi, Coach," all of them called back.

I felt myself smile. Not one of them threw any attitude when the AD had announced my hiring. Not one of them questioned whether or not I'd be able to coach them. On their faces, I saw the passion that I knew was reflected in mine. They were ready. They were eager. They wanted to win, and they had the faith that I'd take them there.

This, right here, was why I'd become a coach.

EPILOGUE

Twenty months later

Kesara and I walked out of the Oakland Arena hand in hand. The excitement from the NBA game still coursed through my veins. It was close to a miracle that I didn't have a game on the only night that Wendell's team was playing the Warriors. I'd missed his rookie year last season, but this year, Kesara had surprised me with courtside tickets to the game. Tavian had been willing to sell me one of his kids to use the other ticket, but there was no doubt in my mind who was going with me.

"You had fun, didn't you?" she asked as we slid into her car. Her grin had flared frequently during the game whenever I caught her eye. She hadn't been to a NBA game before, and I was so glad that she enjoyed it as much as I had.

I let out a laugh at how well she knew me. I really didn't know how I'd gotten so lucky to have her in my life. "It was great, Sara, thank you."

"You're welcome. I'm glad I came with you. It gives me something to taunt Tavian with tomorrow." A mischievous glint danced in her eyes before she looked back at me. "You didn't think Wendell would come over and hug you, did you?"

Her gorgeous smile pulled a wider one from me. "I was thinking I'd be lucky if he remembered me."

That wasn't exactly true. I knew that many of the guys from my team still asked about me. I had two spies feeding me information on the team. Nate, whom I saw occasionally when I hung out with his sister, and Dash, who'd sought me out after not making the cut with his NBA team. He made decent money in the D-League, but in his first offseason, he showed up at my new office, looking for more pointers. We fell into a routine of working out together some mornings, running through drills other mornings, or having him participate in practice with my new team. This was his second offseason with me. He'd improved greatly, verifying my belief that he'd needed another couple of years of college ball to give him a complete game. He had it now, and as soon as I could get his team scout back to look at him, he'd be offered a spot on the roster. Next season, I'd be going to at least two games with former players. I couldn't be more proud.

Kesara nudged my shoulder. She knew I was joking. "Oh, please, you were the single most influential person in his life outside of his mother. I used to watch how those boys looked at you. Half of them worshiped you. The other half seemed constantly amazed by you. You have to know you changed their whole outlook on women, don't you?"

I grinned and leaned in for a soft kiss. My heart started thumping hard, still, nearly two years later. Her kisses were that powerful. I could feel my body respond to her kiss, wondering if we'd make it all the way back to my place before I had to have my hands on her.

Trying to push my need aside for a half hour till we could get to either her place or mine, I thought about her question. "I hope I did." That would make me more proud than watching my players succeed.

She leaned back into the driver's seat not making a move to toward the ignition. A sparkle played in her eyes as a secret smile formed on her lips. It was the kind of smile that sometimes irked me. All-knowing in nature and annoying in how much it taunted me.

When the silence and frustrating smile dragged on, I buckled as I usually did. "What? What evil plot do you have going right now?"

Her eyes flared at my expectant tone. "Evil? Hmm, depends on your perspective." She turned toward me, reaching for my hand. The smile went sinister in a flash. "I just thought I should let you know that we're getting married." She let a laugh escape before leaning in to kiss my stunned mouth. When she'd finished soothing my quivering lips, she sat back and gave me a confident wink. "You know, in case you wanted to buy a new suit."

My eyes blinked and blinked some more before I felt a smile stretch to every part of my body. Yes, a new suit would definitely be in order.

Please enjoy excerpts from Lynn Galli's novels, *Wasted Heart, Imagining Reality, Uncommon Emotions,* and *Blessed Twice,* all currently available.

WASTED HEART

"Somebody's having a good day," a now familiar voice pronounced from the doorway.

The smile I'd been wearing from the prospect of the new case widened when I looked up at Elise. That pesky school of fish swam swiftly through my midsection again, causing a little lightheadedness. She was in a skirt today conservatively an inch above the knee but plenty enticing. For instance, I was having a hard time not fantasizing about how soft the skin would be at the back of her knee. If my friend Des was here witnessing my perusal of Elise, she'd say something crass like how badly I needed to get laid. Crass, but true.

"Hi," I tried for nonchalant, but I'm guessing she saw right through me. "What are you doing here?"

She tipped her head back toward the hallway. "I was going over an investigation on a case that Rachel's taking to trial next week."

"Wasn't Jake on that?" I waved her inside the office to sit in one of my guest chairs. I tried to keep my eyes from staring at her toned calves as she floated into the chair and kicked one leg over the other. Her skirt rode up another couple of inches, and my mouth dried with each revealing hike of material.

Oblivious to my parched state, she responded, "He put in for a transfer to Phoenix to help out the family business now that his father's gone. He wanted to be more available to them."

Jake's dedication helped relieve my dazed reverie. "Amazing how it takes a death to make us realize which things are really important in life."

"You're so right." She sloped into that sexy head tilt again. "Jake asked me to tell you goodbye for him. I think he was a little enchanted with you."

"No." I tossed aside her remark without any consideration. Jake and I had worked seven cases together, and he was never more than affable with me.

Elise studied me for a long moment, not letting up on her sexiness. "Fascinating. You don't believe someone could be enchanted by you?" She was taking great enjoyment from my astonished expression. Before I could react, she stood up to leave. "I didn't really mean that as a question. Good seeing you, Austy."

Sassy, smart, and sexy: the very definition of trouble for me.

IMAGINING REALITY

"Oh yeah! Who's that?" someone yelled above the music.

I looked over and groaned. Jordan Palow stood among the tree stumps of her friends staring at our table. More specifically Elise whose striking looks would catch anyone's attention. Jordan mistakenly believed that she was in a contest with me about who could bed more women. She didn't seem to care that I wouldn't play along. Leering pointedly at Elise, she ignored the rest of us. "You'd make my whole year if you danced with me."

"No thanks," Elise forced a steady voice.

"Aw, come on, hottie. You won't get a better offer."

"Will I do, doll?" my mouth spoke before my brain did. Seduction permeated my skin, rising in waves that I'm certain everyone could see. Why was I doing this? Just because my friend was overwhelmed, didn't mean I needed to step in to make things easier.

Jordan looked astonished. We were barely civil to each other. I traced my fingers over her arm, feeling it flinch before eagerly pushing into my fingertips. I didn't bother to look for the shock from my friends.

She obediently followed my lead to the dance floor. When we faced each other, she snapped her eyes up with a suspicious look. I gave her my most seductive smile, latched my fingers onto her hips, and pulled her into me. With the sound of the thumping beat, I pushed who she was from my mind and began a slow grind with her.

When the fifth song ended, I leaned back and looked into her startled grey-blue eyes. "That was spectacular, doll. We should do this more often." My husky voice made my own skin crawl as I released her and watched her float away from me.

A hand grabbed me before I made it all the way off the dance floor. "You're dancing with me now." My friend Lauren ordered, grabbing my waist to keep me in place. I laughed at her forcefulness. She was so cute sometimes.

She gave me a wink and turned around to wiggle her tush in time with the music. My lousy mood at working over Jordan vanished as I got into the enjoyment of dancing with my friend.

When the next song turned slow, she grabbed my hands and slid them around her waist before looping her arms around my neck. When she pressed against me, she led us in a slow dance. *Hmm, this is interesting.*

"That was nice what you did."

I leaned back and gave her a questioning look. "What did I do?"

"You know what you did. You don't fool me, Jess."

"How much have you had to drink, L?"

"Ha-ha. Play all toughie with everyone else, but I know what you did."

I quirked my eyebrows at her. *No? She couldn't actually know, could she?* "Don't know what you're talking about, shug."

"Yes, you do. You made Jordan disappear so that Elise wouldn't be uncomfortable anymore. You took a woman that you don't like out on the dance floor and made her think she was the only person in the world. You're a good woman, Jessamine Ximena, even if you won't let yourself believe it." Lauren pressed closer, moving our bodies with ease. "One of these days, I'll make even you see it." She tilted up and kissed my cheek before detaching herself to walk away.

Five seconds passed before I realized the song had ended.

UNCOMMON EMOTIONS

Raven pulled her car into the Paul Industries parking lot. Mine was the only vehicle left, so she didn't need to ask where I was parked. "Ahh, modern," she teased of my Lexus.

"Boring but functional and an automatic."

"Is your ankle still bothering you?" She couldn't hide the worry from her tone.

"No, but automatics are much easier with all the traffic around here."

We got out to load my share of the desserts into the back seat of my car. The process took a couple of trips, and we only bumped into each other once. When I surfaced from my last drop off of takeout boxes, Raven stood a foot away. The look in her eyes halted my sidestep.

She held my coat but made no move to give it to me. Her gaze didn't shutter the emotions this time. She took a step closer before glancing at my mouth. When her eyes returned to mine, I knew without doubt that she wanted to kiss me. This was so different from the men who'd dropped me off after a date in the past. They would look at me with determination; they were *going* to kiss me. Nothing in their gazes could be mistaken for this kind of wanting. No, the men let me know what they were going to do. This, this look was of a desire to kiss, a craving to kiss, a near Victorian yearning to kiss me. I felt my breath desert me as suddenly as when I'd fallen off her horse.

Unlike with the men on similar occasions, my heart thumped erratically and something of a ruckus roared through my ears. I felt hot and cold and trapped and free all at the same time. Never once had I experienced this strong of a reaction to anyone. Desire had always been an elusive emotion for me. If I were being totally honest, I'd have to admit that I'd never felt it. Until now.

I wanted this. I wanted her to kiss me like I've never wanted anything in my life. Not because I wanted another woman to kiss me for comparison. No, I wanted *this* woman to kiss me. This incredibly smart, sexy woman.

I should do something. Give her a signal to tell her that she could turn her desire into action. If I looked down at her lips, maybe that would be enough of an invitation. Instead, I stared at those eyes, feeling her breath barely touch my face from her spot inches away. Why couldn't I move my eyes from hers? Give her the simple go ahead, or better yet, tip my head forward and capture those sensuous lips to taste what I knew could become addictive? Perhaps it was my stupid sensibility stopping me; or maybe my concern for her that if we kissed and I felt nothing, as per usual, I'd hurt her desperately. God, I hate being sensible almost as much as I hate being emotionally bereft.

Before I could break the spell and reach for my jacket, Raven stepped back as suddenly as if she'd been yanked by some unseen force. She shook her head and offered my coat, not meeting my eyes. When I took the garment, she waved and hurried around to the driver's side of her car.

"Goodnight, Raven," I called out weakly as the door was closing. Her tires didn't exactly squeal as they left the parking lot, but the escape was no less dramatic.

BLESSED TWICE

There were about a million other things I could be doing right now. Playing tennis, reading a mystery, calling my son at summer camp, working out, rollerblading, base jumping, banging my head against a low hanging beam, and all would be more pleasant than my sixth first date. Cripes, my friend Caroline knew a lot of women. A lot of women who were so wrong for me.

This one's name was Polly, and she worked as a court clerk. After her third cup of coffee—I'd learned never to commit to anything that would last several courses—I could sum up Polly's personality with one word: drama. Or, issues. Or, get me the hell out of here, please!

"And then I was, like, 'what do you think you're doing with my stuff, bitch?' I mean, like, can you believe she was walking out on me and expected to take the one and only gift she, like, bought me in the entire two months we'd been together? I was, like, 'you didn't even pay me rent for two months, you're not taking my Maroon 5 with you.'" Her pretty green eyes stared expectantly at me, asking me to agree.

Still stuck on some of the other intimate details she'd shared prior to talking about a massive blowout over a piece of plastic that costs twelve dollars, I merely nodded then shook my head. I didn't know if she expected me to say, "Yes, I completely agree, even though you're a loon," or, "No, that's just awful, especially since there's no way you could ever replace such a priceless item. Unless, of course, you walked into any music store, or better yet, downloaded the songs so no one can walk out of your life with her love and your CDs."

"You're so easy to talk to," she jabbered on after I'd apparently given the appropriate response. "I can't believe Caroline never introduced us before. I'm having so much fun." Yeah, because drinking coffee is a riot a minute. "So, like, what's your story?"

Well, I've never used the word "like" as a verbal pause, I've never moved in with someone after one night together, and I've never considered a CD worth the effort of an argument. Oh, and I now deem dating a soul draining experience.

"Briony?"

I looked up and felt my stomach plunge as swiftly as if I'd been pushed out of an airplane. M was standing by my table, iced coffee in hand on her way out. She was in casual clothes, showing a hint of midriff, envious calves, and just the barest promise of cleavage. "Hey there, M." I hoped she caught the relief in my tone. Wow, she looked good. No makeup today and her hair was a little more chaotically styled but wickedly attractive. Beyond, actually, more like hot. Yes, hot suited her just fine. Why wasn't I on a date with her? Oh, crap, Polly. "This is Polly. Polly, my friend and colleague, M."

Polly must have picked up on my blatant interest in M, because the next thing I knew, she was telling her, "We'd invite you to join us, but we're on a date."

I didn't know who cringed more, me at the idea that this could really be counted as a date or M at the rude dismissal. My eyes snapped up to hers in apology. Before I realized what I was doing, I made the ASL sign for "help." It was one of a few words I'd learned for when my son spent time with his hearing impaired best friend. This was the first time I'd ever used it, and I never imagined I'd be using it for evil instead of good.

"Pardon the intrusion, but I thought we said two o'clock?" M asked me with the perfect amount of urgency and innocence. "I grabbed a table up front and left all the lecture notes and business plans there. It's a few hours of work, and I've got plans tonight, but if you need a little more time, I understand."

"Is it two o'clock already?" I brought my wrist up to check the time on my watch. "Gosh, I'm sorry, Polly. I didn't mention this work thing because I never thought we'd still be here. You just made the time fly by." Two hours that I'll never, ever get back.

She beamed at my compliment but disappointment showed through. "Caroline said you were a workaholic, but we can work on that." She reached for a hug, which I made lightning quick, and finally, the sixth date on my path through hell was over. Polly banged through the coffeehouse doors with all the drama she'd expressed during her diatribe.

"Thank you for saving me."

"Think nothing of it." M said it like she believed it when I was considering erecting a life-sized shrine and lighting a candle every night. Her eyes darted to the door as her customary introversion returned. "Nice running into you, Briony. Enjoy the rest of your weekend."

"Tell me about those plans you mentioned," I blurted before she could disappear.

"I lied," she admitted with a shy smile. "I figured if I didn't give a limited window of time, she might think she could get us to postpone our work meeting."

Strangely, I felt more relief hearing this than getting out of my date with Polly. "So, you've got nothing going?" She shook her head. I smiled and stepped toward her. "You do now."

I couldn't think of a better way to spend my Saturday than with this beautiful, enticing woman. Not really a date, but far better than anything my friends could set up for me.

LaVergne, TN USA
30 January 2011
214503LV00001B/159/P